D1336490

a30118 023531902b

FRENCH LEAVE

FRENCH LEAVE

The popularity of Somerville and Ross's most famous book, *Some Experiences of an Irish R.M.*, has not only been maintained, but has perhaps actually increased over the years. Its humour and freshness continue to delight innumerable readers.

French Leave is much less well known and has long been unavailable. It is an enchanting novel, displaying to the full Somerville and Ross's gift for dialogue and clear eye for the beauty of the Irish countryside. Edith Somerville's nephew, Patrick Coghill, has written a fascinating essay to introduce this new edition.

The story is set in the 1880s, when it was considered most improper for a young lady from Southern Ireland to go off, by herself, to Paris with very little money but a keen desire to paint. Lady Kirwen, who was a natural Bohemian, sympathised with her daughter's ambition, but the Master of Kirwenscourt wouldn't hear of it.

After a furious row with him on the hunting field, while their friends and neighbours looked on, Patsey Kirwen borrowed £50 from her cousin, Lord Corran, and took, as one might say, French leave.

If Jimmy Corran had realised how achingly he would miss her, he might not have been so ready to lend her the money. But it was done: and Patsey was quickly caught up in the colourful life of the Left Bank. Artistic talent she certainly had: her talent for household economy was more dubious. Despite the help and advice proffered by a lively circle of friends, she was soon in dire financial straits.

And there were emotional problems too. Some curious gossip filtered back to Ireland—to be followed, eventually, by Patsey. The lure of Christmas with her family, love of fox-hunting and a strong dislike of poverty drew her home. She found a most unexpected welcome . . .

FRENCH LEAVE

by

E. Œ. Somerville
and
Martin Ross

TOM STACEY

ST-

First published 1928 by William Heinemann Ltd

This edition published 1973 by
Tom Stacey Reprints Ltd
28–29 Maiden Lane, London WC2E 7JP
England

ISBN 0 85468 340 2

Printed in Great Britain by
C. Tinling & Co. Ltd, Prescot and London

To
My Collaborator

INTRODUCTION

EDITH SOMERVILLE and Violet Martin are part and parcel of my earliest memories; Edith Somerville was my aunt and Violet Martin—better known as Martin Ross—was my cousin. We always knew them as D. and Martin, and it is by these familiar names that I shall refer to them here. D. was born in 1858, in Corfu, where her father, Thomas Henry Somerville, had taken his bride, Adelaide Coghill, on getting command of the battalion of the Buffs then stationed there. In honour of her Greek birthplace, D. was christened Œnone—the opening diphthong of which when used as an initial has proved a stumbling block to many.

Her father retired in 1859, and the rest of her childhood and girlhood was spent at Drishane in Castle Townshend, Co. Cork. There during the next fourteen years she was joined by six brothers, one of whom died in infancy, and one sister, my mother.

Unlike many big houses in Ireland, Drishane, her home, is not isolated by long miles of bad roads from neighbours, but set in a remarkable seaside village, where there is a cluster of " Quality " houses, so that in addition to her own brothers and sisters, there was always a pack of other young with whom to play and share the delights and adventures of a patriarchal life.

Of her own predilections in these formative years, her pencil and her pony undoubtedly held pride of place. One might say that when she was not drawing she was riding. The background provided by her parents, uncles and aunts, is worth touching on. They were a race of enthusiasts who pursued their enthusiasms with passion and determination. Zest was their sign-manual. Their principal hobbies were painting, photography—then in its infancy—spiritualism, music, riding and amateur theatricals.

I can find little or no trace of any interest in politics in those early days; but there are many references to the farmers and country people of the neighbourhood, to whom D.'s father stood in the relation of guide, philosopher and friend, and to whose sorrows and sicknesses, D., her mother and sister administered what practical remedies they could.

In 1875, when she was seventeen, the idea of girls seriously studying art was generally frowned upon, and when my father, who had gone to study in Paris, suggested she should follow him there, there were cries of shocked horror in the family at the suggestion that a young girl should be allowed to work in so notoriously depraved a city. Nevertheless her determination ultimately triumphed, and in 1884, accompanied by her mother, she reached Paris; 1885 saw her there again, but she came home for Christmas that year. She has told me how, soon after, her mother announced that some cousins were coming to stay in the village. Her reaction was fury and frustration, as at that time she was utterly absorbed in her painting and resented anything that might interrupt it. She met these dim and potentially detestable cousins on January 17th, 1886, and though she knew it not, that day history was made, as the young cousin was Violet Martin.

Violet Martin had, in some ways, a very similar background, but with marked differences of emphasis and experience. In her case I can only try to recreate it imaginatively from fleeting references in her writings. She was a younger daughter in a large family, and Connemara instead of West Cork was her country. She knew the same semi-feudal atmosphere, but I think there was a difference. Perhaps because the Famine and its horrors left deeper scars at Ross, her home, than at Drishane. It brought financial ruin to the Martins in their efforts to fend off starvation from their neighbours and dependents, as well as from themselves.

From the nineties onwards the cousins were rarely separated; Drishane was their headquarters and it was principally in Castle Townshend that they wrote their books—thirteen of them, not to mention many short articles—until December, 1915, when after a short illness, Martin died—still at the height of her powers. She was only 53. Of the books they had written three had won immediate fame. The first of these was *The Real Charlotte* (1894), which is rightly considered one of the great tragic novels of the nineteenth century; next came *Some Experiences of an Irish R.M.* (1899). *Further Experiences of an Irish R.M.* followed in 1908. These two books, with their sequel *In Mr Knox's Country* (1915) are masterpieces in comedy—short stories of Irish country life, especially in the hunting field, though by no means exclusively so, all picturing the life they knew so well at every level in the west and south of Ireland, as it was before the First World War. No writers have a finer ear for the idiom of speech to be heard in those parts to this day, or a more vivid touch in describing the wild beauty of that country.

How did they achieve their unique collaboration? I can see them sitting in a sheltered nook in the garden, each with a large MS book and a fountain pen, with two or three fox-terriers in attendance. One thing is certain. Every word they wrote was discussed and turned inside out before it was committed to paper. I am sure their stories and characters were created by conversation. Then gradually the first tentative drafts were written down, sometimes by one, sometimes by the other—but always together. Neither D. nor Martin ever retired alone to write down what they had previously discussed together.

Both had a blazing sense of humour, the golden gift of sympathetic conversation and cast-iron memories, the latter methodically reinforced by immediate recording in notebook or letter any notable phrase or incident encountered in the course of the day. So it is probably true to say that given their conversational method, they contributed equally to the genesis of the book or story. I think it is fair also to suggest that Martin's mind was the finer, and D.'s the more forceful; but D. has told me she could not point to a single sentence in any of their joint books that was not the work of both minds working in harmony.

This intense, unique collaboration, unbroken over thirty years, seemed to survive death. To the end of her life, D. felt herself to be in daily contact with Martin through her spiritualistic faith, and continued to consult her by these means in all matters, especially over the books now being penned by D. alone, but issued, as before, under their joint names. Among them were *An Enthusiast* (1921) and *French Leave* (1928). The former appeared under D.'s name alone, and the omission of Martin's is explained in a note added by D. to her Bibliography, compiled by Elizabeth Hudson:

> That the signature is in my name alone, is due to reluctance on the part of my publishers to accept my views, and has been regretted by me.

She describes *An Enthusiast* in these terms:

> This book appeared not long before the signing of the Treaty that created the Irish Free State. It attempts to give a picture of the closing days of the old order of country life in Ireland, and if sadness is its final note, this does not make the tale less true.

It is a book about a great hope defeated in an attempt at co-operation between Old and New in Irish country life; sad though it is, it is shot through with the wit and sense of character that made the R.M. stories so irresistible.

French Leave is a charming novel that looks back a little way into the past; D.'s note upon it in the Bibliography runs:

> This is a story of the eighties of the last century. It tells of two young fugitives who took, in a literal sense, French Leave of their families—one of them forsaking even Fox-hunting to follow Art—and ran away to France, an effort that was in those days more of an enterprise than can be realised by a later generation.
>
> Some of the incidents are based on the artistic experiences of one of the authors in a Paris Studio. These are entirely authentic, and although they depict the longed-for and highly gilded gingerbread of Studio life with much of the gilt rubbed off, I can vouch for the fact that it was very good gingerbread, and pleasantly hot i' the mouth.

Sustained by her belief in the validity of Spiritualism and of the actuality of Martin's presence, D. wrote on to the very end of her long life, publishing no less than sixteen more books, of which *Mount Music* (1919), *An*

Enthusiast (1921), *The Big House of Inver* (1925) and *French Leave* (1928) are the finest; tragedy predominates in the first three, gaiety in the last.

By a sad irony of Fate, her last book, *Maria and some other dogs*—a collection of dog-stories culled and re-edited from earlier writings and illustrated from old drawing-books—appeared finally complete and ready for issue on her publisher's desk the very morning on which he read the notice of her death. She died peacefully on October 8th, 1949, at the great age of 91.

Patrick Coghill

CHAPTER I

THE girl was very nearly blown. That she continued to run was the result of mental rather than physical effort; the resolve of a fierce soul to give up the ghost rather than its intention. It need not be hastily concluded that—as she herself would have expressed it—she was wrong of her wind; she would have been the first to have repudiated such a slight; but to such as can now recall the costume (that prevailed on high days and holidays) of the young lady of 1884, the fact that her lungs were possibly being strained beyond their power would readily be accepted.

Nevertheless, the girl ran on, regardless of lungs or costume. This hot and thunderous day of late August was a special and intensively high day, being no less than the wedding of her sister, elder and step; moreover, as she was the organist, it may be granted that this was no moment for caution. The church bell was being rushed out of its every-Sunday sedate pace, and was uttering its rather cracked voice in hysterical and unrhythmic bursts, and apart from its warning outcry, the girl was well aware that she was late. This was not unusual with her. The punctuality of amateur organists—especially when they are no more than twenty years old—cannot invariably be relied on; but on this momentous day, to be late was a serious matter, and the girl knew it but too well.

She had started early, in order (as she put it) " to sort the offal in the organ-loft "; a crude, but not un-descriptive reference to the musical stock-in-trade of the choir, and she had not estimated highly enough the handicap involved by the sacrificial splendours that the occasion had demanded. That they had been insisted upon for her by her step-sister, the bride, made their bondage all the more galling. Her mother, who was unconventional, and knew it, and was ashamed of it, had been coerced into asserting her authority. In 1884 those who were spoken of as Elders and Betters, the first always pre-supposing the second, were untrammelled by doctrines of self-determination for their young —especially for their female young. A girl did what she was told, and, as to clothes, wore what her mother wished her to wear, and there was no more about it. Submission does not, however, pre-suppose resignation. There was black wrath in Miss Patricia Kirwen's heart, as, defiant of possible observers, she snatched up her voluminous and trailing skirts, and sped over the grass, scudding, like a ship in distress, under bare poles. But the waistband, of no more than twenty inches, had to be endured. So also had the padded excrescence, like the hump of a camel that has slipped astern, that radiated heat through its victim's already over-heated frame. Possibly it is taxing credulity too high when it is asserted that Patricia was wearing a bonnet. Yet this was indeed the case. Her young, now crimson, face was surmounted by a structure of lace and nodding roses, secured to her head by broad pink ribbons, that, having formed a large bow under her chin, floated right and left over her shoulders as she ran.

She had taken what was known as "the near way," across her father's park, to the church, and there were still a hundred yards of steep grass slope between her and the churchyard gate, when behind her she heard the sound of wheels, and, looking back, saw the bride's carriage, unmistakably the bride's, with horses and servants decked with fluttering white favours, coming along the drive at a pace that ensured their speedy arrival at the church. She looked hastily at her watch.

"Bad manners to them! They've got away ten minutes too soon!" she raged, panting up the final hill. "The Master's going to take no chances about getting Millie off his hands!—thinks he'd rather be sure than sorry!"

She was at the churchyard wicket-gate now. The carriage would have to go round to the main entrance. She took heart, and let her skirt decorously cover her ankles as she made her way at a less violent rate of speed through the churchyard.

In front of the church door was a dense crowd of onlookers, whose ranks opened with reluctance to admit to the church the invited guests. Weddings were weddings in those days, and guests observed all the rigour of the game. Tall top-hats, tight frock-coats, white satin ties, bonnets bourgeoning with tropic decoration, gowns billowing with many-coloured splendour, swelling and swaying like balloons, as their wearers came hurrying from their carriages, casting anxious glances at the sky, that seemed at each moment to come lower and become blacker. The first heavy drops were falling, as Patricia, her bonnet now crooked, and far back on her curly, untidy head, came thrusting her violent way through the crowd.

An elderly hunt-servant, in full professional array, saw her coming, and elbowed a passage for her to the door.

"Hounds, please! Hounds!" he said to the people. "Get forrad, Miss Patsey, get forrad!" he warned her. "They're out o' covert and runnin' hard!"

" So am I, Johnny ! " Miss Patsey responded, her breath coming in wheezing croaks, as she rushed past him and stumbled up the stairs to the organ-loft.

Even as she did so the first long repeated notes of the Lohengrin Wedding March screamed from the organ.

" Who on earth's playing ? " she thought, as she paused behind the organ to drag the hated bonnet into place and stuff the new white gloves into her pocket (for in those days pockets still held their own). " Pretty good cheek to begin without me ! What an awful noise !"

The jerky triumph of the theme (to which it would seem Lohengrin and Elsa must have progressed in a species of polka) was being given forth with the full power of the organ. Every stop was out, the swell creaked with effort, and the boy who was blowing the bellows was working as if he were manning the sole pump of a sinking ship.

" You'll burst the swell-box if you blow so hard ! " Patricia flung at him.

" God knows I'm dead, miss ! " panted the blower, irrelevantly, relaxing for an instant his labours, with a resultant semi-throttled bleat from the over-driven organ.

" Blow ! Blast you ! " came to them, hoarsely, in a man's voice, from the front.

Patricia ducked under the pumping handle and ran round to the keyboard. An unknown young man, fair and long-legged, was seated on the bench, and was playing with an air of intense concentration. The front row of seats allotted to the choir was occupied by other young men, equally unknown to Patsey. The familiar moon-faces of the school children who, with their elderly schoolmistress, formed her usual choir, regarded her, from the back bench to which the strangers had relegated them, with expressions of mingled outrage and bewilderment.

The young man who was playing leaned towards her from the bench and whispered urgently, " Please take on! I can't play the next part—too hard for me! "

Without reply Patricia slid on to the bench beside him, and her long fingers delicately picked up the theme from his and carried on without a check.

" Take your foot off the swell! " she commanded, loudly. She was too angry to whisper, and the roar of the full organ annihilated all other sounds. Then she dashed in half the stops.

" What a pity! " whispered the young man, genially. " It was making such a noble row! "

Who was this horrible man? thought Patsey, ploughing on with Lohengrin, too busy to speak.

He continued to sit beside her on the bench, holding down the upper corner of the page she was playing from, in order to turn over for her.

" I can do it myself! " she hissed. She hated him. His clumsy elbow was almost in her face. He fumbled with the music, uncertain when to turn. " Please get off the bench! "

" Oh why? " He turned on her in reproach, and the music he was holding fell off the desk and slipped down between them on to the pedals.

Patricia did not fail in moments of crisis. She kicked Lohengrin off the pedals.

" Pick it up and go away! "

She was improvising an ending as she spoke, and in the same instant a breathless messenger rushed round the corner of the organ.

" The bride's come! "

The moon-faces, armed with hymn-books, were

already stumbling and pushing their way through the visitors to the front.

"The big hymn-book! Give it to me! Quick!"

Afterwards the young man said, in deep reverence, to his friends, that it had been by the Grace of God that he had noticed on the board what the first hymn was to be and had found the place. Although on all-fours, groping for Lohengrin, he was able to reach the hymn-book and place it, open, in the snatching hand of the organist.

The bridal procession moved up the aisle in the flood of an unwonted wave of song from the organ-loft. The school children's squeaks were inaudible, only a thin squeal, jagged and acrid, like an anæmic flash of lightning, piercing the bellowing of male voices, told that the schoolmistress still asserted herself. The visitors all sang; the disgraced young man, with restored self-confidence, let loose such a sonorous and tuneful baritone request to be led "O'er the world's tempestuous sea," as atoned in some degree for his guilty past.

The organ favoured him; he could feel a certain subserviency to his higher notes that encouraged him. He let himself go, and trolled forth the time-worn hymn as if he were singing a solo in Grand Opera.

"*Thus provided, pardoned, guided*——" He turned to the organist, and aimed the last lines at her.

She ignored him. With the "*Amen*" she had swung round on the bench, her back to the interloper, and was gazing over the curtain that screened the player at the assemblage in the aisle beneath, mentally reviewing them all.

The bride, tall and thin, attired after the strictest order of brides, with four little nieces, veiled and wreathed, as her attendants, drooped, her head held low, beside the bridegroom.

" Trying to make people think she isn't taller than fat old Dick! " commented the watcher. " Poor old Dick! The Master was too many for him! . . . I'm glad he isn't me! "

After this regrettable lapse in grammar her thoughts turned to her father.

" The Master's looking quite affable! . . . He's glad he's disposed of the last of the steps! . . . Pity he didn't put on his pink to match Johnny Ryan and mark the occasion! . . . Mother looks quite smart for once! . . ." (Had Patsey been thinking aloud a softening difference in tone would have been recognised.) " . . . *What* a bustle Miss Murphy's given her! My word! . . . Mother isn't really tall enough for such a huge one! But she looks fine for all that! "

The marriage service, devoid as it then was of the comparative reticence of a later and less barbaric era, advanced, unflinching in its admonishments. The two old officiating clergymen, chips, both of them, of the block that had, not so many years earlier, been hewn from the English parent tree, warned and enjoined in tones of thunder. The listener on the organ bench, being a rebel by nature and by practice, and being also young enough to take conventions seriously, harkened to the bride's murmured promises with resentment and contempt.

" The notion of obeying old Dick! They won't catch *me* ' cherishing and obeying ' ! " She flung up her head, and the preposterous bonnet fell off backwards, hanging by its strings down her back.

The young man, whose eyes had been on her, took a long step towards her, stretching out a hand.

"Let me——!" he whispered, grinning broadly. "I'm your cousin, you know—though perhaps you don't——?" he added.

The well-worn bromide which asserts that the heroine's eyes flashed fire is seldom justified by the fact. Yet it is undoubted that this phenomenon does occasionally occur, and the young man at whom the blue fire of Miss Patricia Kirwen's eyes was directed would endorse what is here stated. He hesitated; the bonnet was replaced by its wearer, who then, turning her back determinately on the intruder, occupied herself with preparations for the further efforts of herself and her choir. But she could not as easily turn a mental back on anyone so unforeseen and pertinacious.

"Cad!" she said to herself. "Shoving himself in where he's not wanted! . . . And how dare he say he's my cousin! . . ."

She awaited, fuming, the final hymn, and when, at length, its moment arrived, the dulcet invocation to Perfect Love was delivered, as far, at least, as the organ was concerned, with a stridency that converted its melting appeals into dictatorial requisitions. She listened to the exhortation that ends the service with growing indignation, as its somewhat one-sided injunctions to the newly made man and wife were declaimed.

"Easy to see that it was men wrote it!" she thought, furiously; and with every stop out she crashed down on the heels of the final word, "*Amazement*," with that startling chord with which Mendelssohn's ever-green Wedding March bursts into existence.

"By Jove, you let them have it hot and strong that time!" murmured the inveterate young man in her ear, as she slammed down the lid of the manual and let herself slip off the bench. " Do wait one minute—I want to tell you—I really am your cousin—at least my mother says she's your mother's cousin. She was going to write and say——"

Patricia surveyed him coldly. " Yes, I remember now. She wrote. Then you're Lord——"

" Jimmy to my cousins, please—if you'll honour me so far? " He bowed profoundly, and Patricia hated him a little more. " I say, wasn't that a cousin getting married? Mayn't I come to the Breakfast? " he hurried on, as Patricia began to move away. " I can send these other chaps to the hotel—that's unless you'd like to have them too? They're quite harmless. You'd like them much better than me, though I *am* your cousin! "

The harmless ones in question were now watching the slow tide of departing guests thronging the aisle below, while they awaited their leader's orders.

" We're not exactly in wedding garments, I know," went on Patricia's new cousin, cheerfully, " but don't you think we might do? Of course, if you'd *rather* we didn't——? "

" It's really nothing to me whether you come or no! " replied Patricia, magnificently. " I suppose you haven't met my father yet? "

" No. Why? Is he a terror? "

Patricia didn't know how to cope with this young man who got inside her guard, refusing to be kept at arm's length. But, she thought, she wasn't going to admit to him that the Master was a terror—though of course he was. She mounted her highest horse.

" I have no doubt my father and mother will be glad to meet you and your friends——"

" And this kit don't matter? You're all such awful swells——"

He had touched a raw spot. The high horse gave an unseating plunge. At Patricia's age such a mount is a precarious one.

" Swells! " she exclaimed with emotion (and therewith the high horse and she parted company). " If you only knew what I've been through with *my* wedding garments! "

" Tell me all about it! " said her new cousin, confidentially.

CHAPTER II

THE wedding breakfast at Kirwenscourt was, for many years, the standard by which to assess the generosity and catholicity of similar functions.

Sir Ingram Kirwen had said to his wife (with his accustomed grace of diction), that she was to make none of her usual damned dunderheaded blunders this time, like she did at the other girls' weddings, leaving out half the people who ought to be asked, and setting the country by the ears. And his wife, who was a Bohemian ingrained and ineradicable (and was undoubtedly dunderheaded in delicate social decisions of the kind), resolved that this great occasion should leave her blameless in all eyes. With this laudable intention, she followed so closely the Gospel precedent of searching the highways and hedges for guests—a generality which, in this instance, must be taken to include the neighbouring town of Templenoe and its suburbs—that, unhappily, few regarded the invitation as a compliment, and many were disposed to take it as an insult.

" Her Ladyship had the whole country trawled! " said Mrs. Morrissey (who, as the pretty and well-dowered daughter of a butter-merchant, married to a doctor, might be said to have a foot in both worlds). " There was Tuppence drinking champagne, for all the world as if it was Tuppence-ha'penny! And to be sure Tuppence-ha'penny wouldn't like that, y'know! "

At what sum, precisely, Mrs. Morrissey estimated herself it is difficult to determine, but although it was undoubtedly more than Tuppence-ha'penny, she—as she would have said—made no bones about talking and making herself agreeable to those of a lower coinage. Thus it was that, having, with salutations to right and left, squeezed her way through the crowded hall into the even more crowded dining-room, she proceeded without hesitation to talk to a tall young man who was, in her opinion, but little removed from the Tuppenny class. Still, in young George Lester's case there were certainly alleviations. In the first place he was very good-looking, in a dark and pallid way, with a wing of raven hair on his forehead, and large brown eyes that, as Mrs. Morrissey said to herself (though approvingly), were like two big burnt holes in a blanket; and, in the second place, he was Going into the Church. Moreover, he had " the name of being very talented."

" Oh, that young Lester's a most talented young man! " Thus had he been extolled to Mrs. Morrissey at a recent tea-party. " He did a sweet sketch of my little Bessie!—and his mother told me he'd painted nature on the bellows for her, and water-lilies on the pier-glass—sweet, she said they were! Oh, he has the reel artistic temperrament! "

Yet it cannot be denied that his presence at this gathering was a surprise to Mrs. Morrissey. After all, she thought, even if he were going to be a clergyman, what was his father but a farmer, one of Sir Ingram's tenants, and a Methodistical old thing too! Though they *do* say he drank very hard one time! Who'd have thought of finding Holy George's son here! *He* was Tuppence, if you like!

But Mrs. Morrissey's thought was without the rancour that it might have held had she been no more than Tuppence-ha'penny.

" Why, Mr. Lester," she began, " I didn't know that you were at home at all! "

The tall young Mr. Lester looked at her moodily. " I'm home for the vacation. I had to drive my mother here. I wouldn't be here only for that."

Mrs. Morrissey, who was short and fair and plump, and quite aware of her charms, looked up at him with a rallying smile, and said archly:

" I suppose you know it's a wedding you're at, and not a funeral? Maybe your mother didn't tell you? "

Mr. Lester's pale face became darkly red. He disliked chaff, which, as its name might imply, is a light matter, and he was a young man who took nothing lightly.

" She did—at least, she didn't—I mean, I knew——" he mumbled, aware of his own inadequacy to cope with such as Mrs. Morrissey.

" Well, maybe you don't know that there's champagne and cake going, over there at the sideboard—where the gentlemen are standing so close! " pursued Mrs. Morrissey, gaily. " But I *do!* And you haven't as much as asked me had I a mouth on my face! "

" I'm sorry—I'll go get some——" Anything, he felt, to escape from this disquieting lady, with her airs and graces, and her chaff that he didn't know how to deal with.

He elbowed through the company, taking small heed of the elbows that met his, elbows that were directly connected with full, flat glasses of champagne, which tossed and splashed in his wake, like waves in the wake of a steamer.

" Here! Steady on! Look out for the lady! "

Mr. Lester's violent course was arrested by another young man, as tall as he, whose suit of grey flannels was conspicuous in the black-coated company.

" Pawdon ! " said Mr. Lester, nervously, " I'm tryin' to get to the——" He was going to have said " the counter," but was preserved from doing so by the shock he received on meeting the blue eyes of the lady for whom he had been told to look out. For, to a youth with the " artistic temperrament " (even though his artistic efforts had hitherto chiefly materialised in nature on the bellows), to look into Miss Kirwen's eyes was—as, later, he said to himself, having recently bought a cheap edition of Keats' poems, and regarding himself as the discoverer of the hard-worked quotation —as though through some magic casement he had seen the blue of perilous seas.

Let it be, as far as is possible, forgotten that Patsey was wearing a bonnet. Let it only be remembered that in those days bonnets " *were worn* " (a velvet-gloved statement that conceals the iron hand of the administrator of Fashion), and that though Beauty herself must submit to Fashion, her triumphs are immortal and belong to every age.

Young George Lester stood still and stared for one dazzled second, then he plunged on through the laughing, gabbling crowd, with the set face of " the charioteer, who, vainly pulling at the reins, is borne along by the horses."

" Who was that chap ? " asked Patricia's newly acquired cousin. " Pretty rough customer—useful man in a scrum——"

" I thought he looked like a poet ! " said Patsey, on whom young Mr. Lester's dark eyes had not failed of their effect. " I suppose he's one of mother's mistakes —you never know *who* you're going to meet here—oh, here is mother—I'll introduce you."

" Tell her I'm one of your mistakes. Do be responsible for me—I'm feeling frightened ! "

"I despise you!" said Patsey, from which it may be gathered that cousinly relations were becoming established.

Through the crowd, talking amiably and vaguely to the guests, who opened a path for her as she came, Lady Kirwen bore down on her daughter. She was short and spare ("My size dates me," she was accustomed to say; "I'm a dump. All my contemporaries are dumps"), with a thin, weather-beaten face and slightly prominent teeth. All that remained of the looks she had once possessed (or Sir Ingram would not, certainly, have married her) were her soft, short-sighted brown eyes, a charming smile, and a light figure, from which not even Miss Murphy's bustle could rob the grace. She was little more than forty, but, accepting the conventions of a period that coerced its women into caps and old age when they were married, she believed herself to have left youth far behind, while her heart was sixteen, and she was deeply ashamed of being still the victim of that infirmity of laughter which in French is well called *fou rire*, that can overwhelm at any moment, and is as unpredictable as it is shattering.

"Oh, darling!" she invoked her daughter in an excited whisper, "an awful thing has happened! I seem to have ordered tapioca instead of rice for the people to throw! Do you think it matters? Will Millie mind? Such masses of people abhor tapioca——" She broke off suddenly and put up her lorgnettes. "Why—isn't this——? Yes, it is! Of course! I remember you now quite well, and your mother said you were coming—Jimmy Corran? You *are*, aren't you? It's such ages since I saw you! You were in a dear little red velvet tunic when——"

"Oh, Lady Kirwen," broke in the young man she

addressed. " Please don't rub it in! I know I oughtn't to be here in these clothes—but your daughter so kindly insisted——"

Patsey turned upon him. " Liar! " she said, which was equivalent to granting full status as a cousin.

" If only the red velvet tunic were handy," went on Jimmy Corran, undismayed, " I'd put it on at once——"

Lady Kirwen's perturbed eyes were still fixed on his face, but it was evident that she was not listening. She turned to Patricia.

" If I *could* find anyone to run to the village and bring me a stone of rice before they start—one doesn't know *what* tapioca mightn't imply——"

Jimmy Corran gave a shout of laughter. " Let me go, Lady Kirwen! Better be sure than sorry—tapioca might be fatal! " He looked at Patricia. " Don't you think, Cousin Patsey, you'd better come too, and show me the way? "

* * * * *

The wedding festivities wore on. Sir Ingram Kirwen, Bart., M.F.H., D.L., J.P., last year High Sheriff for the County, not, in short, a person to be trifled with, or to suffer easily what he disliked, was beginning to think that it was time for them to wear out. He had, all this long day of fulfilment, been congratulating himself on having so successfully got rid of the last daughter of his first family, and there had been four of them, all told. But the process of doing so was becoming no longer a matter for congratulation, had, in fact, become a fair imitation of eternity, and an eternity endured in conditions intolerable to an autocratic gentleman of sixty-five years of age, who had always had his own way.

" These damned women, and their damned dressing

and undressing!" was how Sir Ingram (whose stock of adjectives was, like the moral in the song of the "Widdy Malone," "*not long, but strong*") summarised the interval of arrested enthusiasm that occurs between the disappearance of the bride and her reappearance in "the going-away dress."

The bridegroom, Colonel Richard Villiers, a mature warrior, who, like his newly made father-in-law, had been married before and knew what to expect, was safely and comfortably concealed in the smoking-room, but for the master of the house no such evasion was possible. Sir Ingram's manners, on occasions of state, were as unexceptionable as his frock-coat, and would have been as inadequate a guide to his household character as the frock-coat would be to the costume in which he visited his kennels; but his regard for the duties of a host cannot be said to have lightened his brow or enlivened his conversation. He moved like a courteous thundercloud among the elders of the assembly pressing champagne on jaded matrons, and offering pessimistic opinions on the condition of the country to his fellow County Fathers, since, in their case, to have offered champagne would have been a case of supererogation. But it was well for the bride that she was leaving the home of her youth.

The guests had gathered in two long rows in the hall, provided with handfuls of the rice that had at the last moment been provided. Even at a gathering of Irish people there come times when the stream of talk must run dry, and the dragging final moments of a wedding, when the effects of the champagne have passed from exhilaration into somnolence, are those that test the quality of the most spirited and conscientious guest. The sound of hurrying feet in the gallery at the top of the wide staircase brought hope that sprang up only to fade, as the son of the house—the only son, only vouchsafed after five undesired daughters had darkened Sir Ingram's doors—a heavy schoolboy of sixteen, came down the stairs in a series of clattering leaps, rushed down the alley left for the bride, and was lost in the group of lookers-on, gathered outside the hall-door round the carriage that awaited the bride and bridegroom.

"What was that Gilbert had under his coat?" said a married half-sister, suspiciously. "He was hiding something——"

Her husband, who was possibly soured by long waiting, replied, indirectly, "If ever there was a cub that wanted——"

What the cub wanted was not divulged, as at this moment, in a storm of rice and tapioca, the bride and bridegroom came running along the lane of guests, making, with the best speed they might, for the waiting brougham.

The company swept after them as they fled down the hall-door steps, with Lady Kirwen heading the charge, waving what she believed to be her pocket-handkerchief, but which was, in fact, one of the discarded white silk stockings of the bride, which she had snatched up in the throes of her step-daughter's departure. Johnny Ryan, the huntsman, whipped out his horn and began to blow those thrilling repeated notes that mean "Gone away!" The crowd, waiting outside, cheered, the horses, out of temper from long standing, and excited by the horn, refused to start. One of them got up on his hind legs, the other slewed sideways, letting fly with both heels at the carriage. The coachman lashed at them, shouting; the lookers-on yelled in sympathy and encouragement; a gang of fox-terriers and several red setter puppies uttered their various voices out of sheer enjoyment in adding to the turmoil, while the reiterated notes of the horn kept all things, and especially the horses—old hunters, both of them—at fever-pitch. The brougham had turned, and to those on the steps a singular assortment of foot-gear, attached to its rear, was now disclosed, comprising three ragged white satin shoes, a bedroom slipper, and two large, new, black kid, elastic-sided boots.

From among the group of the household servants gathered at the foot of the steps came a cry, like the shriek of a seagull, that pierced the din.

"Stop! Stop! Them's me boots! Me Sunday boots!"

Following on the cry, an elderly woman, a perfect example of the typical fat and florid cook of the period, came bundling down the steps, and, snatching at the swinging emblems of good luck, succeeded in recovering her property, and thereupon, a boot in either hand, fell to waving farewells with enthusiasm undimmed by the wrong she had so nearly suffered. Above the uproar of cheers and laughter, Sir Ingram's voice bellowed abuse and commands to the coachman, that did not cease until at length the horses broke into a gallop, and the brougham bucketed away down the drive, pursued by the terriers and the puppies, in an ecstasy of excitement and indignation at they knew not what. Patricia, oblivious of her so recently acquired status of leading young lady of the house, girded up her trailing skirts, and ran down the drive, in pursuit of the puppies, uttering fierce commands to the elder dogs to desist from the chase, while she was followed, uproariously, by James Anthony FitzAlleyne, Baron Corran, and his young friends, all offering a fairly successful imitation of a pack of hounds in full cry. Sir Ingram, still purple in the face, and forgetful as his sole remaining daughter of his position, burst his way through his crowding guests back into the house, and going in rapid strides to what young Mr. Lester had so nearly called the counter, poured out for himself a long strong tumblerful of whisky and soda. Lady Kirwen realised the stocking and crammed it as far as it would go into an inadequate pocket, whence it was immediately abstracted by her son, who tied it round his neck.

"Thank God, that's all over now, at last!" said the half-brother-in-law to his wife, his eye on her young half-brother. "Look at Gilbert, I ask you! Didn't I say to you that he wanted licking? Well, no matter—say good-bye now, and let's be off!"

The butler, Moloney, watched, with a sardonic eye, the return of Patricia with the dogs and her attendant youths. He turned to Mrs. Trinder, the cook, who, panting from her recent efforts, was examining her boots to see if they had suffered from experiences for which they were not intended.

"It's a wonder to me how them lads can stir at all, with all the champagne they have drunk!" he remarked with severity. "It's well you got your boots, Mrs. Trinder! When I seen Master Gilbert running, 'Well!' thinks I, '*he's* up to no good!'"

"Sure the devil's busy always with boys!" said Mrs. Trinder, on whom the recent nerve-strain had told.

"Ah, what Master Gilbert! Is it that poor child?" said Kate, the senior housemaid, who had been twenty years in the house, and spoke with authority. "No! But Miss Patsey that put him up to it! Sure she had it in for you, Mrs. Trinder, when you refused her the cutlets, that was over last night from the dinner, for the dogs!"

CHAPTER III

FOLLOWING on a convulsion of so profound a nature as a wedding, it takes a house, that has been rocking from its foundations to its chimneys, some days to recover equilibrium. As in some illnesses, so after a wedding, there are many *sequelæ* to be dealt with. Blessed though may be the relief when the core of the trouble, the Happy Pair, has departed, the survivors are still very far from finding peace or repose.

At Kirwenscourt there was no exception to this rule. The tapioca had already been swept out of the corners of the hall, and shaken out of Sir Ingram's hats (the long array of identically similar, venerable hats and caps, maintained, like old-age pensioners, by elderly country gentlemen), before telegrams began to flow in from the bride, entreating the immediate despatch of articles of toilet, of clothing, of forgotten things, as difficult to find, identify, and pack as they seemed to be indispensable to the continuance of her life on earth. Belated wedding presents continued to arrive, some by post, registered, with the annoyances proper to such; others by train, with even more exhausting attendant formalities. And, most serious of all these post-wedding troubles, there followed also the partition and despatch of those futile morsels of wedding cake that are the meed, primarily, of the givers of presents, and secondarily (yet even more importantly) of those who "expect to be remembered," irrespective of any special demonstration on their parts.

Upon Lady Kirwen and Patricia fell, inevitably, the brunt of these matters, and a week after the wedding found them still confronted by a black and frowning mountain of cake, awaiting distribution. This was the task to which, on a hot and brilliant morning, they had addressed themselves, and it is not easy to say whether of the two, mother or daughter, disliked it more, or was more ill fitted to deal with it. Their packing operations were taking place in what was known as the Old Playroom, a long, bare, carpetless room in a wing at right angles to the main block of the big Georgian house, a room which can be classed in no definite category, either as boudoir, workroom, studio, or dog-kennel, although it partook, to some extent, of the properties of all of these—save, perhaps, the first. It possessed, however, that first element of true comfort in such a room, a superfluity of tables, large kitchen tables as to three of them, solid, submissive to every burden, all heaped with such indeterminate matter as is, in Hindustani, helpfully and compendiously termed "*Boj*"—rubbish that defies classification, whose spiritual home is the ash-heap, yet whose permanent existence is, in such a household as Kirwenscourt, fixed as the stars (and about as likely to be practically useful). Beyond the tables, under a skylight at the end of the room, was a large collection of the articles proper to artists: camp-stools, stacks of canvases, a thicket of sketching and studio easels, a sketching umbrella, open, revealing two broken ribs, a rowdy old lay-figure, clad in a striped Italian rug, with an old velvet hunting-cap on its head, and a pipe stuck in a hole in the corner of its mouth; while a further indication of an interest in art was afforded by numerous sketches of landscape in oils, and water-colours, and scribbles in pencil and in charcoal of horses and dogs, all more remarkable for vigour in style than for accuracy in drawing, that were nailed in all directions on the panelled walls. A rack of rusty tools and a carpenter's bench completed the equipment of the room, Lady Kirwen being one of those unexpected little ladies who, in a former incarnation, might have been a carpenter, and in a future one might develop into an architect. She and her daughter, seated on rush-seated painting-stools, were now established at the carpenter's bench. Beside them were three small, smooth, fox terrier ladies, and two red setter puppies. Ten glowing eyes were concentrated on the cake-packers with an hypnotic power that compelled the relinquishment of occasional fragments, all of which were, with trout-like leaps, intercepted in mid-air by the terriers. Patricia, therefore, fed the puppies, and did so with a lavishness and a disregard of their methods of accepting her attentions that drew a mild protest from her mother.

"Darling, don't give it *all* away—and don't you think you ought to wash your hands?—Think of the people——"

To which Patricia, with that indifference to the canons that should govern conduct which indicates the artistic temperament, replied that the people would never know, and that she would like to take all that was left of the cake to the kennels, and be done with it.

"The whole thing is such humbug!" she declared, picking up one of the silver-printed wedding cards and regarding it with disgust. "The idea of old Millie transfixing Dick Villiers' heart with an arrow!—It looks like a kidney on a skewer!"

"I left it to the shop," replied her mother, vaguely.

" I just said to do them the usual way. Millie thought they were very nice——"

" She would! " said Patricia, intensely. " Millie's an ass! "

" Well, yes, perhaps, partly," agreed Lady Kirwen, meditatively; " I dare say Dick Villiers doesn't much mind that—and she's kept her looks, hasn't she? " She spoke dreamily, as though thinking aloud, and paused, gazing into the future of her step-daughter and the husband whose requirements she so happily fulfilled, with the resigned bewilderment that women of her period must sometimes have felt when they considered the motives that governed their lords in the selection of mates.

Then her thoughts travelled onwards to a point, suggested by the theme, that touched her more nearly.

" There's only you left now, Patsey," she said, pensively. " I wonder how soon I shall be sending off *your* wedding-cake? I shan't have you to help me then, shall I! "

Patsey's mother was quite aware of Patsey's views on the subject of matrimony, and in thus implying that the yoke was for her inevitable, she was possibly, though unconsciously, influenced by a touch of that mild jealousy which must rise in the mare in the shafts when she views, over the hedge, her progeny prancing in freedom.

In this instance the progeny started to her feet as if she had been stung, and her stool fell with a crash.

" *My* wedding-cake! Never! "

The suddenness and vehemence of this declaration were such that the three little white dogs were convinced that there must be a rat involved, and, in their instant scurry to the recognised official rat-hole at the end of the room devoted to the fine arts, they knocked over a recently painted canvas. The disaster stemmed the diatribe on the marriage state that Patricia was about to deliver. The canvas had fallen on its face, and, since the paint was still wet, it had collected an assortment of hairs, chips, and dust that kept its owner occupied for some minutes, and diverted her thoughts from the question of matrimony.

Then she strode back to the carpenter's bench, where Lady Kirwen, her mind evidently far away, was patiently engaged on her task.

"Mother!" said her daughter, severely. "You're doing that box all wrong! You've forgotten the cake! *Don't* think anything more about weddings—tell me what the Master says about my going away. You promised you'd talk to him."

"Dearest child," said Lady Kirwen, returning with a start from reverie, "I haven't forgotten, but there never seems to have been a moment—Papa's out all day —and then in the evening, if he's tired, or been annoyed about anything, it doesn't seem a propitious——"

"I'm sick of waiting for a propitious moment! He's always annoyed about something!" Patricia broke in with the violence proper to her age and to that undeniable tinge of red in her hair. "Now that he's got rid of Millie, why shouldn't he do something for me? Gilbert's housemaster doesn't wait for a propitious moment to send in his bills! I'm his child as much as Gilbert, why shouldn't I have my chance as well as he? I'd show that I was worth while! . . . But no one cares——"

As is not unusual with violent people, when Patricia was angry her voice betrayed her. Now it broke, exasperating her. She walked quickly down the room, and stood staring fixedly at the disreputable old lay-figure. But she saw nothing; her racing thoughts were concentrated on how best to present her case. Then she whirled round and came back and stood before her mother, whose faint protests went by her like the idle wind.

"I know, I know," she cried in a rising crescendo. "I *know* I could paint! I know it's in me, but it'll never come out if I'm to stay here, just waiting till the Master can shove me down some wretched man's throat!"

She glared at her mother with fierce blue eyes, and her mother (who also was something of an artist, though she was too humble to admit it) could only think how enchanting was her young angry face, and how clear the colour that had risen in it.

Without waiting for response, the indictment stormed on. The Rebel, following the recognised precedent for domestic rebels, announced that she would run away, offering to her mother the alternatives of London or Paris, she didn't care which. She demanded to know how it was possible for anyone to develop any talent that they might possess when they were buried in a bog-hole. She accused her mother—quite unjustly, did she but know it—of admiring all she did, and her father of not caring or knowing anything about it—which was perfectly true.

"And how can *I* know if what I do is good or bad? I'm like Adam and Eve—I don't know good from evil—I want to eat of the Tree of Knowledge!"

Here the indictment ceased abruptly, and Lady Kirwen, her eyes on the indignant face of the insurgent whom she had—how, she couldn't imagine—brought into the world, saw a new and less alarming light dawn on it, and realised that there had come a lull in the storm.

Patsey, who had been tramping to and fro before her mother while she harangued her, was now standing quite still, her head up, her clenched fists hanging beside her. Then, as though in sleep, she sat down on the end of the carpenter's bench and fell into meditation so profound that she made no sign of welcome when Dooley, the eldest of the terriers, softly, imperceptibly as a falling feather, floated on to her lap.

Two minutes passed, and to Lady Kirwen, waiting, as it were, in the still centre of the cyclone, unable to guess in what direction it might next manifest, the two minutes felt like twenty. Then Patricia turned towards her mother, and said, thoughtfully, "Yes! I believe I could——" and was silent again.

Lady Kirwen's usually wandering faculties were, for once, assembled into a single cry of interrogation.

"I've been so afraid I mightn't live till I was twenty-one," Patricia pursued calmly.

"My darling! What are you talking about?"

"Grandmamma's forty pounds, of course. I shall have that in November——"

"But, Patsey," protested her mother, "that's in Papa's hands——"

"It won't be!" returned Patsey, confidently. "Not when I'm twenty-one!"

Shock rendered Lady Kirwen incapable of reply, and Patsey continued:

"Forty pounds a year is quite a lot, and heaps of people have told me one can live in Paris on half-nothing."

"Half-nothing!" repeated her mother, dazed, while a prophetic vision of the effect upon Sir Ingram of Patsey's proposition rose, horrifyingly, before her. "I'm afraid it would very soon be whole-nothing!"

Her short-sighted eyes, full of consternation, dwelt on Patsey's face, now glowing with constructive thought. Gradually the point at issue became for Lady Kirwen more remote. " Half-nothing? " she mused. " Is that better or worse than whole-nothing, I wonder? " She continued to gaze at Patsey, and as she gazed she was aware of the fatal tickle of laughter, like a crumb in her throat. She made a desperate effort to arrest it, but Patsey saw the tears gathering in her eyes, and recognised the sign.

" Mother! " she exclaimed, indignantly. " If you're only going to laugh——"

The sound of heavy footsteps in the passage that led to the Old Playroom scared Lady Kirwen's self-control into resuming its precarious sway. She leaned from her stool and caught at Patricia's arm.

" I'll be good, I'll be good! I won't laugh! I'll do my very best for you—— " Hush! Here's Papa! "

CHAPTER IV

THE habit of repression is not easily broken, and the axiom that a man must be master in his own house was impressed very firmly on Sir Ingram Kirwen's household. So, as the door opened, Sir Ingram's young daughter subsided again on to the seat from which the wave of indignation had lifted her, and fell again to her task of squeezing the sticky wedges of cake that her mother handed to her into boxes whose capacity Lady Kirwen only succeeded by an occasional accident in gauging.

At this time of the history of Ireland, those efforts to bring contentment, which have been, for the most part, based on the impoverishment of employers of labour, had not gone very far towards their ultimate achievement of exile for such. In the year 1884 Sir Ingram Kirwen still felt himself to be a pillar of the State, and strictly fulfilled the duties and obligations that he conceived to be proper to his rank and his rent-roll. Unfortunately for Patricia's aspirations, he did not hold that his duties to his daughters extended further than was involved in providing them with creditable husbands. Dick Villiers, he told himself, might be a little long in the tooth, but he was a good fellow, thoroughly creditable and, if you came to that, Millie was getting on a bit too, and to marry her off—off his hands, in fact—had been an affair that had for some years engaged his anxious attention. In Sir Ingram's opinion, unmarried daughters were superfluities, if not disgraces, to any right-thinking parent. But Millie (with God's help, and with that hint to Dick Villiers about her mother's money) was safely disposed of, and there was no hurry about Patricia. She had taken after his side of the house—she was a right-down damned-good-looking girl—there was no fear of her!

So Sir Ingram felt, temporarily, at peace with the world, and could stand, his hands in the pockets of his roomy frieze shooting-coat, viewing the—for him—symbolical operations of his wife and daughter with undisguised approval.

" Well, girls! Packing away! Packing away! That's all right! " he said, benignantly, regarding his wife and the now sole daughter of his house and home with the satisfaction that arose, unknown to himself, from the peculiar implications of their task. " Don't send all the cake away out of the house, Maud; keep a bit for Patsey to put under her pillow, to dream of a husband on! "

" It would be a nightmare if I did! " declared the sole daughter, defiantly.

Sir Ingram laughed indulgently. He liked—or thought he liked—to see a girl show spirit. He was proud of Patricia, even though on her arrival (following on four step-sisters) she had been regarded as a reprehensible error on the part of her mother. But Gilbert had followed with all due speed, and Patsey had atoned for her mother's fault in turning out good-looking.

" Much more of this job to do, have you? Why, bless my soul, you'll break down the mail-car if you send away any more to-day! "

Lady Kirwen had been trained by time and expediency to recognise her husband's jokes, and she greeted the *jeu d'esprit* in connection with the mail-car with suitable appreciation.

"By the way, Maud," Sir Ingram continued, "Jimmy Corran's just walked over from the hotel. He said his friends were going, and he had come to say good-bye. I told him not to be in such a devil of a hurry to go away, and I'd send a trap over for his things, and we'd put him up for as long as he liked to stay. He said he'd be delighted. He's down in the hall now, looking at the paper. I've given him a loan of a gun, and I told him to take Flora and go out on the hill and see if he couldn't pick up a grouse, but he said he didn't think the old bitch'd work for him——"

"That's very nice, dear," responded Lady Kirwen, amiably and at large.

"What's very nice?" said Sir Ingram, with some pardonable irritation. "That Flora won't work for him? Upon my honour, Maud, I don't believe you listen to a word I say!" He turned to Patricia. "See here, Pat, your mother'll finish this job. Do you go and put on your hat and take Corran up over Slieveroe. Flora will work for you all right. He might pick up something there. I'd go myself only I've got to meet Casey at the office."

Patricia slewed round on her stool quickly.

"Is that about the mountain being poached? I saw Casey before breakfast, and he told me he heard shots there early this morning. What's the use of taking Jimmy there? The birds won't be in it!"

Sir Ingram pulled his long moustache, which, once red, was now growing grey; his thick orange eyebrows came down like blinds over his eyes. He did not approve of Patsey's interest in what he held to be the masculine domain of sport, but, since it had refused to be crushed, he could not ignore it; he felt it like a spur, irritating and stimulating, and on this absorbing topic he could not keep silence.

" Did Casey say who he suspected? "

Had Sir Ingram been demanding the originator of the Gunpowder Plot his manner could not have been more portentous. Patricia was pleased with the effect she had created. She nodded her head gravely and replied:

" Casey said the shots were somewhere between Slieveroe and Derrygoole."

" Ha! " broke in Sir Ingram, triumphing in a suspicion made certain. " That psalm-singing blackguard Lester! An old poacher himself, and now his son's at it! And he has the damned impudence to ask me for a bit of mountain—for sheep, he says——" He turned suddenly on his wife. " Didn't I see that young hound here at the wedding? It beats me to think what the devil made you ask the feller into the house? "

Lady Kirwen's mind, stirred by the word " mountain," had wandered away on such a travelling theme as her soul loved, and was planning an expedition. " My thick boots," she was saying to herself, " and just an apple and a biscuit in my pocket——" She returned with a jerk of mind and fingers, upsetting the contents of the box that she was packing on to the floor, where they were fallen upon by the dogs as instantly as is, we are assured, in the desert, a dead camel by vultures.

" Ask who, dear? "

" That poaching Long Tom of a son of Lester's! I give you credit, Maud, for asking the wrong people and forgetting the right ones whenever it's possible to do so! " He turned on his daughter. " Birds or no birds, go and do as I tell you and take your cousin out on the hill with the gun. Have you no manners that you leave him hanging about by himself? "

A definite command was, as a rule, for Patricia a

certain incitement to mutiny. But the hill, on a lovely September day, and old Flora (who came easily first) and Jimmy Corran were quite good company.

"All right. I don't mind—if Mother doesn't want me?"

With alacrity she stood up, and swept the cake-crumbs from her lap, and swung away down the long room to the door, followed by a train of dogs.

"If you meet that young scoundrel," Sir Ingram called after her as she was leaving the room, "tell him——"

Patricia turned in the doorway, interrupting the valediction. "I'll tell Jimmy to put a charge into him! Will that do?"

She slammed the door and ran down the passage to the corridor over the front stairs. As she ran she said to herself, not for the first time, "How does Mother stand it?"

From the hall below the smell of tobacco rose. She looked down over the rail of the corridor, and saw Jimmy Corran, with a newspaper in his hands, his lengthy person apportioned between two armchairs.

The inveterate larker that is immanent in most young creatures, from boys and girls, to puppies and kittens, woke in Patsey. With the same instinct that suggests to a puppy to dash from a hiding-place on a playfellow, or to a kitten to stretch a clawed arm from under a sofa to provoke attack, she slipped into a neighbouring bedroom, filled a tumbler with water, and returning stealthily to the corridor, leaned far out over the rail and poured the contents of the tumbler on the prostrate form below.

The aim was good, but one of her dogs had preceded her, and had warned the proposed victim that she was near. Thus it chanced that he was rising from his place at the moment of the assault, and of the descending shower a sprinkle only reached him.

During the week that had passed since the wedding, Jimmy Corran had not failed to establish on a firm basis his position as a cousin, even though one only of the second degree. It is an elastic relationship, that is just sufficiently removed to impart a touch of adventure to companionship, and yet is near enough to justify a freedom that is half-way to the brotherly love enjoined by the apostle. When, therefore, it is added to these considerations, that this recently discovered second cousin was no more than six-and-twenty, it will be understood that he took up Patricia's challenge with enthusiasm. He was already half-way up the central flight of stairs before his assailant had started to run for safety. He caught her before she reached the door of her room, for which she was making, and snatching at her wrists, held her in a strong grip.

" Now then! I've got you! It was a good try, but not quite good enough! You've got to say you're sorry! "

" You may thank Dooley for saving you! " retorted Patricia, breathless, and fighting hard to free herself. " Anyhow, your hair's all wet! Now we'll see if the wave is permanent! And," she added, " I'll never say I'm sorry, for I'm not! "

" Then you've got to be punished! People who won't apologise when they do this sort of thing to their cousins ——"

Without finishing the sentence, he loosed hold of her wrists and caught her into his arms.

" Now for the punishment! "

The victor's laughing, good-looking face bent over hers, delaying the kiss that was to be at once the penalty of unprovoked attack and the meed of victory. It delayed too long. The clawed arm of the *embusqué* kitten never struck swifter than did Patsey's freed right hand at her captor's triumphant face. As she struck she heard Gilbert's voice at hand, and put forth a cry for help that did not fail of its errand. Gilbert, a skilled and unscrupulous player of football, tackled his adversary from the rear, acting on the principle inculcated by that wise monarch of whom it is said:

" '*In battle-day*,' *the King replied*,
'*Nice tourney-rules are set aside!*' "

The little dogs joined in the scrimmage, barking, springing, and snapping impartially at the combatants, while the red setter pups, in whom discretion in moments of crisis is ever uppermost, watched from afar, their tails between their legs, uttering whimpers of nervous agitation.

" Pax! Pax! "

Jimmy Corran, spent with laughter, was on his back on the floor of the corridor; Gilbert was sitting on his chest; two terriers were licking his face, the third had pushed her sharp nose into the pocket of his jacket, and with histrionic growls was worrying his tobacco pouch. Patricia, who had burst free early in the struggle, was holding the tumbler, refilled with water, over the head of the vanquished. She, as he had done, delayed the delicious moment of triumph. She leaned over him, and saw with pride the red marks of her fingers on his cheek, and was preparing to let a torturing preliminary drop fall upon it, when her ally leaped to his feet.

" Get up, Jimmy! " he hissed. " Look sharp! I hear the Master coming! "

CHAPTER V

OUT on the hill was early September at its best, and that in the south-west of Ireland is, as the south-west of Ireland would say, " a big word." The blaze of the sunshine was softened by the lightest of thin winds, that brought up from the lower lands the scents of honeysuckle, and blackberries, and late-blossoming gorse, to blend with the heather and peat scents of the hill. The yellow of cornfields glowed through the haze. If one stood still, the hum and whir of reaping machines sounded faintly, and added to the high peace in their suggestion of labour. The small town of Templenoe was lost; a pool of smoke hung in its place; beside it was the lake, Lough Eskaheen, which means Beautiful Water, deeply blue, spotted with specks, like flies, that were the boats of fishermen. Beyond the hills that hemmed it in on three of its sides, a long narrow band of sea caught the sun, flashing like the blade of a bright sword.

But fair as was the prospect, it cannot be said that it received the appreciation it deserved from the expedition launched by Sir Ingram. It was now past two o'clock, they had tramped the hill since noon, and at each moment, for all three of them, the ling and heather seemed to be taller and to make worse going, and the steep slopes of the mountain grew more steep, and the luncheon that they had forborne to eat until some success had been achieved, became more desired. Even the horseflies had lost energy, and were kicked up from their repose in the heather only to sink into it again. A brace of questing hawks squealed and circled high up in the blue air, complaining of the lack of sport, and old Flora, the red setter, whose luck had been no better than theirs, had fallen into depression, and was moving slowly ahead of her party, making no pretence of doing her duty as a gun-dog.

A ring of grey boulders that lay in a dip on the crest of the hill, once, presumably, a place of grave Druidic ceremony, now spoken of lightly, with patronising facetiousness, as "The Nine Stony Gerr'ls," was the point to which Flora was leading her young charges. She had assured herself that there were no birds on this beat, and she was accustomed to have her lunch served at the Stone Circle. She turned her wise, greying head at intervals to see if her lead was being followed, and, entering the Circle, was proceeding, as was her wont, to seat herself by the flat altar-stone, when a ridge of hair rose along her back-bone, and with a rolling, growing growl she set an unseen enemy.

From behind the altar, summoned by Flora's menacing voice, a long body rose gradually into view, surmounted, finally, by the pale face and black hair of young Mr. George Lester.

"Then the Master was right!" thought Patricia. "What luck to have caught him!"

Full of the pride that is no doubt felt by the special constable when he makes his first arrest, she advanced upon the poacher, and said in tones of ice:

"May I ask what you are doing here? I suppose you know this is private property?"

Mr. George Lester's pallid countenance became livid with alarm. Muttering that he thought he was doing no harm, he stooped down out of sight behind the sheltering altar. He rose into view again with a bag in his hand.

"Then he *has* been poaching!" Patricia thought, with increasing satisfaction. "That's where all the birds are, of course! Now he'll have to produce the gun, and then——!" She felt proudly that she was going to equal her father in the slaughter of this shameless poacher. She and Flora, in like suspicion and indignation, moved round the end of the great altar-stone in order to keep an eye on the suspect.

The young man, having slung the bag over his shoulder, had knelt down again and was occupied with something on the ground.

"Taking the cartridges out of the gun!" Patricia said to herself. Then, in what she felt to be a successful imitation of Sir Ingram's judicial severity, she said:

"Will you kindly tell me if you have a gun there?"

He was kneeling with his back to her, and he turned a scared face over his shoulder. He had not known she was so near.

"Oh no! Not at all," he said, stammering. "It's only"—he hesitated—"only a sketching easel——"

Gilbert uttered the cracked and discordant cackle of the schoolboy whose voice has broken, an offensive sound that was now barbed with the triumph of a younger brother in seeing the discomfiture of a sister. Such a laugh from Abel would have justified the act of Cain, but Patricia was too thrilled by this change in the situation to notice it. In an instant she had discarded the role of special constable in favour of that of fellow-artist. The lack of birds, the shots that Casey had heard that morning, were swept from her mind (though not from that of young Mr. Lester, who was thanking Providence for an escape), and her ardent apologies for a mistake culminated in a request, even an entreaty, to be allowed to see Mr. Lester's work.

"You know I sketch too!" she declared, gazing at the still shaken young man with eyes alight with artistic sympathy.

What the matron of Templenoe had spoken of as young George Lester's artistic "temperrament" was not proof against the entreaties of this being with those unforgettable eyes (whose unmistakable resemblance to perilous seas he again endorsed) and the voice that, as he subsequently defined it to himself, when it wasn't frightening the heels off a fellow, was coaxing the heart out of his body.

"Really?" he faltered. "You would like to see what I've done? But I assure you, Miss Kirwen, 'tis meezerable—'tis not worth your looking at it at all——"

He was, nevertheless, fumbling with a long drawing-book as he spoke. Disregarding the protest, Patricia seated herself upon one of the flatter of the Stony Gerr'ls, and took the book from George Lester's hesitating hand. What was lacking to her in technical knowledge was made up for in self-confidence and decided opinions. She entered with zeal upon the examination of the drawings.

The first few pages of the book were devoted to studies of flowers, which had probably provided the material for that Nature on the bellows that had been eulogised to Mrs. Morrissey.

Patricia thought them very bad, as, indeed, they were. She hurried on. Landscape followed. Heavy and sodden greens, blues, and yellows, rubbed, and washed, and worried, until an adequate representation of a bruise had in many of them been the result. The artist was standing beside the critic; his strong bony hands were clasped; he muttered elucidations of the geography of the sketches, its accuracy being the point which he appeared to find most important. Patricia, for all her youth and usually voluble enthusiasm, was hampered by candour, and knew not what to say. She murmured that the technique of water-colours was a mystery to her, while she was sensible of the mounting wave of self-reproach that can inundate the soul of one who has recklessly volunteered art-criticism, and—like the typical infant—can find no language but a cry.

The landscape ceased and blank pages supervened.

"There's a few things at the other end——" The words came in a short-winded jerk, and Patricia, sympathising, yet with a sinking heart, reversed the book.

A change of quality as surprising as it was refreshing was instantly apparent. The pages were filled with figures and caricatures in pen and ink and pencil, and it was quite evident where young Mr. Lester's talent lay. Patricia's praise, generous if rather undiscriminating, flowed in a warm and bubbling stream, as page after page was turned, and the drawings progressed in strength and competence. Brief, but less nervously delivered, biographies of the subjects were offered to her.

"Those are some of the chaps at College"—"That's an old lad who comes begging around our place at home"—"That's Doctor Armstrong. He's one of the examiners——"

"He's awfully well drawn!" said Patsey. "But what an upper lip! Surely it's *rather*——"

George Lester, staring at his own drawings over the critic's shoulder, forgot for a moment his shyness, and, in defence of his drawing, relapsed into his native idiom.

" Lip!" he repeated. " He's a lip that'd trip a goat!" Then, horrified at such a solecism, " I mean, 'tis very long—I think that's all there is in the book, Miss Kirwen," he went on, incoherently, and tried to take it out of her hands. But Patricia had already turned the page.

" Oh, but who are these?" She began to laugh. " Why, I know some of these people! Isn't that the Dean?" She uttered a cry. " Oh! How awfully good! Look, Gilly! The Master! Isn't it the very image? Mr. Lester, you ought to go in for this sort of thing! I think they're splendid!"

Mr. Lester became crimson. He clasped and unclasped his hands, mumbling deprecation of Patsey's praises.

" But you *ought* to take it up seriously—go and study in London—or Paris—as I mean to do!" she added, with a touch of defiance that alarmed her hearer, who could not know that it had been inspired by his drawing of her father.

He bent down and again tried to take the book from her. " Indeed, there's nothing more worth your while ——"

" I'm going to see it all!"

She held the book firmly and turned the page. " Colours! How exciting!"

The page was filled with vividly coloured female heads, drawn from all points of view, full face, three-quarters, profile, all renderings of the same subject, and all distinguished by enormous eyes of cobalt, stimulated by emerald-green. Most of them were crowned with a structure purporting to be a bonnet, in which brilliantly pink roses and a large bow of pink ribbon were salient features.

Gilbert had come near to see the caricature of his

father, and was now crouching on the stone beside Patricia, looking at the book with her.

"By Jove, Patsey!" he cackled. "Talk about 'penny plain!' 'You're tuppence coloured,' and no mistake!" Again he gave vent to a hoot of derision, and this time Patricia, who had been finding suitable comment on the portraits of herself a difficulty, shelved the comment and avenged the insult by snatching the cap from Gilbert's red head and sending it skimming across the circle of the Stony Gerr'ls like a woodcock flying down wind, and the next instant, with a double push on his shoulders, she had tumbled him backwards off the stone into a bush of heather.

"Now, Jimmy! Sit on him! It's your turn!"

And then, to the surprise, even to the horror, of young Mr. Lester, Lord Corran, Miss Kirwen, and Master Kirwen indulged, for the second time that day (though this he did not know, and would scarce have believed), in what appeared to him to be a senseless and unseemly struggle. He didn't quite know what to do. Possibly, he thought, it might be best to assume unconsciousness. So he continued the interrupted packing of his sketching materials, while, from Master Kirwen, pantings and bad language, varied by cracked squeaks, told that punishment for him had taken the form of being tickled by the implacable fingers of his sister.

"Well!" thought young George Lester. "If these are what they call Quality manners——"

He had finished packing his things just as the struggle in the heather ended. He stood up, and Patricia, flushed and rather blown, stood up also, and thanked him effusively for having shown her his drawings.

The cobalt and emerald-green orbs were looking

straight into the brown pools that were set deep in George Lester's head.

"I enjoyed seeing your book so *very* much!"

George was thinking "I made them much too dark—they're more the colour of a wave when it curls." He murmured aloud that she was very kind, and he bowed low over the hand she gave him, and he shouldered his load, and went away down the heather with the easy swing of a lad bred to the hill, a steady step that could not have hinted to anyone that, as a matter of fact, he felt as if he were walking on air. She had looked straight at him and had told him his work was splendid . . . that he ought to take it up seriously . . . that he ought to work in London or Paris. . . .

Jimmy Corran, who had found himself considerably bored during the interlude of art-criticism, said, while they stood and watched young Mr. Lester's retreating figure, that when Patricia shook hands with him the honour had been too much for him, and his knees had bent under him, and he had curtseyed. Gilbert said: "All very fine his pretending to be an artist! Why has he got leather patches on the shoulders of his coat? And Flora was smelling that bag of his! I'll bet there were birds in it this morning!"

Patricia defended her fellow-artist from both calumnies with her accustomed warmth in controversy, and proceeded to deliver an oration in which praise of his talent was judiciously qualified by criticism.

"Figures are his line," she said, authoritatively, "but his colour is bad—muddy and muddled."

She was pleased with this phrase and repeated it more than once.

Jimmy Corran said, "Quite so. I agree. With a dash of suet about the gills."

" I didn't mean him himself," said Patricia, descending, with some heat, from the rostrum to the arena, " and what's more, you know perfectly well I didn't! "

" I thought that, as an artist, you were criticising the gentleman's complexion," said Jimmy Corran, deferentially; " the description seemed to me excellent."

" *Now* let's have lunch! " said Gilbert.

CHAPTER VI

IN the 'eighties of the nineteenth century it can hardly be denied that daughters were at a discount. Like the dogs, cited in that Canaanitish woman's magnificent effort of special pleading, they were permitted to eat of the crumbs that fell from their brothers' tables, but if no crumbs fell, the daughters went unfed. It may be conceded to Sir Ingram Kirwen that he had been legitimately embittered by the successive arrival of five daughters before an heir to the throne had been vouchsafed, and his oft-stated view that education was unnecessary for wives, and was the ruin of servants, was held by many others of his contemporary gentlemen of position, who, possibly, had had less to annoy them in the matter of superfluous daughters than he.

His theories were undoubtedly justified in the case of the four daughters of his first marriage. The first three had glided off the paternal stocks with the docile submission to authority of a successfully launched ship. And what education had they had, Sir Ingram would like to know! Much help this trash of Women's Colleges (just then coming into notoriety) would be if it were left to them to find husbands for the unfortunate girls whose parents were fools enough to send them to them! A five-and-twenty pound governess had taught all that was necessary for good-looking girls like his (with a share of their mother's fortune). And look at the result! All married well as soon as they came out; all, of course, except Millie, and she, after all, hadn't quite the looks of the other girls, and she had a touch of that High Church nonsense that she picked up in England, that made her not every man's bargain—Dick's a sensible feller, she can bow and scrape as much as she likes for all he'll care! And look at her now! Plenty of money, and every prospect of finding herself a rich widow some of these days!

These reflections and observations of Sir Ingram's were being presented by him to Lady Kirwen in what was known as Her Ladyship's Garden, where she was engaged in grubbing out the weeds that had sprung up among her dahlias during the week of rainy weather that had followed on the first few perfect days of September.

To be strictly accurate, Sir Ingram's remarks were addressed to the latter half only of his wife, that portion which—since she was on all-fours—may, in the language of the stable, be spoken of as her forehand, being hidden from view beneath her luxuriant dahlia plants.

"Well, but, Ingram," Lady Kirwen had responded from the depths of the dahlias (in that confounded irrelevant way she had, that showed she hadn't been listening to a word a man was saying), "you know Patsey's one idea is to be able to go away to learn to paint—Paris, or anywhere."

"If you'd come out of that I might hear what you're trying to say," said Sir Ingram. "How can I carry on a conversation with your bustle and the soles of your shoes?"

Lady Kirwen crawled backwards into the open, and sat down on a garden seat near where her husband was standing.

"I'm sorry, dear—but you never saw such obstinate ——"

"Well, attend to me now, and never mind your

weeds." Sir Ingram tried to be patient. "What's this you were saying about Patsey?"

"Only that it seems such a pity she shouldn't be able to develop her gift for Art. It really *is* exceptional, Ingram. She must have got it from Grandmamma," Lady Kirwen's large, other-worldly eyes looked away beyond the gorgeous orange globes of her dahlias, into the past. "Mamma's mother, I mean. She used to paint her little dog—Cuddle was its name—over and *over* again, *most* beautifully. It skipped two generations, unluckily for me!"

"*What* skipped?" shouted Sir Ingram, cross because confused, confused because cross. "What the devil has your Grandmother's dog's skipping got to say to anything?"

Lady Kirwen was seized with one of her most inopportune and agonising attacks of *fou rire*. She laughed and snuffled and wept, while Sir Ingram stared at her in a foaming silence which tried his self-control almost beyond his power.

"Oh dear!" gasped his wife at last, mopping her eyes. "I only meant that the turn for Art missed Mamma and me. But Patsey——"

"Upon my honour, Maud, you're enough to drive a sane man crazy—laughing like a fool at nothing at all!" interrupted Sir Ingram, with indignation that was not without justification. "And you may tell Patsey she can put Paris, or anywhere else, out of her head. What with this wedding, and Gilbert's school bills, and these damned Land Commissioners cutting down rents every five minutes, I've no money to waste on nonsense like that! What's more," he added, "I wouldn't consent for a moment to letting her go away by herself—perfectly unheard of!"

"You know there's that forty pounds a year that Mamma left her," ventured Lady Kirwen. "That would be some little help——"

"Help!" echoed Sir Ingram. "You might as well say forty pence would be a help! No! Let her set to work and get married, and her husband can take her to Paris as much as she likes! What's the good of my asking Corran into the house when she makes no more of him than if he were her brother? There he is, a dam' nice young feller, pots of money—with that long minority of course—a nice title, good looks—what more does she want, I'd like to know?" He struck the ground with his stick and walked away a few paces; then he turned back to where his wife sat. "I can see he has a great notion of her! You must have seen it yourself—any fool could see it! I can hear them thumping away at the piano together, with their duets, or whatever it is they do, whenever I go through the hall! Thank God I can't hear them in the study! If you were any good at all, Maud, you'd point out to her she may never get such a chance again! Why, my God! It's no more than your *duty* to point it out to her! Aren't you her mother!"

"I've always thought so, dear," replied Lady Kirwen, meekly.

Sir Ingram looked at her sharply. Was she going to laugh again? He was never quite sure if she were or were not laughing at him. Not that—as he had often said to himself—there was any reason why she should, except that she was twenty years younger than he was, and that makes a man uncertain, and you never quite know where you are with women—idiotic things seem to amuse them. But he was fond of his wife, and feeling that he had now made quite clear to her his views as to Patsey's future, he proceeded to light his pipe, and mentioned, amicably, between puffs, that he was taking out the hounds, cubbing, on Thursday, to Derrygoole—" that covert on Lester's land, you know. I'm giving Jimmy a mount. I'm having the young entry out for the first time. It's a good place to enter them. Plenty of foxes—there was a big litter o' cubs there—and I've had the rides cleared. Tell Patsey if she likes to come out, she can have a horse—Derrygoole I'm going to—don't forget to tell her. I'm going down to the kennels now."

He swung round, and strode away; at the gate in the glossy escalonia hedge that enclosed the little garden, he turned.

" Tell her she can ride that brown mare I bought from Keating the other day. By the way, you're going to Dublin, ain't you, on Thursday? "

" No, dear, to-morrow."

" Well, I shall be away all day. Patsey can tell the men what she wants. Let her tell them in good time. They've got to get away by four o'clock. The sun's up at five. Don't forget now, Maud! "

The Master retired. Lady Kirwen pulled on her gardening gloves again, and had resumed her campaign among the dahlias, when she was attacked in rear by the three little dogs, and emerged to find her daughter standing behind her, in, as Lady Kirwen soon found, as autocratic and uncompromising a mood as that of her sire had been. The Master's message was badly received.

" How kind he is! He just wants to get that mare tried! They told me in the yard this morning that the hounds were going out on Thursday, and that Jimmy was to ride Merrythought. *I* wanted to ride Merrythought. He goes better for me than anyone——"

(Patricia's fault was not self-depreciation, which is, after all, often a nuisance to other people.)

" Papa says he believes Jimmy's a very good man on a horse," said Lady Kirwen, mindful of the duty recently laid upon her.

" How does he know ? " struck in Patricia, and rushed on with her grievance. " So then I told Foley I'd ride Little Tim, and Foley said the Master had said Gilbert was to ride Little Tim, and he wouldn't let him ride the new mare as she'd buck him off. It's nothing to me how hard she bucks, but I don't believe she's ever seen hounds—I'll have to start *hours* before the others to keep out of their way. They've not had her out exercising—and she'll probably kick one—and then I shall be cursed in heaps and sent home! That's always the way with the Master. He gives you something with one hand, and while you're thanking him, he hits you over the head with the other! "

Lady Kirwen, unlike her family, was bored by horses, and during Patricia's complaint she had allowed herself to drift into reverie, from which, as Patsey's harangue ended, she came forth with a start, aware only that Sir Ingram had been the point of its peroration.

" I spoke to him about Paris," she began, apology in her tone. " I'm sorry to say he says it's quite impossible. You know the rents aren't being paid well, and then there was the wedding, and now there's my wretched tooth-business in Dublin—I'm going up to-morrow, you know—I don't know *what* it mayn't cost—and the man may keep me for ages; and there's any amount of other horrible things that there's *no* money for at present——"

Patricia gazed at her mother in a silence that was too full of anger to be resolved into words. Her face went red up to the bright curls that, obeying the decree of the fashion of the moment, lay on her forehead. Then she said:

"I'm one of them, I suppose!"

"One of what, darling?"

"Of the horrible things! Pity the Master didn't put me in a bucket of water before my eyes were open! It isn't fair to bring people into the world and then do nothing for them!"

"Dearest child, you shouldn't say that nothing is done for you. Papa always lets you have horses and dogs, and he lets you hunt, and—and——"

"And nothing else!" broke in Patsey. "Dog-boy, and rough-rider, and under-groom! That's all I am! Don't worry, Mother, I know you can't help it. Come on, you dogs, I'll take you out for a walk! That's my job! I may as well do that as I can't do anything else!"

The little dogs who, feeling themselves neglected, had been moodily coiled under the garden-seat, and had been even more bored than Lady Kirwen, burst forth at the summons, silencing her with their clamour, springing and snatching at Patsey's hand, that encouraged them of its own volition, in spite of its owner's pre-occupation with her wrongs.

Lady Kirwen watched Patricia swing in long strides along the garden path, as Sir Ingram had swung and stridden a few minutes before, and thought how alike they were in how many things. Patricia was tall, like him. "Fair, and foxy, and as fine a man as ever broke bread, God bless him!" was what the country-people said of Sir Ingram. And Patsey had taken after his side of the house, the Kirwens, whose eyes had been blue, and whose hair had been what the ladies of the family preferred to call auburn, ever since the world began.

There may be some who would find interest in hearing how this child of the 'eighties was dressed; if for nothing else, for the satisfaction of feeling how superior in all the qualities that matter is their own attire. (And this, as everyone knows, is a confidence that is imparted anew, yearly, with every change of fashion.) Therefore let it be recorded that on Patricia's head was what Fashion, at that period, was accustomed to call a "sailor-hat" (though why thus named was known to none, least of all to sailors). She wore a blue-and-white linen shirt, with a starched stand-up collar, and a black tie. Her skirt reached to her slender ankles, its waist measurement was, at most, twenty-one inches; it was made of coarse white homespun flannel; the blue-and-orange stripes of the "blazer" that she wore over it made as brilliant a note of colour as Lady Kirwen's dahlias themselves. Little Lady Kirwen, who was artistic, said to herself that Patsey always looked her best in blue, and it was ridiculous to say her hair was red.

"She's wasted here!" she thought, sitting in dejection on the garden-seat, forgetful of the weeds that were under-planting the dahlias, wishing that the small fortune that she had brought into the Kirwen family had not been imperceptibly absorbed into the Kirwenscourt Estate overdraft.

CHAPTER VII

MEANWHILE Patricia and the dogs had taken a short cut by jumping the sunk fence at the foot of Her Ladyship's Garden, and had gone on through a wild shrubbery of rhododendron and laurel to the wood that lay between the house and the head of the lake. The thought of the lake had come to her, with its promise of healing solitude. She told herself she would take the punt and paddle out into peace, and think things over.

There was no peace in the wood. She ran down the path to the boat-house attended by a maddening horde of flies, flies of the variety whose persecutions are hardest to bear, since they do not appear to wish to gratify any appetite save that for inflicting torment.

The punt was afloat, chained and padlocked to a post by the boat-house. Patricia extracted the key of the padlock from its theoretical hiding-place in the wall of the house; she loosed the punt, in which the dogs had already established themselves, and, getting in, pushed off from the little landing-place.

The punt swished through the reeds that nearly closed the channel from the backwater where the boat-house stood, to the open water of the lake, pressing down the water-lily leaves that made a green pavement under her keel. It was a very still, grey afternoon. The reflected hills broke in brown ripples on either side of the punt's round bows, the little white cottages on their lower skirts vanishing in the depths under her, to rise, shaken and wavering, but none the worse for their im-

C

mersion, as she passed on. The lake was a large one, four miles or more in length, and from one to two miles wide, and although Patricia could see, far off, the boats of fly-fishers, this end of the lake, round which lay her father's demesne, was, this peaceful afternoon, hers alone.

She shipped her oars, and shifting the stern cushions to the bottom of the boat, placed herself on as much of them as she was in time to wrest from the instant occupation of her dogs, and took a match-box from her pocket. Then, very carefully, from the pocket of the blue-and-orange coat she drew an envelope. There were two Virginian cigarettes in it, and with a feeling of luxurious freedom from molestation, she lit one of them and began to smoke.

"Good luck to Jimmy!" she said aloud. "The Master mightn't be quite so fond of him if he could see me now!"

She blew an exulting puff of smoke in the face of the nearest dog, and the nearest dog being Dooley, who never forgot that she was the eldest, and was disposed to stand upon her dignity, withdrew, sneezing, and in a huff, to the bow, and turned her back upon the rest of the party, implying that she was not amused.

Patricia lay on her back, and enjoyed her cigarette with zest that possibly owed something to the fact that in her father's eyes for a woman to smoke was an offence so heinous that he would no more have prohibited such a crime than he would have thought it necessary to forbid her to commit a murder.

The calm was complete. The thin smoke of the cigarette went up unwaveringly towards the low grey sky. Patsey watched a pair of gulls flying in from the sea to try their luck in fresh water, and sensed, with an inner and wordless self, the perfect grace of their stooping curves, while she pondered over the inconsistency of things. This smoking, for instance. Forbidden to Gilbert at school, winked at, in his case, at home; for her, an unpardonable sin. It was but another of the senseless limitations by which she had found herself hedged in ever since she had left the schoolroom. There, making every allowance for her three and a half years' seniority, she knew she had been a better man than Gilbert; year for year she had beaten him on all points; but now it seemed as if each year widened his freedom and narrowed hers, quite irrespective of their powers or capacities. Patricia was not the only girl who in those far back years was dashing herself against the bars of her cage, but she was certain—as, I suppose, are most sufferers from prejudice and injustice, especially those sufferers who are young—that in no cage were the bars so strong and so close together as in that which enclosed her, of which her father kept the key.

As she lay there, the boat resting quite still on the silk-smooth water, only moving when she, out of the restlessness of her mind, jerked herself this way or that on the cushions, she tried not to think of her father, or to let herself dwell on the point of view from which he regarded his female dependents. This was, after all, an abstraction, the point for her to consider was how to get out of her cage. She forgot her cigarette, and it went out; lost consciousness of the shimmering peace, the quiet loveliness that lay all round her. All the arbitrary prohibitions and hindrances that fate was using her sex to impose on her scourged her as with whips. Once, her mother, straying back from one of her mental rambles to actual things, had said, dreamily, that there were over-dogs and under-dogs, and it all came down to being a matter of muscle. Patsey had said, on fire in a moment, " I'm not an under-dog! And what has muscle to say to my going to Paris? " But to this enquiry Lady Kirwen had made no reply, since, having moved away in her mind, she was wandering in the Louvre, and remembering how she had always had neuralgia in picture galleries.

Dooley, sitting on high in the bows, had begun to repent of her huff, and to regret the cushions, of which she perceived her juniors had secured nearly entire possession. She therefore uttered a warbling and humorous yawn, that expressed a mixture of boredom and restored good temper.

Whatever might be Patricia's pre-occupation she was aware of the dogs and subservient to their wishes.

" Very well, then, we'll go home," she said aloud, in response to the yawn. She picked up the oars, and began to pull as if she were rowing a race, while her stinging thoughts kept pace with her like a swarm of wasps.

Jimmy Corran was standing on the boat-quay, with a gun on his shoulder, as Patricia arrived there.

" I thought I might have a try for a duck. I suppose you wouldn't like to paddle me down to the island? " He saw her flushed face. " I say! Perhaps you've had enough? You look as if you'd been going it! Why? "

" No reason at all," Patsey said, shortly. " I'm all right. Get in. Dogs, go home! "

The exhortation was not needed, as the three ladies, having sprung ashore, had already started at full gallop for home, remembering the servants' tea-hour.

Jimmy Corran, unlike the dogs, did not obey the order he had received. He made as if to hand her the gun.

" You hold the gun. I'll row."

Patricia was standing in the stern, keeping the boat's nose to the quay with one oar. She took no notice of the gun, and looked at him with a flash of the blue fire for which he had played.

" I suppose you think I can't? "

His answer was to step into the boat and seat himself on the aftermost thwart, picking up the other oar as he did so, and placing his gun on the bottom of the boat.

" Now then! Give me that oar! "

" I'll go ashore! "

Jimmy Corran, most of whose life had been spent at school and college in England, was not immune from the common weakness of those who know least of Ireland, the ambition to imitate the manner of speech of her peasants. Therefore he now said, sweetly, " Ah, sit down, little gerr'l, and give me th' oar! "

" I wouldn't try to talk in a brogue if I were you. People will think you're an Englishman! "

She was so well satisfied with this taunt that she didn't realise her cousin had pushed off, and the punt moved out with a suddenness that forced her to sit down. She handed him the other oar, and silently accepted the position of passenger, though not without a touch of the resentment that a hint of coercion ever roused in her. " If he thinks I'm going to talk to him, he's mistaken," she thought, looking away from him, sideways, down the lake, " I wish I had gone ashore with the dogs."

He was a strong rower, and the little punt soon cleared the reeds and was out in the open water, springing forward in successive bounds, smashing holes in the silky surface of the lake. Depression fell again on Patsey. In the silence her mind went back to her father's ultimatum. She hardly noticed that the punt was now out in the wide part of the lake, and that Jimmy had stopped rowing and was looking hard at her.

"Look here, what's the matter?"

"Everything!"

"Is it my fault? Have I done any——?"

Patricia cut him short. "No, of course not! I shouldn't care if you had!"

He began to laugh. "Your father's asked me to stay on for a bit and have some cubbing, and your mother said she hoped I would—*she's* always nice to me—I was wondering if you objected?"

Patsey said nothing.

He took out his cigarette-case and offered it to her. "Come on! Smoke the pipe of peace!"

She eyed him suspiciously. Was he patronising her? Condescending to the weaker vessel? Her nerves were all on edge, and the mood of indignation held her.

"No, thanks. As a matter of fact, I've one of yours in my pocket now."

"Well, keep it for an earlier opportunity and have another!"

He struck a match, and offered it, flaming, to her, with the open case. He had an engaging smile; his grey eyes asked for friendliness.

Patsey said to herself: "Well, it's not his fault. He can't help being a top-dog——"

She took a cigarette and lit it, and handed back the lighted match.

"That's more like it!" said Jimmy Corran, watching her. "Now, what's the row?"

Patricia looked at him doubtfully. She tried to decide if he would be stupid or understanding, mocking or sympathetic. Even if he mocked it would be a comfort to fight him and let loose something of what she was feeling. She blew two or three whiffs of the cigarette. Then she said, doggedly, " I want to go to Paris."

" Paris? What on earth for? I've been there once. I thought it was a dull hole."

" I don't care how dull it is. I want to paint."

" Well, can't you paint here? "

He looked across the polished levels of the lake to the west. The clouds had broken and were setting the stage for the sunset. A saffron glow was flowing down through a long slit in the grey heaven, hanging like a veil of pale fire across the end of the lake, touching here and there a narrow path along the water toward the boat.

" You won't see anything in Paris to beat that."

" You don't understand, Jimmy," Patricia said, wearily. " It's to be *able* to paint that—and heaps of other things——"

" Well, then, what's stopping you? Why don't you go? "

It was the question of one who knew no limitations. Its innocence, or ignorance, touched Patricia's sense of humour. She looked at him almost compassionately.

" It's easy to see you're a man! "

" So I had supposed, but why specially now? "

She paused before replying. She thought of his freedom, his strength, his money, his power to order his life as he chose.

" Because when you want a thing most awfully you've only to stretch out your hand and take it. There's no one to put handcuffs on you! "

Her voice shook a little, and she turned her head away so that he should not see the unshed tears that had started to her eyes, the quick tears that betray a high-strung temperament, and are provoked as easily by anger as by grief.

She smoked fiercely for a few moments, and Jimmy Corran felt a warm gush of what he told himself was pity flood his soul. What hard luck! . . . Why shouldn't she do what she wanted? . . . That old bully of a father of hers! . . . He felt a tremendous wish to comfort her—just to sit there in the stern beside her (there wouldn't be much room, but that wouldn't matter)—and put a frankly cousinly arm round her, and tell her what happiness it would give him to be able to help her. Would it be safe (he wondered) just to lean forward and take her hand? He had decided that he would take the risk, but at that moment she turned towards him again, and, by Jove, how lovely she was, with the western light in her face, and her eyes like, yes, like blue stars! Why hadn't he taken her hand? (Which was something of a *non sequitur*, yet not entirely.)

The cigarette had brought appeasement, and had given just the touch of occupation and distraction that she needed to steady her.

" Fancy what the Master would say if he saw me smoking! " she said, with a laugh that was a little strained. " You'd catch it almost as much as I should! I wonder what he thinks girls were created for? To be told not to, I suppose, no matter what they want to do! "

" But look here," said Jimmy, picking up the oars and beginning to row (feeling that the moment for pity and consolation had passed, but, please God, it would come again). " Go on about Paris. What's the difficulty? Is it want of money that's stopping you? "

" Why, of course it is! The Master says he can't afford it. If I were Gilbert—a boy—he'd afford it fast enough! "

They had by this time nearly reached the little

island, a dark green thicket of laurels, furze and arbutus, mounted on a low cliff of limestone. Pale, isolated boulders, outliers from the island, were dotted about in the shallows, mauve-grey above water, topaz-brown when one saw them through the brown lake water. As the boat drew in to the shore a couple of wild duck rose with low quackings from a mass of reeds, out of range. Jimmy put up his hands, and followed them with an imaginary gun as they flew fast and straight across the island and down the lake.

" Lost those lads! Never mind, they're not the only ones! I'll get ashore now." He stood up. " See here, Patsey, if it's only rotten money that's stopping you—I've got money to burn—honour bright I have! Let me lend you what'll see you through—I'm your cousin, you know! I told you that the first day I met you, but I believe you've forgotten it! No—shut up! I won't argue. I'm going ashore. You go and stir up some more of those blooming ducks out of the reeds back there and put 'em over the island to me——"

He picked up his gun and stepped from the punt on to a rock; then, with the sure lightness and poise of a dog, he leaped from one boulder to another until he reached the shore. He climbed up the low cliff and moved on, looking for an opening in the bushes.

Patricia had waited to make her protest until he was safely on shore, but words had failed her until the moment when the bushes were closing behind him. Then she called after him :

" Nonsense, Jimmy! You know that's impossible! Out of the question—of course I couldn't't——"

From the green depths of the thicket came the monosyllable, unmeaning, ugly, yet dear to youth, seemingly indispensable: " Rot! "

CHAPTER VIII

It would seem, sometimes, as though ideas and aspirations were air-borne—like the microbes of those diseases that are specially favoured by that Power of Darkness who is, we are told, Prince of the Power of the Air—and develop simultaneously and without contact in various bosoms.

Patricia Kirwen, from the time that she was able to clutch a pencil in her infant fist and scribble over her picture-books, through childhood, and youth in the organ-loft (where all the hymnals were enriched with portraits of the clergy), up to her present age of twenty years, had never wavered in her resolve to express herself in terms of paint. And now, young George Lester, destined by his father for the Irish Church, had spent his summer vacation in systematic avoidance of his theological studies, and in passionate struggles in portraiture and landscape in the exciting and intractable medium of water-colours, alternating these efforts with the poaching excursions that he found almost as exciting, and far less of a strain than Art.

The hardy microbe of Revolt, carried by viewless currents across the gulf fixed by convention between young George and Patricia, had established itself in both their youthful breasts in direct conjunction with the equally vigorous and inveterate microbe of Art. The encounter in the Ring of the Nine Stony Gerr'ls had brought about a crisis in young George's development. " She said I had talent! " he told himself, gazing at his summer's work, pinned round the walls of his attic bedroom, trying to see the best in it, condoning its faults, assuring himself that he would do better next time, that he now saw exactly where he had gone wrong. Then she had said he should " Take it up seriously!" What could she have meant by that? Those caricatures maybe? Was it that they were too joking-like? Yet they were what she had seemed to like best. She hadn't minded the thing of Sir Ingram at all. Wasn't it a mercy she had taken it so well? The eyes that she had turned on him! Young George Lester's head swam, and something inside him—his heart, he supposed—seemed to turn over and melt when he thought of how he had, for one wonderful instant, looked intensely into her eyes and held that lovely glance in his. " I'll meet her again, somehow," he told himself. " I might find out then what she meant—she'll not mind me asking her. There's no—no——" he cast about for a phrase that should express his feeling, and remembered one he had read in the *Templenoe Observer* last week—" no 'aristocratic hoity-toity-ness' about her! Yes! That was it! Not a bit of it at all she had!"

He swept over the leaves of his sketch-book until he came to the page that had led to so abrupt a closure of the exhibition. He stared at the heads that covered it, analysing them, pointing out to himself their faults, their hopeless inadequacy. He shut his eyes and saw Patricia's face as he had seen it last, up on the top of Slieveroe, at the Ring of the Stony Girls. He could see it quite clearly; she was stooping over his book, she was like a rose in shadow, she had an aureole like a saint from the sun behind her shining through her hair, and the blue sky for a background—oh, if he could paint that! He opened his eyes and looked from the picture in his mind to those on the page. " I'll do better next time," he said aloud. He tore the leaf from the book, and striking a match, set alight the corner of the page and held it, watching it curl and twist as it burnt, until only a little triangle of paper remained. The rest was in crisp ashes on the floor at his feet. He had held the page face downwards while it burned away. It hurt him to destroy his work, but he held himself to his intention. It was a sacrifice, a burnt-offering. " When I saw her again, I knew they weren't worthy of her. Never mind! I'll try again——" Then he groaned. How could he hope to do better without teaching? What chance had he? he asked himself. He felt as though he were walking between two high walls of rock, that led, inevitably, to a dreaded future, a future for which he knew himself to be supremely unsuited. Yet he could not turn and go back, because behind him there was an all-powerful being, armed with what George visualised as a thick stick. (But this was inadequate as an allegorical representation of his father, because Holy George's weapon was more potent than any stick, however thick, being the key of the money-box.)

" Geor-gee! "

A faint cry reached him from, as it were, another world, his mother's voice, calling him from vision to the reality of high-tea.

" Come down, dear, to your supper! Father's in and waiting——"

George put away his drawing-book, with another groan that expressed in some degree his resentment with life in general and his father in particular, and went down the steep and narrow farm-house staircase to the room, known as the parlour, in which the family meals were eaten, and, speaking generally, the family life was lived.

This particular parlour was the pattern of many such in Irish farm-houses of the better type. It possessed two windows, many degrees too small in proportion to the wall-space. Between the windows was a venerable table-piano, now practically dumb and toothless, but still serving its country and working its passage in the capacity of sideboard (as an old hunter will end his days doing farm work). On it were displayed an ornate electro-plate tea-pot, flanked by its vassal vessels, urn, cream-jug, and sugar-basin; on one side of these was an enormous Bible, of the type that is described as a Family Bible and is dedicated to voluminous family records; on the other was a ragged stack of old music, thrown in—perhaps it may be more accurately said thrown out—with the piano, at the auction where it was purchased by Mrs. Lester. Facing the piano, at the opposite side of the room, was a mahogany cupboard with a mirror-back. At the farther end of the room a small and shabby writing-table shared the available space with a black horsehair-covered sofa, that had the air of defying anyone to have the temerity to sit on it, a challenge which, to judge by its austere polish, had never been accepted. On the ginger-brown walls were a print of " The Choristers," a highly coloured advertisement Farming Calendar of the previous year, and two woolly enlarged photographs, in florid German gilt frames, of the Master and Mistress of the house. Lesser photographs, in various stages of decay, were disposed on the mantelshelf in decorative support of a black marble clock, and on either side of the small fireplace were two aged armchairs, very much the worse for wear, that suggested a pair of dilapidated tramps squatted beside the smouldering turf fire. Probably a stranger would, before noticing these details, have been struck by a peculiar, dull, and disagreeable odour that pervaded the room; this was provided by goat-skins, which lay, like islands, on the floor, at intervals dictated by worn spots in the underlying drugget.

In the middle of the room was a large dinner-table, and at the end of the table, facing the door, Mr. Lester was standing when his son came into the room.

Mr. George Lester, senior (commonly called Holy George, owing to his adoption, in middle life, of a form of extreme, even aggressive Protestantism, after a youth not distinguished for piety), was a shortish, strongly built man with a large nose, a thick grizzled beard, and a dictatorial voice of that variety of high tenor that can express disapproval with peculiar poignancy.

This gift was apparent in his greeting to his son.

" Come on, George, come on! What's keeping you? Here I am waiting on you to say grace."

" You could begin without me," George replied to his father, sulkily.

" And leave you eat your food like a heathen, I suppose! " returned Mr. Lester, proceeding, without drawing breath, to a prolonged sanctification of the coming strong tea, soda bread, and boiled eggs.

During the observance young George remained standing, very erect, with an unbowed head, as a gesture of protest. Mrs. Lester's head was suitably bent, but she looked up from under her brows from son to father, and as she seated herself on the iron-hard, horse-hair-covered seat of her chair, she broke into instant conversation as if to prevent a resumption of hostilities.

" When I was in town this morning," she began, while she poured out and passed to her family large cups of a liquid resembling in colour and quality liniment of iodine, lightly tinged with milk, and seething with soft sugar, " I met Mrs. Morrissey in at the Medical Hall. She told me the doctor was after being sent for to Kirwenscourt, Master Kirwen wasn't at all well. Casting off his stomach all night they said he was."

" That'll do him no harm," young George commented sardonically. " I expect it was owing to him, after the cake I saw him eat at the wedding! "

" I suppose it was more of it the child got," responded Mrs. Lester. " The doctor said Sir Ingram was only laughing at him and told him he should be pulled out of bed to go hunting to-morrow, no matter what way he was! "

Holy George looked up from his egg.

" Did you post that letter of mine yesterday, Minnie? " he said to his daughter, a fat little girl of about twelve years of age, who had been applying herself to her supper in a silence inspired partly by hunger, and partly by a just appreciation of her father's mood. Her round cheeks now turned a deep crimson.

" I—I posted it this morning going to school, Father," she faltered.

" On earth what good it is me to give an order to any one of you I don't know! " exclaimed Holy George, in a single indignant breath, his small bright black eyes looking like vindictive boot-buttons as he directed his gaze at his erring child, while a dripping spoonful of egg was arrested in mid-transit, as though his arm were paralysed by shock. " What good is it, I'd like to know, to teach you the Gospel command ' Honour your father and mother,' when you think no more of me telling you a thing than the dog? "

Minnie, feeling herself unable to reply effectively to this enquiry, and feeling that it was advisable, if possible, to introduce a fresh subject, withdrew her round brown eyes from the encounter with the reproving boot-buttons, and fixed them lower down on her father's face.

" There's the track of the egg on your beard, Father," she suggested, in a light conversational manner, which was, unfortunately, taken by Mr. Lester to be intended for what he called " impidence."

" And what is it to you if I have? " he demanded. " Isn't it enough for you to forget my orders and to leave an important letter lying in your pawket, without giving me impidence into the bargain, and taunting me with what doesn't concern you? "

He pulled a large bandanna pocket-handkerchief out of his pocket and scrubbed his beard fiercely, his eyes still searching Minnie's countenance for a hint of the crime of which he accused her.

" The child meant no harm, George," put in Mrs. Lester, quickly, " and she was greatly upset about the letter."

Her mother's defence of her unnerved Minnie, causing her to realise the pathos of her position, full of good feeling and repentance, yet misunderstood and unforgiven. She burst into tears, and, rushing from the room, pounded upstairs to her own bedroom overhead, where she could be heard sobbing loudly, and stamping on the floor between the sobs.

" That's temper! " said her father, with the satisfaction of one who has proved his case. " Annie, I beg you'll go up presently and point out to her that it is better to rule her spirit than to leap over a wall—no—I mean to take a city—— What are you laughing at, sir? ' He turned angrily on his son.

" Oh, nothing, sir," said George, " I was only thinking Minnie wasn't very likely to want to do either, so it wouldn't be much of an inducement." He pushed back his chair. " I have enough eaten, Mother. I'm going out. You might leave a drop o' milk on the dresser for me—I'll get it when I come in——"

His father watched him as he left the room. His expression was hostile, but he said nothing. He pushed his cup and saucer over to his wife to be refilled, and rising from his place took it from her, and walking to the fireplace drove it in among the photographs on the chimney-piece while he filled his pipe. Then, without turning to Mrs. Lester, he began to speak.

" 'Tis an extremely annoying thing about that letter. I wouldn't be surprised if I had trouble over it—yes, and bad trouble too."

" Is it the letter Minnie didn't post till to-day, George? " Mrs. Lester asked, leaving the table and bringing a work-basket with her to the fireplace. " What was there that was so important in it? "

Mr. Lester sat down and stirred up his pipe and kicked the sullen sods of turf in the fire. He disliked a direct question.

" 'Tis possible you mayn't be aware, Annie, that before a man puts down poison on his land—his own land, mind you—he has to give public warning to that effect? "

He paused, and pulled at his pipe with loud smacks, and Mrs. Lester, who was stout, careworn, and affectionate, and considered that her own province of the kingdom of home gave her quite enough to do, replied, " Well, indeed, George, I never thought about it at all."

Holy George, nodding his head at this confirmation of his low opinion of the female sex, resumed.

" I have an adver-tisement in the *Observer* this week, stating that I have poison laid on my land in Derry-goole, but that'll not be out till to-morrow——"

" But, George," Mrs. Lester looked at her husband, while she bit the end of a piece of cotton preparatory to threading her needle, " what harm was it the child above not posting the letter? "

" I'd be thankful, Annie, if you'd not interrupt me," said Mr. Lester, who, as an occasional lay-preacher at a Methodist chapel (with which—despite his membership of the Church of Ireland—he had what may be described as a flirtatious connection), was unaccustomed to interruption, save possibly an appreciative groan; " I'm coming to that in good time."

It was, perhaps, in order to give his wife a lesson in patience, or it may have been a device of artistry to stimulate her interest, that Holy George here paused in his narration, and again having recourse to his handkerchief, filled the pause with a long and mournful blast on his nose.

Mrs. Lester threaded her needle, and applied herself so contentedly to her sewing that the artist in Mr. Lester began to fear that the device had failed of its effect, and that a change of method was advisable. He stood up, and looking down at her industriously bowed head, said portentously:

" That letter Minnie is after forgetting to post was to warn Sir Ingram Kirwen that there is poison laid outside the wood. I heard yesterday that his hounds would be in it to-morrow morning, and I wrote at once. That letter won't get to Kirwenscourt now till after they're started. And there, you may say, is the end of me getting the bit of mountain I asked him for—and my lease, maybe, refused renewing——"

Mrs. Lester's scissors clattered into the fender, and she let her work and her hands fall on to her lap. Her large brown eyes expressed to the full the consternation for which Mr. Lester had, so to speak, put his cards on the table.

" If the hounds go in that wood," he continued, with a confirmatory nod at each word, " in the morning they'll all be dead corpses! Like the Assyrians," he added, meditatively, " but it won't be the Angel of the Lord that smote them, only the dead sheep that I have there, filled up with strychnine! "

" George! " Mrs. Lester gasped. " Can't you stop them going in it? "

" How can I stop them and it nine o'clock now, and they starting at five o'clock in the morning, or maybe four? It was the letter was to stop them," replied Mr. Lester, almost with triumph, so complete was his case against his daughter.

Mrs. Lester gazed fixedly at her husband for a full half-minute before she spoke.

" Why, then, they *shall* be stopped! " she declared. " If I have to stop them myself! "

" Ah, what nonsense you're saying! How would you get to Derrygoole Wood by four in the morning, and it a good six miles from here? "

" If it was no more than for the sake of them poor hounds alone I'd walk all night! " said Mrs. Lester, undauntedly. " But I'll not do that (for all they say the fox never sent a better messenger than himself)—no! But I'll send Georgie! Georgie will ride there on his bike! And if Sir Ingram doesn't treat us fair after that, there's no gratitude left in the Race of Man! "

CHAPTER IX

YOUNG George Lester had very often had more disagreeable things to do than the mission with which his mother had entrusted him. It was the fourth of September, the hour was half-past four o'clock of a very still morning, and the dim and all-pervading greyness that is like a whisper in the air, foretelling the dawn, part hiding, part revealing, appealed to his imagination and turned his errand into an adventure. George was a Romantic, and he found something at once mysterious and stimulating in gliding, swift and noiseless, along the smooth bog-road by the lake, with all the world asleep round him, himself alone intensely alive, riding against time to avert a peril.

A white mist hung low over the water. The reeds, on one side of the road, and the drifts of bracken on the other, that had spread downwards, linking mountain with lake, were netted with gossamer. Here and there the glistening threads had spanned the narrow road; George thought, as he broke through them, of how he had broken the tape when he won the mile at the College sports, and felt that the omen was good; to-day, also, he was going to win.

He saw no moving, living thing, except once a coot, that sped from the bracken to the reeds, nearly under his wheel, and once a cormorant, that rose near the shore of the lake through the mist, and sped in strong direct flight down a long valley toward the distant sea. He rounded the end of the lake, where was a rough stone quay, with a boat, piled high with peat, lying off it, and then the road turned away from water and mountain, and took a line through grassfields and cornfields and patches of potato " garden," that had as yet hardly more colour than a black and white engraving. But the light was growing, and presently he could see Derrygoole Wood, a blotch of darkness on the grey horizon. In a farm a cock crowed. Very far away behind him, on the farther side of Lough Eskaheen, he heard, faintly, cur-dogs barking.

" That's the hounds," he said to himself. " They're coming the southern road. I'll meet them at the cross-roads."

He rode on at speed. The wood soon became black and definite, and in very few minutes he had reached its scattered outposts of Scotch firs. The road George was on ran along the eastern bounds of the wood, and met the southern road about mid-way of its expanse. At this point the two roads became one, which, cutting across the depth of the wood, went on to the west.

Under the deep September shadow of the trees George could see nothing. His father was tenant of a farm that adjoined the wood on its southern frontier, and part of the covert went with the farm, giving certain rights of cutting litter and of shelter for cattle. George knew the wood well. He had often met the hounds here and run with them on foot; on one of the rare occasions when his father let him have one of the farm-horses that could jump, he had had a good hunt out of it, and he had shot woodcock in it many times, without very scrupulous attention to the fact that among his father's rights shooting was not included.

In this the southern side of the wood was the way-in usually taken by the hounds, and he knew that it was at this side that the poison had been laid. He rode on a little way past the junction of the roads and went for a short distance along the road until he came to the gate into the wood. Then he got off his bicycle, and resting it against the gate, he climbed on to the fence facing it, and sat there to wait for the hounds.

" A beastly job I have! " he thought. " Old Johnny Ryan'll be raging mad, and God knows what the Master will do to me! . . ."

He lit a cigarette and considered the position. Would Miss Kirwen be out? he wondered. . . . Wasn't it a queer thing that she and he had the same tastes, Painting and Hunting, Art and Sport? . . . He might never have the chance to meet her again, let alone speak to her, friendly as he'd found her. . . . Well, that was the difference of it, he supposed, trying to regard the question of Class Divergence with philosophy. He heaved a sigh, partly genuine, partly artificial, as being demanded by the occasion. George was twenty-two, and, as has been said, a Romantic, and this, obviously, was a suitable moment for a sigh.

And just then something crept over the fence of the wood just above the gate where his bicycle stood, a small animal that moved very slowly and lay down in the middle of the road.

George stiffened like a terrier, staring hard.

" A fox, by Jingo! " he thought. " Dead to the world! " Then, in horror, " God! It's poisoned! "

The little fox, a cub, lay on its side; slight convulsive movements shook it for a few instants, then they ceased, and it was still.

" Dead! " said George aloud, his heart falling like a stone. " What the hell am I to do now? "

He went over to the cub and touched it gently with

his foot. There was a little foam on its clenched jaws. It was dead.

" Poor little beggar! " said George. " But maybe it's as good for you to die that way as another! I d'no which I'd rather myself—I'd take the chances of a run, I think! "

As he stood there pondering over the complicated question of sport, forgetful, for the moment, of his mission, he heard in the stillness the distant very faint sound of a horse coming towards the wood along the southern road.

" It can't be the hounds yet," he thought. " It's some fellow coming to the meet. I'd best send him back to stop them——"

He walked quickly out of the shadow and down the road past the spot where the two roads joined. The horseman was still little more than a speck, and it was two or three minutes before he discovered that the rider was a lady, and that the chance to speak to Miss Kirwen again had come sooner than he had expected. He stood in the middle of the road and held up his hand. His heart was thumping so hard that it seemed to him he would not be able to make his voice steady.

" Wait a moment, please! " he called to her.

He could see her face clearly now. She pulled in her horse beside him.

" What's the matter?—Oh, it's *you*—Mr. Lester, isn't it? "

" Miss Kirwen," began George, in his shaking voice and his respectable Protestant brogue, " I beg your pawdon, but—but——"

" What is it? What do you want? "

George cleared his throat. He was very pale. ("What's

the matter with him? " Patricia thought. " He looks as if he had seen a ghost! ")

" The wood's poisoned! " said George, hoarsely. " I'm after meeting a dead fox on the road——" He caught his breath, and put a hand on Patricia's mare's withers to steady himself. He said to himself that it was meeting her suddenly like this and having such a beastly thing to tell her that made him act like a fool this way.

" What are you saying? A fox poisoned? " Patricia stared at him, aghast.

" Me fawther wrote to warn Sir Ingram," George went on, hurriedly, " but the letter wasn't posted in time——"

" We must stop them at once," Patricia said, her mind racing. She thought of her father, and saw, as if in a mirror, his arm swing up, and his hunting-crop come down on the head of the bearer of this ill-tidings. " The Master would kill him dead! " And hard on the heels of the thought came bitter disappointment. No other covert near—the puppies out for the first time—Jimmy mad keen for the gallop she had promised him. (Hadn't she squared Johnny Ryan and Mick, the whip, not to stop the hounds if by a stroke of luck they got away with an old fox?)

" Your father ought to be ashamed of himself! " She hurled it at George. Yes! The Master would be justified in killing him on the spot.

" Would *you* go back and tell the Master? " said the wretched George. " I think I should go and throw the dead fox some place it wouldn't be found——"

But he did not move. Patricia was gazing, not so much into his eyes, as through them (" out through the back of me head! " he thought subsequently), and, as he stood, riveted by her gaze, he saw a spark rise in those blue eyes that he could never have dared to dream would ever thus be lost in his.

He did not know that at that moment the devil had entered into Miss Kirwen.

Patricia began to laugh.

" Look here! Have you got a bit of string? Quick!—Think! " she adjured him. The words hit him like bullets from a revolver.

" I don't know—I don't think so," he stammered, in bewilderment for which he might be forgiven. " But—yes! I wouldn't say but I have a fishing-line in the tool-bag on me bike—I'm not sure——"

" Where's the fox? " Patricia cut in on the heel of his hesitations.

" Back there on the road through the wood——"

" Show me where it is! "

" This way," said George, swinging round, and setting off for the wood, running his hardest.

Patricia struck the mare, who, made angry by the blow, caught up to the runner in a few plunging bounds and ramped beside him, pulling hard, till they came to the place where the dead fox lay.

" Listen! " Patricia said, swiftly. " I'm going to run a drag with that fox! Tie your line to my thong, and then tie it round the fox's neck—and tie it tight—and oh, for goodness' sake, hurry! "

George thanked Heaven, with a piety worthy of his father, for that bit of fishing tackle in his tool-bag. He was a handy man with his fingers, and in less than two minutes he had cut off a long length of line, had made it fast round the neck of the fox, had doubled it, and tied it to the thong of Patricia's crop.

" Well done! Well done! " she said, breathlessly. " Now, when I get away, you stand here till you see the hounds, and then holloa—yell! Just yell as hard as you can! They'll go to you, and then you cheer them on after me before they can be stopped! I'll start a little higher up. Come on! Bring your bicycle! Get on, mare!"

She started at a trot, and stopped about twenty yards farther on. George had begun to enter into the spirit of the game, much strengthened by the undreamed-of glory of such conspiracy. He snatched his bicycle and followed her. She flung him his orders. She told him when he had laid on the hounds he was to ride "like blazes" (yes, like blazes, she had said! Even in that tense moment George felt this was comradeship indeed!) for the turf-quay at the corner of the lake. "I'll go round outside the wood—I'll meet you there, and you must be ready to chuck the drag into the lake, and I'll whip the hounds back. D'you understand?"

"But won't they see you? It's open country!"

"I'll chance that—I've a good start—this mare's fast, and they're a good bit behind still——" She looked radiantly at the confederate. "There'll be the father and mother of a row if I'm caught!" she said, with ecstasy. "What a spree! Mind you do what I tell you! Give me the fox! Now for it—good-bye!"

She dropped the fox, and galloped away up the road through the wood, the fox's body dragging and bouncing behind her, like a dinghy in a heavy sea behind a racing yacht.

During the seven or eight minutes that then passed over George's head it seemed to him as if suspense were turning his hair white. At last the jogging jingle, the admonitions, and the whip-crackings that tell of the approach of a pack of hounds, came to his straining ears. They came in sight; the scarlet of the men's coats glowing in the dull light under the trees, the hounds a twinkling shifting crowd about the horses' feet, with the young entry, to whom a certain indulgence was extended, frisking frivolously around their elders.

George's breath was coming short. He said to himself with solemn intensity, " I'll not fail her! " He waited till the leading hounds were within fifty yards of him, then he took off his cap and began to holloa.

He was almost frightened by his success. The hounds swept down on him like a storm, old and young with equal enthusiasm, full of the joy of their first day in the field, and entirely resolved on accepting any pretext for enjoying themselves. George capped them up the road on to the line with screams that drowned the curses of Johnny Ryan, and the roars and whip-crackings of Mick, the whipper-in. Let them curse him as much as they liked—he had not failed her!

He was on his bicycle and away down the road by which he had come, riding " like blazes," to keep tryst with her, before the Master and the few riders with him had reached the wood, while Johnny Ryan and Mick, finding it beyond their power to stop the rejoicing pack, and seeing that the miscreant who had started them had escaped, saw nothing better to do than to set spurs to their horses and to thunder away after the hounds.

What Sir Ingram, a person, even in his calmer moments, of emphatic diction, said, on this alteration of his programme, need not be particularised. Jimmy Dangan, who had no cut-and-dried theories on the subject of cubbing, caught up his reins, and remarking to the world at large that this was what he called a good egg, gave his horse a stab of the spurs, and set off at full speed in pursuit of the disappearing forms of Johnny Ryan and his underling.

CHAPTER X

WHILE her accomplice, full of glory, was spinning along the road, *en route* for the turf-quay, Patricia was discovering that the job she had undertaken so light-heartedly, at (it may be remembered) the instigation of the devil, was very far from being an easy one. She knew the country, not intimately, but, she thought, sufficiently. The course on which she had determined was to skirt the farther side of the wood, taking it right-handed, and then to make her way as best she might for the turf-quay at the corner of the lake.

" About three miles in it, and all grass," she thought, as she galloped up the muddy road. " That ought to suit Jimmy very well—if only it will suit me and Miss Keating! "

She had left home very early that morning—in order to keep clear of the hounds—with the brown mare (now, in compliment to her former owner, known in the stables as Miss Keating), whose views in regard to them were as yet undefined. She was clear enough of them now, Patsey thought, but could she keep her lead?

An open cattle gap into a big grassfield, at the western end of the wood on the right, was encouraging, and was helpfully followed by a succession of similar gaps in the next few fields, that told of the mild ramblings of the dairy cows that were now rousing themselves from repose to stare at her. But although the going was good, it was not the only point to be considered. It had soon been evident that the drag was causing the youthful Miss Keating considerable anxiety. She felt herself being pursued by a mysterious creature that followed close behind her in uneven leaps, and from which, gallop as she might, it was impossible to escape. She was a big strong young mare, and, once or twice, when the pursuing thing, checked by some obstacle, bounded into the air and all but struck her quarters, it was well for Patsey that she had a mouth so light that she yielded to the restraint imposed by no more than a large ring-snaffle and a martingale. Fortunately, also, George had allowed a fairly long tow-rope, but the strain on Patsey's arm was heavy, and it is little to say that she shared the anxieties of Miss Keating with regard to the drag, if from a different angle.

The first jump they came to was a low wall, lightly built of single stones. Had it been a five-barred gate, Miss Keating, who was by now feeling seriously alarmed, would still have cleared it with a foot to spare. The fox's little body whizzed through the air behind her taut on the tow-line, clearing the wall as effectively as the mare herself. Some low banks and another " stone gap " or two followed, and after each jump Miss Keating's agitation became more acute, and her resolve to fly at full speed from the pursuer became more fixed. A marshy field, in which the going was heavy, presented to her rider a chance of checking the mare, who was now rapidly becoming uncontrollable from terror, and Patsey succeeded, though not without considerable difficulty, in stopping her before the next fence, a tall bank blind with bracken and briars, was arrived at. Thankful for a moment of respite, Patsey looked about her, hastily taking stock of her position. Things might be worse, she thought. The lake was now in sight, not more than about three-quarters of a mile away, and there was no sign as yet of the hounds.

"I'll give them a check," she said, hauling in the line until the cub, which was not very much larger than a good-sized cat, was in her hand. It was coated with mud. "The wretched little thing's getting heavier and heavier every moment," she said to herself; "it's a harder job than I thought. I wonder if I were a fool to——" She stopped suddenly, and her heart gave a shattering jump. Surely that tiny musical thrill in the air was the cry of the hounds! "If the Master catches me he'll leather the life out o' me!—and I wouldn't blame him!" she added. She laughed. The touch of danger restored her self-confidence. She tucked the muddy little body under her arm, and with a kick and a shout set the mare at the bank. But the check had had a damping effect on Miss Keating's spirits. She charged the bank with an apparently good heart, but her nerves were shaken, and at the last moment she swung off to the near side, and Pat, hampered by the fox and its harnessing, could not keep her straight. She dragged her back, the mare prancing and showing temper, and was about to send her again at the bank, when the drag slipped from under her arm and fell on the ground. Feverishly she pulled the excited mare to a stand, and gathered up the loops of fishing-line. She had just secured the little muddy drag again, and was setting the mare's head straight for the jump a second time, when a figure sprang into view on the top of the bank.

Miss Keating's shaken nerves caused her to greet this appearance with a deep curtsey, followed by what was the next thing to a buck, but an angel from heaven would have been far less rapturously greeted by Patricia than was young George Lester.

"Oh, thank Heaven you've come! Take this beastly thing over the fence for me—the mare's refusing——"

George leaped off the bank.

"I'll run it for you down to the lake," he said, quickly, "I saw you coming—I can do it easy——" He was detaching her thong and crop from the drag while he spoke. "I'm used to cross-country running."

In the fields behind them they heard a man's voice shouting.

"What's that?" gasped Patsey.

"Only a chap driving cows——" He checked himself. "Listen! Isn't that——?"

Faintly, and still far away, but unmistakably, came the cry of the hounds.

George snatched up the drag and was over the bank as easily as a hound, Patsey's incoherent gratitude following him as he started across the ensuing field at a run, swift and steady, the drag following with a docility that it had not hitherto displayed.

"Now, my lady!" said Pat, vindictively, setting her teeth, and delivering with her crop and doubled thong a whack comparable to a blow from an umbrella, alarming and humiliating, if comparatively painless. Miss Keating, in suitable recognition, sprang with kangaroo agility off her hind legs, and executed a heraldic flourish in the air, then, dashing at the bank, with head up and ears pricked, she sailed from field to field without as much as a kick back at it.

Pat sat down in her saddle, enjoying herself for the first time, and telling Miss Keating what she thought of her. Then she ranged up alongside of the runner.

"Sure you can do it?"

"Rather!" George threw back over his shoulder, his fear of her forgotten in the joy of effort.

He was a fine runner, and made no more of the banks than did Miss Keating, who, her fears now composed, had steadied, and was jumping perfectly, and as if, as was indeed the case, she loved it.

" They're coming on! " Patsey called to George. " The hounds sound much nearer, and I can see a couple of horses far back! "

" Righto! " said George, " I'll put it on a bit! "

He quickened his pace, his long even strides lengthening with a superb ease.

" Oh, well run! " Patsey, cantering smoothly, quit of the drag, encouraged him. " If you can only keep it up, we'll do it! "

George laughed. Keep it up! He would run like this all day—with her beside him!

" There's the turf-quay! " he called in a few more moments, checking for an instant on the top of a bank. " There's only one more field to the road now——"

In another three minutes they had reached the quay.

" Have I time to run it about the reeds a bit? "

Patsey looked behind her. The two leading horses were still half a mile away, a third was not far behind them, the hounds, thanks to the brief check, about midway between the confederates and the coming avengers.

" Yes, I think so—but be quick! "

She watched George with growing approval and admiration, as he splashed to and fro among the reeds and sedge.

" He knows what he's about! " she thought. Then she saw him run to the quay. He dragged a flat stone from its wall and tied the string of the drag round it, binding it to the small wet bundle of fur which was all that now remained of the ill-fated little fox. Then clambering out to the end of the quay, he hurled the weighted body far out into deep water. It went down with a splash.

Pat drew a long breath.

That was that, anyhow! But now what should she do?

" Miss Kirwen," said George, hurriedly, " the best thing you can do is to ride back along the road to the wood and follow them up. Please give Sir Ingram me father's message. I'll get away home—the hounds'd wind the odour of the fox on me, maybe! "

He tore his bicycle out of the ditch where he had left it, and whirled away at full speed as the leading hounds topped the last fence but one before the road.

Patricia had scant time for consideration, and decided without delay that the advice her fellow-conspirator had flung to her could not be bettered. A thin fringe of alders shut off, to some extent, the fields she had just crossed, but she knew that in another half-dozen seconds the hounds would be on the quay. " That check didn't hold them long enough," she thought, peering between the stems of the alders, " I'd better go——"

The two hunt servants were now crossing the fence next behind the hounds; the third rider had improved his position and was near enough for Patricia to recognise Merrythought's white face as he rose to the bank which the two red coats had just jumped.

" Jimmy's safe enough! Even if he knew, he wouldn't care! "

This comforting reflection, however, could by no stretch of imagination be applied to her father, who might, for all she knew, be following the others. Shielded by the fringe of alders, she started at a fast trot along the road which George Lester had recommended. She was about half-way to the wood when she saw a few riders coming towards her at a gallop. She pulled up to a walk, and in a very few seconds she recognised that Sir Ingram was heading the charge.

" The Wars! The bloody Wars! " thought Patsey, who had learned from Johnny Ryan some phrases useful in emergencies. " Here's the Master! Now for it! "

She moved Miss Keating to the side of the road and pulled up.

In a very few thundering strides the Master's huge chestnut horse was being dragged to a standstill beside her.

" What have you been at? Where are the hounds? " shouted Sir Ingram, his face much the same purple-crimson hue as the old red coat that he kept for cubbing.

" I heard them a few minutes ago—down near the lake," replied Patsey, steadily, though she could not disguise from herself that she was frightened.

" Then what are you coming this way for? "

Pat thought of her late collaborator's advice.

" I—I was going to follow you up."

" You're telling me lies! " roared Sir Ingram. " I've just heard it's a damned drag, and I'll get to the bottom of it! I believe that blasted young Lester is in it—he was seen here this morning! "

Patricia's inheritance of a hot temper, which is a useful supplement to courage, asserted itself.

" I don't tell lies! The wood's poisoned—I was looking for you to tell you so! "

" Then it *was* that blackguard who laid the drag! " blazed Sir Ingram. " He'll be sorry for himself before I'm done with him! "

" He came to warn you the wood was poisoned. I met him. He asked me to tell you. And "—Pat faced her father, towering over her on his great red horse—" if you want to know who laid the drag, it was I! "

" You!—You!——"

Doctor Morrissey, who was one of Sir Ingram's attendant riders, said afterwards, " Upon me soul, I was on the point of rushing at him and opening a vein! He appeared to me to be on the verge of an apoplectic seizure! "

Pat, white but resolute, stood her ground. " Yes, I did! I did it to save the hounds—and—and——" her temper mastered her, she would show him she wasn't afraid of him, " —and I did it for fun! "

" For FUN! " The Master's bellow shook the air. " You dare to say that to me! If you weren't what you are—and that's an impudent young she-devil——" here Sir Ingram averted apoplexy by releasing some further disparaging comments on his daughter's sex—" I'd thrash you within an inch of your life! "

Pat's colour came back in strength.

" Thrash away! I don't want any advantage! "

She dared her father, stung to deeper rage than she had known in her short life by the abuse with which he had assailed her in public.

Sir Ingram's right arm went up. His heavy crop was in his hand, and Dr. Morrissey and Patsey's recent brother-in-law, Colonel Dick Villiers, who were of his retinue, pushed forward in horror. Sir Ingram's explosions of temper were as celebrated and as feared as the outbursts of Mount Etna, and he was regarded with awe as being capable of any act of violence.

But when the crop descended it came down on the chestnut's ribs. The big horse, startled and indignant, gave a tremendous plunge, and put an end to further conflict by going away down the road at full gallop. Dr. Morrissey, Gilbert, and the two farmers who were of the party, followed the Master, but Colonel Dick, who was a good-natured little man, and had suffered acutely during the scene, rode up to Patsey.

"By Jove! she's a good-looker!" he thought.

Her eyes were shining with tears of anger, and the clear and brilliant scarlet that can go with her type of colouring burnt in her cheeks.

"Look here, Patsey," said kind Colonel Dick, nervously, "don't mind the Master! He don't mean it—and, you know, Patsey—I say you know—it—it wasn't the thing to do!—and—and, anyhow, why the deuce did you go and *tell* him you did it? That was where you went wrong, you know! And then, why on earth did you go and tell him you did it for *fun?* That set him mad, you know!"

"Well, but I *did* do it for fun—partly—and I wanted Jimmy to have a ride—and really, Dick, it was the surest dodge to get the hounds away—that *was* the chief reason——"

Her voice was shaking with the strain of the past battle, and the rage with her father that was in her soul. "Dick," she went on, after an instant in which she tried to steady herself, "will you and Millie let me go and stay with you? Mother's away——" Her voice gathered strength. "I won't stand being spoken to as—as I was just now! And before those men!"

("By George!" said Colonel Dick, recounting the affair to his Millie when he went home to breakfast. "She held up her head and looked at me like a queen!"

"You should have had sense enough to have told her she was very silly, and must have known quite well how angry Papa would be! " his Millie had replied, tartly, being of opinion that men made far more fuss over her young step-sister than was good for her.)

Colonel Dick, however, did nothing so spirited or so sensible. He assured Patricia of a warm welcome whenever she liked to come to him and Millie, and continued to pour into her wounds the best equivalents for oil and wine that he could muster, until, as they neared the lake, they were met by Jimmy Corran.

Dick Villiers, despite the low opinion of his intelligence held by his wife, was—as he frequently remarked—not such a fool as he looked. " These two don't want *me!* " he said to himself; and with an explanatory statement that he wouldn't object to a bit of breakfast, and a final soothing injunction to Patsey to keep her tail up, he rode away.

It was full morning now, with the delicious crisp clarity and brilliance in the air that only those can know who have seen the sun rise on a fine morning in early September.

" When did you find out it was a drag? " Pat asked presently, in the course of mutual explanations.

" A fellow turning cows had seen you, and shouted to Johnny Ryan—I bet you found it a hard job? "

" The very worst! " agreed Pat. " I was pretty near done when George Lester met me and ran the last bit for me."

" Oh, he did, did he? " said Jimmy, without enthusiasm. " It was *your* show, though! You gave us a jolly good gallop! I don't care a blow if it was a drag or no! " He paused and looked at her. " I expect the Master was pretty mad, wasn't he? "

Pat said nothing. What had her father said to Jimmy when he met him, as he must have done, at the turf-quay with the hounds? Had he described her to him in the same refined terms?

Jimmy, watching her, saw her face darken. He guessed what was in her mind. That old Master was a proper old savage. . . . But, after all, he was her father . . . it wouldn't do to abuse him to her . . . it wasn't the done thing. . . .

"Jimmy," said Patricia, suddenly, after an interval of silence during which her mind was whirling from one alternative to another, planning, making decisions, whipped to speed by the lash of anger, " do you remember that afternoon we were out on the lake in the boat? "

" Yes, rather! Quite well! Let's do it again! "

Patsey held steadily to her point.

" You said then," she went on, " that you could lend me some money——"

" Rather so! Only delighted," broke in Jimmy again.

" Well, if you mean that you really can, I'll take it! "

She looked straight at him, her light, bright eyes dilated, her breath coming quickly. " I'll pay you back, of course, as soon as ever I can——"

" Oh, rot! "

" Yes, I will! Please, Jimmy! I'm in earnest! "

" Well, we needn't worry about that till you've got the money anyhow! How much do you want? Say the word! How will you take it, when will you take it, where will you——? "

" I'm *not* joking—I do really want it—I don't know how much exactly—fifty maybe. But can you spare it? It seems an awful lot—— Oh, *don't* laugh, Jimmy! I'm in dead earnest, and I *will* pay you back—I'll—I'll *make* it—earn it, I mean—I know I will. Anyhow, I'll have forty pounds of my own next year——" She checked herself, and said anxiously, " But I'm afraid I'll have to have it soon——"

" I fear I haven't got it about me," said Jimmy, assuming an air of apologetic gravity, while he patted his pockets successively, finally bringing forth a handful of shillings and coppers, " but if you *could* wait till we got home?—Or would you like four-and-eightpence to go on with? No?—I say, Pat, I'm sorry! I'm only playing the fool—I tell you what, you can leave it to me in your will! That'll be something for me to look forward to! "

How could she expect him to take her seriously? What a baby she was, and, by Jove, how good to look at!

CHAPTER XI

COULD Lady Kirwen have realised in any degree how serious, from Sir Ingram's point of view, had been Patsey's misdeeds, and how terrible the resulting scene, it is certain that she would have abandoned her appointments with her dentist (with the unrepining submission to the will of Providence that is not unusual in such case), and would have rushed home to fulfil her normal function of buffer-state between her husband and her daughter. But

> " *When storms are none and pyrates flee,*
> *Why play the Bells of Enderby?* "

And with no warning sound of those fatal bells in her ears, Lady Kirwen had put forth, as cheerfully as the circumstances permitted, for her first *séance*, at, as it happened, almost the moment of the return from the chase—if a drag can be honoured with such a name—of her angry husband.

Although Sir Ingram's wrath cannot be said to have subsided, yet, by the time he had reached home, it had begun to cool down, as far, at least, as Patricia was concerned. The Lesters, father and son, were in another class; there was no cooling down in that connection; more, as it were, banking down of the fires until a more convenient season. It was not so much that the Master condoned his daughter's conduct, as that an unfamiliar and decidedly uncomfortable feeling of compunction for what he now felt had been his rather too outspoken expressions of displeasure, was beginning to assail him. If Dick Villiers and those other chaps hadn't been there it would have been a different thing, he thought, but, damn it all, a man can't always pick and choose his words. Considering the gravity of the offence he had done well to be angry. Yes! His only regret was that he had expressed his reproof in quite so trenchant a manner. He said to himself that he had spoilt Pat—given her horses and all she wanted—that was the fact—mighty few girls had had the luck she had always had! After all, it was no harm to check her for once.

Thus consoling himself, the Master pulled off his hunting kit, and getting into the heavy frieze, leather-patched Norfolk jacket and breeches, and the gaiters and ponderous boots, that were his daily wear, he thumped majestically downstairs and sat down to breakfast.

" Where's Lord Corran, Moloney? "

" His Lordship's having a bath, Sir Ingram. He said not to wait for him, and Master Gilbert's changing."

" And Miss Patricia? Why isn't she down? "

" Miss Patricia's breakfast went up to her from the kitchen, Sir Ingram—she sent down for it."

Sir Ingram's brow clouded. He responded to the information with no more than a grunt, but since his mouth was already engaged with more practical matters, this was as much as could be expected at the moment. He had magnanimously determined to show some degree of clemency to the sinner, even to extend the sceptre whose touch should bring forgiveness, and he was rather anxious to get it over and resume ordinary relations—" get all square before Maud comes home " was how he put it to himself. Maud was an easy-going little thing, but she could give you a nasty nip if you fell foul of her puppies—women thought nothing of right or wrong where their blessed pups were concerned! No sense of proportion!

Meanwhile Miss Patricia had no smallest intention of touching the sceptre, or of accepting forgiveness. She told herself that she did not ask for the Master's forgiveness, and, for her part, she had no intention of forgiving him! He had blackened her face before her companions of the Hunt. He had disgraced himself as much as her. She said to herself that she wished her mother had heard him. . . . But her mother was nothing but a door-mat for him to wipe his boots on. . . . Only that she was never at the door! Always outside it, running through the wood, like the Red Queen! Angry as Pat was, she found herself laughing, as she thought what an inadequate little door-mat her mother was. . . . But her mother would surely have gone for the Master if she had heard him this morning! . . . Patsey began to boil up again. She wasn't going to stand it! . . . And before those men! . . . A nice story to go through the country! . . . What fun for Dr. Morrissey!

Patsey was at the difficult middle-age of youth, when the creature is too old to endure despotism, too young to have learnt toleration. Why should the fact—the unfortunate fact—that he was her father give him a right to insult her in public? . . . or in private either, if one came to that? . . . She lashed herself with remembrance. It must be admitted that filial affection as between Patsey and her father was a negligible quantity. But affection for fathers of the school of Sir Ingram (a large and flourishing one during the first half of the nineteenth century) was a matter more of the Church Catechism and of theory than of practice (the practice being summarised in what may be called Lip-Service; in other words, a morning and evening peck at the male parent's jaw).

Patricia was her father's daughter, not only in looks, but also in other matters less advantageous. Temper, for instance, not improved by the often-impressed fact that a father's choleric word is flat blasphemy in the mouth of his offspring, specially his female offspring. And Obstinacy. A quality not infrequently as troublesome to its possessor as to others. And Courage, which also can have its drawbacks, especially when it nerves its possessor to revolt. In fact, Kate, the senior housemaid, had many sound reasons for suggesting that Miss Patsey was a fright, and since Kate had been twenty years in the house, she might be expected to know what she was talking about.

* * * * *

The dining-room breakfast had at length faded to a finish, the last relay of eggs and bacon had found its early close, and Moloney, having seen Sir Ingram forth on his way to the farm, and gathered that the two younger gentlemen proposed to indemnify themselves for early rising by slumber on the sofas in the billiard-room, felt himself at liberty to proceed to the kitchen, there to debate the questions as to the cloud on his master's brow, and the possibly allied non-appearance of Miss Patricia.

It was one of the many appointed moments when a sustaining cup of tea was available, and Mr. Moloney was not above such solace. He took his accustomed seat at the head of the table in the servants' hall, with the air of assured authority of a barndoor cock among his ladies, and accepting the cup that was immediately proffered, he remarked to the company at large, but more especially to Kate:

"Will anyone tell me what ails Miss Patsey? Is she sick that she couldn't come down to her breakfast?"

Kate ignored the glance, and addressed herself to another cup of tea. The situation was still obscure, and she did not choose to reveal ignorance.

"She's not sick at all, Mr. Moloney," ventured, after a pause, an under-housemaid. "I carried down her tray, and she didn't leave a bit after her."

Mr. Moloney's query had been pointed at Kate, and the temerity of the underling in replying did not please him.

"That tells nothing," he said, repressively. "And she having the dogs above, no doubt."

"She sent orders to Mr. Foley to have the black horse in the dog-cart in an hour's time, and Denis to go with her," remarked Mrs. Trinder, the cook.

"She'll be apt to have no lunch so," said Moloney, "it's past eleven o'clock now."

"I'll send a sup o' broth up to her if that's the way," said Mrs. Trinder. "I'll go bail them dirty dogs got more of her breakfast than herself did! Wasn't it enough for her to be away out o' the house before four o'clock this morning, without going driving now again?"

"She'll not drink it!" said Kate, darkly. "There's something over her——"

She was interrupted by the jangling of a bell on the wall over her head, and the underling rose to respond.

"That's her bell now. No, stay here, you, Bridget, I'll go myself."

No one as well as Kate knew the extent of the disorder in which Patricia could plunge her room, but even Kate stood aghast and speechless at the chaos that met her gaze.

" Oh, Kate," Patricia began, " I want you to pack this box, please—those things on the floor there—I'm going to stay with Mrs. Villiers."

" Are you going to stay for long, miss? I'll never get all them things into that little trunk." Kate advanced upon the trunk. " Sure you have it half full already! " she said in just displeasure. " Surely to goodness, miss, you don't want all them boxes and books taking up all the room? "

" Don't touch them! Those are my painting things! "

" Then I must get one of her Ladyship's trunks so," said Kate, severely. " Are you going for so long, miss? If you might have told me last night I'd have——"

" I don't know—I can't tell you! " broke in Patsey, exasperated, looking at her with wild eyes, beginning to realise that to abandon the paternal roof was easier to decide upon in a hurry than to achieve. " I'll take the small box in the cart with me—I'll have to settle about the rest."

She moved in quick strides about the room, opening drawers and presses, taking folded things out, stuffing them, unfolded, in again, trying to make the momentous decisions consequent on involved packing, with a mind distracted by the difficulties and complications that she was raising up for herself, yet obstinately resolved on overcoming them.

While she watched Kate, the thought came to her that it was advisable to leave a note for her father, if it were only to let him see she wasn't going to stand—— Her temper began to boil up. She got pen and paper and wrote.

" *Dear Papa, from what you said to me this morning, I*

can see that you will have no objection to my going away." She paused, and thought: " I'll just make it clear about the drag." " *The drag was entirely my idea, and not young Lester's. Patricia.*"

She gave the note to Kate, with directions that it was to be given to Sir Ingram when he came in to lunch.

Dooley, the eldest dog, lay on the bed, her head only visible in the welter of garments, flung there, for consideration and selection, by the packers. Her eyes followed Patricia's every movement. She said to herself, " If I lose sight of her for an instant, all is lost! "

Patsey, conscious of the gaze, and of what it implied, tried in vain to veil it with the superfluities of her wardrobe, but, from beneath the drifts of apparel, the little head rose like a cork to the surface, and the eyes resumed their watch. There comes a moment, as Dooley knew, when human resistance fails. She was aware that this could not be relied on as a certainty, but the thought kept hope alive. She watched Kate narrowly as she locked the trunks, and waited, tense with anxiety, until Kate, always a faintly hostile power, had left the room to summon men to carry the luggage downstairs.

Patsey was very tired, and had seated herself on the sofa on which Kate had set apart for her a top-coat, gloves, and hat, that had all boded evil to the small wise watcher on the bed. Now, rising from among the discarded evening dresses, she met Patsey's eyes, and knew the yielding in them. She dropped off the bed and stole to the sofa, and laid her head on Patsey's knee, and Patsey, from sheer force of habit, patted an invitation. In an instant the little supplicant had sunk into that accustomed place, and was pressing her head in dumb entreaty against the adored breast.

Her intuition was not at fault. The moment had come.

Patsey snatched a collar and lead from a shelf behind her.

" Yes! You shall run away too! " she whispered, putting the collar on Dooley's neck. " I can't leave you behind! Goodness knows what will be the end of it for either of us! I've said I'd do it often enough, and I will—but it's not going to be an easy job! "

There came a rap of strong knuckles on her bedroom door. " They've come for the boxes! " Her heart gave a lift, excited and apprehensive. " I'm for it now! " Then she called out:

" Come in! I'm ready! "

CHAPTER XII

YOUNG George Lester bicycled home from the turf-quay at the western end of Lough Eskaheen at the highest rate of speed of which he or his machine was capable, and knew it not. His thoughts were whirling faster than the wheel. He felt as if he were treading air, yet with the physical satisfaction of the strong swift drive at the treadles. Everything had gone right. If he had thought for a month he couldn't have planned it with more wonderful perfection. All had been miraculous, from the moment when she had gazed at him, and, while his whole being was throbbing in response to that gaze, had asked him—how bewilderingly—for a bit of string! Not for his heart, not for the devotion of a life-time—just for a bit of string! But it hadn't seemed like bathos at all. Anxiety to be able to satisfy her was all he felt. And then his blessed, his ever-to-be-canonised tool-bag had produced exactly what was wanted, and all was well! She had trusted him, had told him what to do, and he had done it—yes, and had done it well! It was his guardian angel, he felt sure, that had inspired him at the right moment " to go meet her " in the fields. (His guardian angel being, most probably, Irish, like George himself, would doubtless have used the idiom familiar to his ward.) Hadn't she thanked Heaven for the sight of him? He whirled in at the narrow gateway that led to the front door of his father's house, his mind misty with bliss.

It was not until he was leaning his bicycle against the

wall by the door that he began to consider what he was going to tell his father. The mission had been his father's, but it was his mother who had laid it on him, late last night, waiting to speak to him, half undressed, at the top of the stairs; an absurd figure, which he had instinctively tried to memorise in terms of caricature, in her white petticoat-body, with her jolly bare arms, like bolsters, and her short red flannel petticoat, that made no attempt to conceal her equally jolly and still more bolster-like legs. Now, since that mission that had resulted in such wonders, he seemed to himself to have moved on to another plane, where events of epoch-making importance occurred, where—he cast about for expression—where a man could call his soul his own, and didn't have to answer dictatorial enquiries as to whether it were saved or no! Yes! He had come to man's estate!

As he hung his cap on a peg in the passage into the house, he felt that he had had as much of that sort of thing as he could stand. He looked at his watch. It was half-past eight. He told himself that his father would have gone out about the farm as usual—that same was a comfort anyhow—and Minnie would be away for school at Templenoe. The house would be empty, but that was no harm. Mother would give him a bit of breakfast; he was jolly hungry. The thought of the fine breakfast that he was going to eat enforced still further the feeling of confident manhood that he had brought home with him. With his mother he knew that he need not try to conceal the elation that was singing in his heart, and fizzing in his head like—like champagne, he supposed (he didn't know much about champagne, having been brought up strictly "blue-ribbon," though he had tasted it on the memorable day of the wedding at Kirwenscourt). But his mother would understand. . . .

George walked with confidence into the parlour to summon his mother, and there, to his surprise and dismay, found his father.

Holy George rose to meet his son.

"Well, George, well? I was waiting in to see you. Did you meet them? Were you in time?"

It was only then that young George remembered how far from adequate had been his delivery of the message entrusted to him.

"I—I didn't meet Sir Ingram, Father," he said, nervously. "It—it was Miss Kirwen I saw—I told her——"

"Her? Is it the youngest lady of all? And what good I ask you was that? Did anything happen the hounds?"

"Nothing! Nothing at all! There was a dead fox there, I saw it die on the road, and she—I—we—we ran a drag with it. It was to get the hounds away before they could go in the wood. I didn't see Sir Ingram at all."

In Holy George's unregenerate youth he had learned enough of the art and practice of fox-hunting to be aware that there were methods of conciliating an irascible Master of Foxhounds more efficacious than that of laying a drag out of one of his best coverts.

"A *drag!*"

The almost treble note on which he uttered the word imparted a special poignancy to it.

"That puts the cap on it! What in the name of—of Pity possessed you to commit a folly the like o' that? Didn't your mother tell you to meet Sir Ingram himself and tell him dogs were coming after rabbits and would be hunting my sheep, and I was forced to put down poison and the notice'd be on the paper to-morrow? She did, I know. You and your sister between you have made a nice hand of it for me! I that was looking to get a strip of mountain from him, let alone my lease that wants to be renewed in November! It'd be no surprise to me if we were all turned out on the road! And there'll be the end of you and your college training! And no loss to the Ministry you'll be! There'll be one fool less doing the Lord's work! That's something, anyhow!"

Holy George's voice, when raised to the note (F sharp in the treble clef) which he had standardised for denunciation, had a power to madden that was only equalled by the prolonged shriek of a stationary engine letting off steam.

Young George, hungry, excited, his ears, no less than his temper, lacerated by the long scream of vituperation, felt suddenly a rush of rage that swept away the flood-gates that youth, and habit, and his mother's sedulous training had erected to keep his soul in subjection.

"Very well, then, there'll be one humbug less in this family to talk cant!" he shouted, his face scarlet, and his eyes alight. "I'm obliged to you for meeting me half-way! I had made up my mind the same way already so we'll not fall out over that!"

Mr. Lester, subsequently, in narrating the scene to a chosen ally, said he knew now what Balaam felt when the ass turned about and rebelled against him. "And this is a very different case, mind you!" he had added, remembering how entirely in the right he had been, and how quite in the wrong Balaam. "Though indeed, if I'd had a staff in my hand, like Balaam, it would have gone hard with me not to strike him!"

What, however, Holy George had not thought it necessary to mention, even to the ally, was that, failing the staff, he had been unable to refrain from slapping his son's face. Not a violent slap, but a reminder, irresistible to an autocrat, that revolt cannot be tolerated.

In what was, at that moment, young George's condition of mind his response to the correction would probably have been regrettable, but very fortunately for both father and son, before any reprisal was possible, Mrs. Lester, to whom in the kitchen the noise of battle had reached, at this moment burst into the room and flung herself between her husband and her son.

" What's all this? What are you about, Georgie, roaring and shouting this way? I heard you back in the kitchen itself! For shame on you! I didn't think it of you——" While she was upbraiding she was interposing herself, like a ruffled hen, between the Georges, encircling the younger, placing, as it were, a shielding wing round him, or—to vary the metaphor—riding him off towards the door. " There now! Go on out o' this! Go out to the kitchen now, and I'll give you your breakfast. You're tired. He doesn't know what he's saying." She turned on the elder George. " Don't listen to the child! "

Young George, still burning with unquenched anger, turned round on this indignity, but, before he had time to speak, his mother, catching him by the shoulders, hustled him out into the passage, and slammed the door.

CHAPTER XIII

JIMMY CORRAN'S natural desire for sleep, after unnatural early rising, healthy exercise, and a satisfactory breakfast, was not gratified with the speed which happy experience had led him to expect. He rolled over and over among the heights and hollows of the enormous old billiard-room sofa, and propped himself with supernumerary cushions, but Sleep, that shy bird, that flutters from the grasp of the old, and closes with soft unhesitating wings the eyelids of the young, ignored his summons.

What did Patsey want with fifty quid all of a hurry, like this? Surely she wasn't bolting off to Paris to paint the Lord knows what this afternoon? She wasn't like herself, riding home. Old Ingram must have given her a bad doing over the drag! A wicked-tempered old devil he is too when he gives his mind to it! Jimmy rolled over again. The sound of Gilbert's breathing, low and regular, like the ticking of a small clock, came to him across the billiard-table, and was exasperating. Why couldn't he go to sleep, like that young waster?—not a bad boy, but a mighty poor performer on a horse—not a patch on Patsey! He recalled the morning when she had tried to pour water over the balusters upon his head. What a smack she had given him when he tried to kiss her! Her face came before his eyes, brilliant and defiant. He wished he had kissed her. She had scored off him that time, but the very next chance that came his way . . . He reflected on this point for some minutes. It did not conduce to sleep. . . . His mind returned to the question of the loan for which she had asked. It was the last thing he wanted to do to help her to get away out of the country. . . . Just, too, as he had been thinking of taking that little house of the old boy's down by the kennels, and bringing his horses here next month. . . . Quite a nice lot of hounds the old boy had, to give him his due, and well turned out too, and a good sporting country. . . . But if Patsey weren't here . . . Wouldn't that rather wreck it? . . . This thought afforded him subject for considerable meditation. The more he thought about it the more indispensable to the success of the project seemed the presence of his recently encountered cousin. Yes, by Jove, it wouldn't be much fun jogging home, after a long day, with old Ingram, or old Dick Villiers, or even Johnny Ryan! . . . Now Patsey was good company . . . Patsey . . . extraordinarily blue her eyes had looked this morning . . . that time when he had chaffed her about the money . . . she had been dead in earnest about it. . . .

He began to wonder how soon she wanted it. Perhaps he ought to try and get hold of her now and find out? He felt stimulated by this thought, and pushed himself on to an elbow and looked at his watch. Half-past eleven. Well, it was obvious he wasn't going to succeed in getting to sleep.

He swung his long legs off the sofa and stood up. He was conscious of a sudden keen desire to see Patsey, and have it out with her about the money—give it to her, of course, if she wanted it. But how sickening if he were to be the one to help her to get away! What a blasted fool he had been that afternoon in the boat! Shoving money down her throat! Going to Paris to paint. That was what she said she wanted it for. Such rot! As if she didn't paint well enough as it was!

By this time he had arrived at the hall. The dining-room door was open, and he saw Moloney moving about in the room. " I'll have a drink," he thought, " and I can send her a message."

Miss Patricia was going out, Moloney said. Out? Where? Moloney didn't know. She had ordered the dogcart. He believed there was luggage—it looked like she was going away to stay. Moloney had thought his Lordship might know. She didn't come downstairs since she and his Lordship came in this morning—Jimmy put down his glass.

" Will I give your Lordship another——? "

" No, thanks, Moloney. Do you always put in more whisky than soda water? "

" Oh, m'Lord! " expostulated Moloney, faintly flattered.

After this it was that had come that strong rap on Miss Patricia's door. She opened it.

" The things are all ready—— Hullo, Jimmy, what is it? "

" I wanted to speak to you. May I come in? "

" They'll be coming for these things in a minute. Come down to the Old Playroom." She thought, " Good Jimmy! I expect it's about the money——"

She walked quickly down the long passage, with Dooley running close at her heels. Jimmy followed her, and felt, somehow, as though he were seeing her for the first time; noting how well she moved, how flat her back, how straight and slender her neck, how bright the coil of hair that lay on it. What a murder it would be if this girl went away out of the country just as he was beginning to—to realise her properly!

Arrived at the Old Playroom, Patricia seated herself on the end of the carpenter's bench, as was her custom, and waited for Jimmy Corran to open fire. He was standing in front of her, regarding her attentively. She did not have to wait long.

"May I be allowed to ask where on earth you are going?" He couldn't keep indignation out of his voice. "You never said a word about this game—I mean, bolting off like this—this morning!"

"I'd had enough rows!"

"I wouldn't have made a row!"

"Why, you're beginning to make one now!"

Jimmy began to protest. He told her it was absurd to go off like a rocket just because she got into hot water with the Master, as if, as far as he, Jimmy, could see, that didn't happen to every living soul on the place every second day! And what harm did it do her, he wanted to know?

"Rockets don't go off in hot water. Anyhow, it scalded me!"

"Well, scalding or scolding, what's the odds? It's not worth thinking about—and—and it's beastly unfair on me, Patsey! Just as I was looking forward to some jolly hunting with you!"

"You can have it without me just as well. It's no use your scolding me too, Jimmy, it's settled now. I'm going over to Millie and Dick to-day—I dare say I'll not stay there long. But I'll not come back here!" she added, with a flash in her eyes.

Jimmy put his hands in his pockets, and his head on one side, and regarded her.

"That's so, is it?"

She nodded.

"Do you mean you're really sticking to that—that"

(he swallowed an adjective that expressed his feelings) " scheme of going abroad? "

She nodded again, watching his face, on which gloom was fast gathering.

" Well, then, I suppose you'd better have this——"

He took his cheque-book out of his pocket, and laid it beside her amid the *débris* on the carpenter's bench. An ink-bottle and a pen were at hand. He knelt at the bench and opened the book.

" Not if you don't want to lend it to me! "

His reply was to look up at her, his grey eyes—that, like his hair and moustache (for in those days a moustache was valued), were of a startlingly light tone in contrast with his sunburnt skin—cloudy and vexed.

" Will fifty be enough? " was all he said.

" Heaps! "

Jimmy grunted, a grunt hopeless and indignant.

" Do you know how to cash it? Have you an account at a bank? "

" Nonsense! Of course I have! I've had an allowance for ages—since I was eighteen. I'm 'passing rich on forty pounds a year'! "

" Good God! I'll make the cheque a hundred."

" I won't have it if you do! I could never pay you back—and I've heaps just now, masses! I got my quarter last week, luckily! No, please, Jimmy! "

She snatched at the cheque before he could change the figures, Jimmy caught her hand, and, standing up, seated himself on the bench beside her.

" You're such a baby," he said, with more tenderness than he knew in his voice, holding her right hand, with the cheque in it, in his. " Talking rot about paying me back! Didn't I tell you you could leave it to me in your will? "

He pressed her hand, leaning over her, conscious that something new had come into his relation towards her. To neither of them had there seemed anything either compromising or unusual in the affair just completed, but now, unexpectedly, the air had become charged with the feeling that something irrevocable had happened, that had involved them each with the other; a feeling that with Jimmy Corran set his blood galloping with expectation, unformulated, yet delightful, but that half scared, half angered Patricia, so that she tried to release her hand from his grasp.

" I could never pay you back—I won't have the cheque," she stammered. " I'll not take it! I'll chuck the whole thing! "

" I wish to God you would! But not for that reason!" he said hotly. He felt himself torn between the desire to keep her and the dread of disappointing her. " Look here! Take it just for the present, but don't make any hard and fast plans till—till——" (he grasped at the first straw that came handy) " till you've seen your mother. Please, Patsey, dear—just to show there's no ill feeling! "

" Well," said Patsey, slowly, in reluctant agreement, putting the cheque in her pocket, " if you do really feel like that about it——"

Then a sudden realisation of what he was doing for her, helping her, freely and generously, to carry out a plan that she knew he hated, came upon her. She was over strained and excited. When she looked up at him he saw that there were tears in her eyes.

" Jimmy, don't think I'm not grateful! I'll never, *never* forget how kind—how good——"

Jimmy put his arm round her and drew her close to him.

" Are you—are you really grateful? Patsey, listen, I want to tell you something—no, don't go away—I won't let you go—just let me tell you——" He turned her face towards his with his other hand, his eyes met hers, and knew, as Dooley had known, the yielding in them. . . . He lengthened the dizzy moment of anticipation, and, as once before, delay proved dangerous, and the kiss that might have made all Patsey's plans of none effect delayed just a moment too long. For half-a-dozen seconds all that she had been through, all that was still before her to do, had become a load too heavy for her to carry. Paris had gone far away and was hedged with difficulty, and Jimmy had suddenly changed from being a playmate, and had become a haven of refuge—or was it a danger? She wasn't sure which he was. She found herself shaking, and afraid of the new look in his face that was so near hers. And she was very tired.

> " *If goodness lead him not, yet weariness*
> *May toss him to my breast.*"

Another instant, and weariness might have betrayed her, and the delaying kiss have sealed her surrender, but a step sounded in the passage, the door was being opened.

" Let me go! " she said in a low voice, jerking herself free from his arms and standing up.

Moloney came into the room.

" Your things are in the trap, miss. It's ready, and waiting in the yard, by your orders."

Disapproval was written all over him.

It spurred Patsey's contrary spirit to persistence.

" Very well. I'm coming. I've left a note with Kate for you to give Sir Ingram."

She walked quickly out of the room and downstairs, followed by the two men; she stood and patted the black horse's nose, while Dooley, and other small matters, were being established in the cart.

Kate watched the departure from the kitchen window, full of thwarted curiosity, as well as of the proprietary affection that a servant, such as she, of the elder sort, could feel for a child of the house, noting the set of Patsey's lips, the lift of her chin, as, with a smile that in its effort to seem unforced had become defiant, she shook hands with Jimmy.

"Isn't she the dead spit of the father?" Kate commented to her ancient comrade in arms, Mrs. Trinder. "She'd die down dead before she'd let on what ailed her! If she was breaking her heart this minute she'd have a grin for you! Didn't I hold Sir Ingram's leg for the doctor that time he broke it, and not a roar out of him!"

"But where is it she's going at all?" asked Mrs. Trinder. "And she leaving the young lord after her!"

"Sorra know I know!" answered Kate, heavily; and when Kate acknowledged herself defeated, Mrs. Trinder knew there was no more to be said.

Patsey climbed into the dogcart and picked up the reins and the whip.

"Denis, you can sit at the back and hold Dooley. Good-bye, Jimmy! Good-bye, Moloney!—Come up, old Sweep!" She gave the black horse a touch of the whip, and drove away at a sharp trot.

Moloney turned to Jimmy.

"I'd be thankful if your Lordship would give the note to Sir Ingram. I'm afraid he'll be greatly put out when he gets it!"

Jimmy grimly accepted the mission, his mind engrossed in stormy debate as to whether he had himself or Moloney to thank for having, as he said to himself, put everything in the soup.

CHAPTER XIV

OLD SWEEP, the black horse, was well aware that he had, as he put it to himself, to "go along" when Miss Patricia had the reins, and, still more, the whip, in her hands. She gave him no time to regard with feigned consternation heaps of stones that from long standing had passed into institutions; nor, if a pig were to be faced, could he conveniently turn and fly for home, as was his practice when Lady Kirwen was in nominal control; still less could he exercise his faculty, comparable only to that of a spirit-level, to detect a hill, and thereon to relapse into a walk and what would seem to be profound slumber. Miss Patsey was a fright, Sweep thought, having heard the same comment often enough from Mr. Foley and Mr. Ryan, and there was nothing for it but to go along.

Carron Hill, which was the name of Colonel Dick Villiers's place, was what was called "a good eight miles"—which, freely translated, meant a bad nine—from Kirwenscourt, and when Patricia pulled Sweep to a halt in front of the hall-door, his black coat was streaked with sweat and flecked with white lather. He was so thankful to be permitted to stand at ease that he ignored the agitating roars of a gong that assailed him through the open door, and he even refrained from the attack that he was accustomed to make upon the roses and clematis that decorated the pillars of the porch.

Now that Pat had arrived at her brother-in-law's house, which now was also that of Millie, a trepidation, unusual to her, and all the more discomposing for that, began to make itself felt. Old Dick was all right, but what would Millie say? Millie had always backed up the Master—Millie wasn't a bad sort—she didn't jump on people—she was too tepid for that, but she could sometimes give a scratch, a tepid scratch, but a scratch for all that, and now that she was a married lady it was impossible to say what capers she mightn't be up to.

Patsey had always rather looked down on Millie, as an elderly person (Millie was thirty-seven) given to good works (missionary bazaars, crewels, crochet), reading serious novels seriously, and paying long visits to her mother's relations in England. To be scratched by old Millie would be rather hard to bear, and Patsey realised suddenly that she had undoubtedly laid herself open to be scratched.

She descended from the dogcart, and Dooley leapt in a rainbow curve from Denis's custody at the back, and rushed into the hall with the customary enthusiasm of the visiting dog, only to rush out again with a shriek, being seen to the doorstep by a large lady cat. Led by the shriek came Colonel Dick, and to admit that the sight of his young sister-in-law filled him with consternation is to impute no slur on his hospitality.

"Why, Patsey?—Patsey?—You here?—God bless my soul! You ought to be in bed after being up since cockcrow!"

"So ought you, Dick, if it comes to that!" retorted Patsey, telling herself she was in for it now, and there was no use in funking. "I told you I was coming, and here I am!"

"Well—well—well," said the Colonel, sparring for wind, and averting his eyes from the suit-case on the step at Patsey's feet. " All right, all right! Come in and have a bit of lunch—Millie's there——"

(" They don't want me! " thought the visitor, picking up Dooley.)

" Go round to the yard, Denis," went on Colonel Dick, " and put the horse up, and go in and you'll get your dinner——"

(" He said nothing about the luggage! " thought Patsey. " They won't have me! ")

In the hall she met Millie, advancing from the dining-room, dinner-napkin in hand.

" Why, Patsey dear! " Millie began; and then, in tones of alarm, " Oh! You've got Dooley! I'm afraid Dick's beloved Mrs. Bounce won't approve of that! She's got a family! "

" I'll keep her in my arms," said Patsey, her brain beginning to whirl with alternative plans. (" I can't stay here! That's very clear! " she thought.)

" We only got home the day before yesterday," continued Millie. " We're rather upside down still! *Rather* a brief honeymoon, wasn't it? Only a scrap over a fortnight! *I* could have done with a little more London, but I didn't wish Dick to miss the cubbing. Papa relies on him so! "

" I've a nice lot of cubs for him! " broke in Colonel Dick, with a precipitancy that suggested anxiety to keep conversation on strictly neutral ground. " I'll take jolly good care *they* don't get poisoned! Now then! Sit down, girls, sit down! Patsey, what may I give you? "

" I'm afraid there's not much choice—just cold beef, dear," Millie interrupted, rather coldly. "We've hardly settled down yet." She eyed Patsey, noting the absence of her usual colour, and the violet shadow under her eyes. " It *is* nice of you, Patsey dear, to come so soon to see us—though I must say you look very tired, and *I* think you ought to have rested and done nothing! Another day you must bring Papa over to lunch, and Jimmy Corran—I hear he's *so* nice—when Dick and I have shaken down a little more."

"Well, er——" began Pat slowly, her thoughts flying, "I shan't be at home—not for some time—I'm going to join Mother in Dublin—I can catch the four train at Ballylickey, can't I?"

"Oh, *that* accounts for the luggage that you had in the trap!" exclaimed Colonel Dick, relief betraying him to the admission that he had observed the suit-case.

"Quite! Doesn't it?" said Pat, her colour rising, and with it her temper. "I changed my mind since I spoke to you, Dick."

"Oh—ah—yes!" fumbled the Colonel, rising and hurrying to the sideboard. "Have a small whisky-and-soda, Patsey, you'll have a long day of it! Why, let me see—you'll have a thundering long wait at the junction—it'll be eleven o'clock to-night before you get into Dublin!"

"What an hour to arrive!" Millie interposed, disapprobation in her voice. "Surely you're not travelling *alone?*"

(In the year 1884 to travel alone was a measure of freedom not very generally extended to young ladies of Patricia's age and status.)

"No!" said Pat, defiantly, "I shall have Dooley with me!"

Millie ignored the defiance.

"It seems very late to arrive!"

"It isn't so much that it *seems* as that it *is!*" said Pat, with a laugh. "But that can't be helped. I shall wire to Mother to expect me when she sees me—not before!"

Millie said nothing. Later, when discussing the whole affair with the Colonel, she said that she hadn't argued the point with Patsey, as she had dreaded one of her bursts of fury.

"Kind father for her!" struck in the Colonel, chuckling.

"A man's a very different thing!" Millie replied with severity, which was certainly indisputable; and the Colonel, who valued the privileges of his sex, the more that renewed matrimony had already taught him that some of these were in danger of being curtailed, would have been the last to deny it.

CHAPTER XV

THAT other mutineer, young George Lester, whose mutiny had, so far, gone no further than the preliminary engagement with his father, now found himself in the unsatisfactory position of having no method more effective of emphasising his revolt than sulking. This, however, he did very thoroughly, even to the extent of refusing to join the family circle at the midday meal (a refusal that did not extend to the repast subsequently conveyed to him by his mother, in his bedroom, to which he had retired).

There young George Lester sat, in solitude, on the edge of his bed, moodily devouring, while his thoughts beat in barren circles, finding no outlet, ever returning to the same point, like wild things in a cage. That his father should strike him was no new thing. He had told his mother what had happened. " I won't be treated like a child! " he had said. " And you may tell Father I said so! " It had maddened him at the moment, and he promised himself he wouldn't forget it, but it was not the central point of his meditations, which was the financial problem of the future.

His father had threatened to take him away from college. Well and good! He had agreed to that, well pleased that the enemy's first shot should be a blank cartridge, and that he had as good as told him so. No objection at all to getting out of that affair, thank you! He had been shoved into it against the grain, now he was quite ready to take his hand from the plough! It was incidentally pleasant to think how his father would ram that text down his throat, and how little he would care! That particular plough was not his game! They had pushed and persuaded him to agree to it. His father out of piety—or so he supposed. " I don't think it's humbug with him," George said to himself, " but it's precious hard to be sure!" His mother, quite frankly, to make a gentleman of him. But that wasn't the sort of gent he wanted to be! Oh for freedom! For money! Not a lot, just enough to get away—to be an artist! That was the same as being a gentleman, a king of the world! Anyone's equal! The equal even of—well, why not? She had treated him as an equal, this morning . . .

He couldn't sit still. His thoughts, imprisoned in that narrow cage, tore at him like wolves. Oh, to get clean away—no more sermons, lectures, commentaries. To have Freedom, and—what was this his mother used to say?—" to follow me own Figgairy O!" That was it! His own vagary. To feel no longer like a square peg in a round hole. But it all came back to the same thing, the same blank prison wall: shut in, because he had no money.

He sat bolt upright. Why, what a fool he was! He *had* those few pounds in the bank, to be sure! Not many, faith! So few he had nearly forgotten them! But some one of his friends might be fool enough to back a bill for him. He ran through the list of his acquaintance, feverishly. Would any of them——? *Could* any of them——? Well, anyhow, he would see what, exactly, he had of his own in the bank. Those few odd shillings that he had earned now and again at college, giving a lift with their work to bigger asses than himself—and there weren't many, he said, with a bitter grin—he had them all put away in the bank as fast as he had got them. That was the only decent thing he could say for himself. It must have been that something told him one day he'd want it badly. How much was in it at all he didn't know—he hadn't looked at his bank-book this long time—where the mischief was it now? George rooted in his small chest-of-drawers. Half the drawers jammed in his haste. He dragged at them with fury, and the little chest-of-drawers, rather than yield, danced a sort of polka with him on the bare boards of the bedroom.

At last, in an old davenport, the bank-book submitted itself to him.

Cash, to credit, eleven pounds fifteen shillings and ninepence.

"What good is that to me?" George thought, despairingly. "It'd hardly get me there, let alone keep me any time at all——"

Could his mother help him? His hot thoughts dwelt on her for a space. Poor Mother! Hadn't she to go to Father for every penny she wanted? Even the egg money from her fowls she had to account for! It was a bloody shame! She would give him the skin off her back—George knew that well—but that wouldn't be much good to him! . . . How damned unfair it all was! Why should his father have the right to treat him and his mother as if they were his negro slaves?—Especially him! He hadn't asked to be brought into the world, but here he was, thanks to his father (George, like most men, considered his mother's share in the matter was comparatively negligible), and at least he had a right to choose what sort of life he wanted, and how could he do that without money? That was what stumped him all the time! By jingo! he had better look out ("he" was Holy George); if he, George the younger, found any cash lying about, he'd stick to it all right, and not think twice about it!

George heaved a gusty sigh, and stamped across his narrow room to the window. He looked out across his father's land to the dim line of hills. Derrygoole Wood was just discernible, a blot a little bluer than the faint blue of the hills. What a chance it had been! What fun! What marvellous, marvellous luck! Was it all to end there? . . . In one of the nearer fields he saw his father's big figure, superintending the collection of the last of the sheaves of oats. Thank goodness, he was out of the house—George could go downstairs without fear of meeting him! Mother would be there, and he might talk to her for a bit.

There was no one in the parlour. He looked into the kitchen, and " the girl " informed him that the mistress was just after going out to walk down to the town on a message.

George went back to the parlour, and looked about for the newspaper—anything to take his mind, for a moment, off all this. It was lying on his father's writing-table. As he took it up he saw that the principal drawer of the table was half open. An unfinished letter lay on the blotting-paper pad; beside it, open, was a bill for artificial manures, with a brilliantly coloured landscape heading, which caught his eye.

" He must have gone out in a hurry," George thought. " It isn't often he leaves his drawer open—I suppose it was a cheque he was to write for the artifeecials——" As the words passed through his mind, they brought with them a suggestion that turned him rigid as stone.

The long blue cardboard cover of the cheque-book was in view, just inside the drawer. . . . George stood and looked at it. Then he began to laugh. The thing, of course, was impossible, but what a sell for the Father to find out that it was thanks to himself leaving the drawer open George was able to cut the whole concern! . . . Supposing he was to tear a cheque entirely out of it. . . . Of course, the last one in the book would be the one to take—if one *did* take it—the way it might be months before it was come to, and no one, hardly, could be so exact to know by the numbers how many cheques were in the book. . . . The signature would be no trouble at all; it was as like his own as two peas, only for the flourish, and that'd be no trouble. . . . It'd likely be a month, anyhow, before the Father'd know the money was gone. . . . Mr. Day at the bank would be safe to think it was all right, with term at college beginning next week. . . . He could cash it in Dublin. . . .

Indignation bubbled up in him again. If only he was treated as any other man of his age was treated, and given a proper allowance instead of having his bills paid for him, as if he were a baby, or wrong in the head! . . . How can a chap live any sort of a decent life if he has to go whining to his father for every ha'penny he spends, and maybe not get it, and have his face slapped into the bargain! . . .

Gradually he drew nearer to what had seemed the impossible, almost ludicrous thing, that was, really, so possible, so simple, so—yes—so justifiable! After all, it was only the same—no, it wouldn't be as much, even, as what his college bills came to, and he was determined he wouldn't go back there—not if the end of all was that he had to enlist!

* * * * *

George was back in his little room, contemplating

the blank cheque, that had been the last one in the book that lay on the table before him.

What price the Ten Commandments? The Fifth? Well, he could honour his mother all right! If the bank would honour his father's signature, that would be all right too! . . . Then what about the Eighth? . . . Hang it all, this wasn't stealing! Only taking what he had a jolly good right to. . . . Here! Where's the pen? . . .

He had covered a sheet of notepaper with copies of his father's signature, made from the last letter that he had had from him, before he had satisfied himself. His eye and his hand were wont to work together. When at last the cheque was filled and signed, Holy George himself would not have disowned it. Young George sat, looking at his handiwork, until the ink was dry. Then he folded it and put it into a pocket-book, and put the book into a breast-pocket. He had filled the cheque for five-and-twenty pounds.

CHAPTER XVI

PATSEY and Dooley caught " the 4 " at Ballylickey, and the guard, who was an old and valued friend, put her into her first-class carriage (for Patsey, at this stage of her career, it was unthinkable that she could travel by any other class), and made no difficulty about Dooley, save a recommendation to " tidy her up " (which meant to hide her under the seat) before the ticket-collector came round, for he was a cross man that'd excess the Angel Gabriel if he got the chance.

The long, ill-lighted platform at Kingsbridge Station, with its string of outside cars and four-wheeled cabs, lined up against a dark wall, was at no time calculated to raise the spirits, and it seemed to Patricia the most entirely horrible place she had ever seen. She had slept, with Dooley on her lap, for the later hours of the journey, utterly tired, mind and body, and to wake up to the dreary hustle of the station gave her courage its first definite shock.

" Have I been a fool? " she thought, as in one of the four-wheelers she was slowly bumped over the rough " setts " along the quays, on her way to Finnegan's Private Hotel. The windows of the cab kept up the continuous scream that was the peculiar accomplishment of the Dublin four-wheeler of the era that preceded motor vehicles; the horse was lame; Patsey's porter had, probably in fulfilment of a compact, bestowed her and her luggage upon the last and worst cab in the rank. Its driver, surly and insolent, acknowledged the receipt of his fare—which Pat's ignorance had nearly doubled—by extending his open hand, with the silver coins in it, as if to invoke the judgment of Heaven, while he remarked, with a derisive piety that was based upon the determination to be offensive, "Holy and Merciful, Lord God Almighty!"

The door of the hotel had opened, and a small but competent boy appeared.

With the words, addressed severely to the cabman, "Enough said!" he swept Patsey and her luggage into the house, and, banging the door on the continuing invective, observed that he knew that one well, and he was a thrick o' the loop and a holy terror.

It was nearly midnight. One dim jet of gas fluttered in the hall of the hotel, which was a small and humble one that Lady Kirwen felt it her duty to patronise, since its struggling proprietress had at one time been her maid, and did not permit the obligation to be forgotten. The boy, yawning dramatically, lighted Patricia up the steep stairs with a candle of which nothing remained but the wick, flaming in the socket of the candlestick.

"How can Mother stand this hole!" thought Patricia, dragging herself and Dooley after the guide. "Not for the sake of forty Finnegans would I stay here!"—from which it may be gathered that Miss Kirwen had not as yet visualised her proposed future as an art-student, living on forty pounds a year.

She was received by her mother with anxiety and bewilderment.

"What has happened? Why have you come? Is there anything wrong? You told me nothing in your wire ——"

"I had a row with the Master. You mayn't send swears in a telegram."

Her mother groaned. " What about? "

Pat gazed at her with tragic eyes, ringed now with black and set in a tragic face. She made no answer, and letting herself fall into an armchair, lay back, her long legs stretched in front of her. Her hat fell off; even her bright hair looked limp and tired. Her mother looked down on her with dismay.

" . . . and poor little Dooley too! " Lady Kirwen went on. " My darling, *why* have you brought Dooley?"

" He hasn't fought with Dooley," said Pat, with a shaky laugh. " Only me—Mother, I've been going hard since three o'clock this morning—I'm half dead! I'll tell you everything to-morrow——"

And, having announced this intention, Pat sat bolt upright, and beginning with her meeting with George Lester, gave her mother a minute and complete history of all that had happened, drinking, the while, the tea that Lady Kirwen's tea basket had made possible, and smoking one of the cigarettes that Jimmy Corran had poured into her coat pocket as she was getting into the dogcart.

Lady Kirwen, with faint, helpless moans, listened despairingly, and accepted with resignation her daughter's concluding declaration, that she was going to Paris, to work there " as long as the money holds out." She made but two coherent comments, one being that Jimmy Corran must be paid—though Heaven alone knew where the money was to come from, unless, yes! she might sell some of Aunt Austin's pearls!—and the other, that " The First Mademòiselle " (which suggested the Court of a later Louis) would be a good person to write to in Paris. Didn't she keep a *pension* for ladies only? The second one wasn't so reliable, was she?

" I liked her much the best," threw in Pat.

" She certainly was far less troublesome about her food," agreed Lady Kirwen, reflectively. " But didn't we hear that after she left us she had some affair with a married man? "

" Oh, bother the mademoiselles, Mother," says Pat, irritably, " do attend, I was just coming to Millie and old Dick—I'd forgotten them——"

It is not likely that Patricia had also forgotten the moment in the Old Playroom when all that had led up to it was so very nearly obliterated. But she had shunted it off the main line of action. The hesitation, she told herself, had been only momentary, only because she had been dead tired, not worth even hinting at to Mother—of course she had to explain about the money, that was different——

So Lady Kirwen (being, as has been said, a Bohemian at heart) abandoned opposition, and ran away too. She pacified her conscience by writing to inform Sir Ingram—having replied to his telegrams with an assurance that Pat was in her safe keeping—and then she and Patricia fled to London by the night mail, before the letter could reach him and enable him to interpose his commands.

It is hard to say which of the runaways, mother or daughter, enjoyed most the ensuing ten days that the sacrifice of a selection of Aunt Austin's pearls (removed from the bank to take up humiliating existence in a Dublin pawn-shop) had made possible. The mutinous couple spent them in shopping, sight-seeing, and great contentment, regardless of such thunders of the House as Sir Ingram, who was no great hand with a pen, had succeeded in despatching by post on receipt of his wife's letter from London.

" *Only for the trouble I'm having with Lester and dis-*

temper among the young hounds I should go over to London and insist on Pat coming back with me and you. I am very much anoyed——"

It was regrettable that the suggestion of anti-climax imparted by Sir Ingram's slight mistake in spelling should have appealed to Lady Kirwen's unmanageable sense of humour.

" We needn't *telegraph* to Papa," she had said at last, mastering her shaking voice, and trying in vain to keep the note of conspiracy out of it. " A letter will do—and —and " (her voice trembled again) " I might tell him where the dictionary——"

" Now, Mother," Patsey said, impatiently, " *please* don't begin again! "

Patsey, like her father, had little sympathy with the victims of their risible nerves.

Lady Kirwen went down to Victoria with Patricia, having provided her with such a variety of " things that she might find useful " as would have satisfied the requirements of the White Knight in Wonderland, and saw her off with a gaiety and an ardently expressed envy that Patsey, being young and excited, took at their face value, and knew nothing of the tears that hid the departing train from her mother.

* * * * *

A wild night. Raining hard at Newhaven, and blowing a bit too. Patricia found the ascent of the narrow gangway up to the deck of the cross-channel boat a far from easy matter, and the fact that she was carrying a heavy green carpet-bag (for carpet-bags were still in existence in the year 1884) did not facilitate her progress. In the carpet-bag, it may at once be stated, was Dooley. Patricia, determined that only death should part them, having devised this method of saving her from the horrors of the " galley " in the steamer, and the barbarous dog-boxes in the trains. On the wet, dark deck, a struggling crowd, the concentrated steamer crowd, fiercely self centred, and terrible with suit-cases, whose struggles have the reckless disregard for others exhibited by wild elephants in a *keddah*, or big fish in a net, swayed and strove, and made progress to the cabin and lower regions an almost insuperable difficulty. The carpet-bag in Patsey's right hand grew, like St. Christopher's burden, every minute more heavy. The hat-box in her left developed a fresh projecting corner at each step, the retention of the umbrella under her arm became more and more precarious. At each moment she expected a protest from the incarcerated Dooley; almost she hoped for it, as an assurance that her charge had not been smothered in the crush. Again, as when in the Dublin four-wheeler, she said to herself, " Am I a fool? "

The pressure had become almost intolerable; she contrived to turn her head, and looked over her shoulder to make a protest to those behind her who were so brutally shouldering forward. As she did so she felt a hand groping for the handles of the carpet-bag, and a voice, a voice that brought her back in a flash to home and Templenoe, said in her ear:

" Allow me, Miss Kirwen! "

Patsey's soul started in amazement, her body being too tightly wedged to do so. George Lester was wonderfully beside her.

" You! *You!* " was all that she could find to say.

" I saw you going up the gangway. Please let me carry this for you——"

He took the carpet-bag from her hand, and contrived

to slip behind her so as to take some of the weight of the crush off her.

Suddenly the ground opened under her feet, and she found herself going downwards, held erect by other people's backs. Then came level ground, and release from the worst of the throng. She was swept unresisting into a backwater, and found George Lester was still beside her.

"Where are you going? Are you really going to Paris after all?—like me!" she added.

George looked at her with what seemed to her a strange expression; triumph was in it, and something that was appealing, almost scared.

"Yes—I got away! And to think of you going there too!" Without waiting for her reply, he went on, "Miss Kirwen, this bag is entirely too heavy for you—if I might be allowed to help you off the boat with your things?" He spoke with hesitating humility.

That Miss Kirwen should have accepted the offer was an act contrary to all her theories of independence, and her confidence in her own strength. The familiar Irish voice, so gentle and lingering, so incredibly unexpected, had made her realise how lonely she was, how far away from home, and how consoling among all this herd of hard, self-engrossed strangers, to meet with someone who knew her, who wanted to help her.

She found herself accepting his offer gratefully.

"But haven't you things of your own?"

"I haven't but just one small thing—it'd be a pleasure—I'll be here to meet you when we get in; I'm back in the second-class." He stopped with a gasp. "My God! what's in this?"

George forgot his shyness, and almost dropped the carpet-bag in not unnatural alarm at its suddenly becoming restive.

"Hush! Dooley's in it! My little dog—I'll take her to the cabin—I've got a berth—I'm smuggling her!" She began to laugh in the spring of her spirit in finding a fellow conspirator, and one whom she had already proved to be good at need. "Then I'll look out for you here——"

She was gone. George stood, rapt, marvelling, thanking Heaven for the chance of being useful to her, almost forgetting the weight of shame that had oppressed him ever since that indisputably questionable episode in connection with his father's cheque-book. He had come very near to making confession to his mother. His conscience was such a nuisance; anything to quieten it; and he had such a good case, it would be a relief to expound it and set forth his defence. Even though his mother might not at once be amenable to argument, she would never willingly betray him, and it would give him a consoling feeling that his guilt was, as one might say, shared. Yet, on second thoughts, it might be risky. She could not help being transparent; it was not in her to keep a secret. Maybe he'd better wait and say nothing. When he had the cheque cashed, and the money safe, he might write to her—his father was always out when the post came in—he would put his case convincingly, and she might be able to hold his father down when the murder was out and the row began. After all, his father had slapped his face. He owed George something for that. (From all of which it may be gathered that George's conscience was not entirely unmanageable.)

For ten days after the encounter of father and son an armed neutrality had reigned at the Lesters' farm. George had made no sign of contumacy; had fed at his father's table, responding briefly to his mother's observations, addressed ostensibly to him, but aimed at his father, as to his approaching return to college, and the preparations about his clothes that she had still to make.

Together with his conscience, temporarily battened down and under hatches, George had inherited something of the iron Irish Protestant backbone that had come to him and his father by direct descent from one of those Cromwellian soldiers whose stock, prosperous, upright, bigoted, and contentious, has penetrated most of Ireland, contributing with potency to her welfare and to her rebellions, if not to her pacification.

Holy George ignored his wife's hints. In his heart he was as determined as ever that George's hand should not be taken from the Gospel Plough, and in view of that determination he felt it to be regrettable that he should have smacked the face of a future clergyman; apology, even, might be due, but not until young George should have seen the error of his ways—stupidity first, then "impidence"—and acknowledged his faults; then, perhaps——

In the meantime young George had, very quietly, proceeded with his preparations for abandoning the plough. He had written to the Professor of French in his Dublin college, from whom, incidentally it may be mentioned, he had hitherto learned nothing. Now, however, he acquired from M. Dupin quite a considerable amount of useful information. M. Dupin, who had a fancy for George, had read his letter with interest, and had sympathised with him in a desire to desert Dublin for Paris ("For any reason, *parbleu!*"). M. Dupin had arranged about his passport, and had communicated with an English colleague in a Paris *Lycée*, and, between them, the way had been made comparatively straight, even for such a youth as young George, bred for the

Ministry, and adventuring, tongue-tied by ignorance of language, manners, and customs, into a foreign city.

Thus it was that, at the end of ten days, the younger George packed his small portmanteau, and strapped it on to the back of his bicycle, and without a word to anyone, not even to his mother—but that was only because of her transparency—bicycled to the station, and went to Dublin by the early mail. Arrived there, he had time, before the start of the North Wall boat, to visit his friend, M. Dupin, for final words of counsel, to cash the cheque that had, for these past ten days, stung like a mustard-leaf in his breast-pocket, and to sell his bicycle; and then, having burnt every boat, he betook himself to that office where the ends of the earth lie, submissive and accessible on the counter, and took his through ticket for Paris.

Paris! The very name shook him to the core (wherever that conventional seat of emotion may be). As the train banged and cantered in changing rhythms, from Holyhead, down the long line, to London (and London was exciting enough too), he thought of how he and a fellow-student, idling in Grafton Street, had seen in a window a picture of a lady, opulent of physique, exiguous of costume, and how the fellow-student had remarked respectfully, " Sum'chous female! I'll bet she comes from Pawris! " George had no taste for ladies of the Parisian type (if indeed the diagnosis of the fellow-student had been correct). He told himself that he had another and very different ideal, one that inspired to high thoughts and endeavour. The Paris that he was bound for was the place where (for she had told him so) he would find Art, the Real Thing. This was the Paris for whose sake he had taken his hand from the plough; not that of females however sumptuous.

To be quite exact, George's actual destination was Number One Hundred, Rue de la Grande Chaumière, in the Quartier Latin. He had written it out clearly to show the cabman. A room had been engaged for him by M. Dupin's English colleague, a studio had been suggested, just round the corner. The colleague had promised general friendliness, and with nearly forty pounds in his pocket (for he had got a good price for his bicycle), he told himself, after anxious calculation, that he would have nine hundred francs, as near as made no difference, and with that he could certainly live for—what was this Dupin told him he ought to be able to live on? Well, what was the good of talking? He'd just have to make it last as long as he could—besides, hadn't Dupin's pal said he might give lessons in English and earn a bit that way? . . .

Stretched on the hard berth, in the small and gloomy second-class cabin, young George lay in the rigid stillness that is a precaution, if not a preservation, in such circumstances, while his mind revolved in ceaseless activity. The wide wings of Hope fanned his hot thoughts; vision after vision formed and faded, yielding place each to a more dazzling successor, until—but by the time his first picture was in the Salon the steamer was in mid-channel, and the night was stormy. The profound depression that precedes sea-sickness fell upon him, and with the certainty that his father would prosecute him for forgery, George's mental sufferings gave place to physical ones.

CHAPTER XVII

"*The livelong night in Branksome rang*
The ceaseless sounds of steel;
The castle-bell, with backward clang,
Sent forth the 'larum peal."

THIS may, possibly, be an excessive description of the actual state of things at Kirwenscourt on Sir Ingram's return from the farm to luncheon on the fatal day of the drag, but it presents, on the whole, a reasonably correct impression of the general atmosphere there.

Sir Ingram had come in brimming over with the clemency towards his erring daughter that he had magnanimously determined upon for reasons that, after due consideration, had appeared to him sufficient, and that were not entirely dissociated from anxiety to effect the reconciliation before she should have time to write to Lady Kirwen.

When, therefore, with the sceptre metaphorically extended, he marched into the dining-room and asked for Miss Patricia, to be told that she had driven away, with luggage, in the dog-cart, with the black horse, and Denis Brian, and where to Moloney didn't know, what has been alluded to above as " the 'larum peal" uttered no uncertain clang.

" And why the hell did no one ask her where she was going? " yelled Sir Ingram, who, in such a moment as this, found mere shouting quite inadequate as a method of disclosure of his mood. " Here am I keeping a pack of dumb, dam' fools——"

Jimmy Corran, coming into the room at this moment, noted the happy alliteration with respect, but, noting also that it betokened a state of high storm, would have been glad to have retired till calm was restored. In this, however, he was frustrated by Moloney, who, regarding him thankfully, as being of the nature of a lightning conductor, said:

" Here's his lordship, Sir Ingram, I expect he can tell you——" and slipped out of the room, carefully shutting the door behind him.

" What the devil's all this about Patsey, Jimmy? He says *you* know." The bereaved parent proceeded, in scarcely less infuriated enquiry, " They say she's gone away, and taken luggage? What's it mean? Where's she gone? "

" Well, sir," began Jimmy, nervously, " I—I believe she's gone to Carron Hill—to—to see Mrs. Villiers—I'm not sure—that's what she said she was going to do——" (He thought, " If the old boy finds out about that cheque——")

The old boy, however, caught at the suggestion of Carron Hill, and began, with rather less violence, to discuss the possibility of an invitation by the morning's post from Millie, having been the explanation of Patsey's sudden departure.

" I was greatly annoyed with her this morning," he said, still angry, but simmering down. " I wouldn't have believed it possible she'd have put a hand to such a disgraceful business! I spoke to her when I met her——" Sir Ingram cleared his throat and hung fire for a moment, " h'm, h'm—rather sharply, perhaps, but I've been thinking—in spite of what she said to me at the time——"

(" By Jove, I've got to give him her note! " thought

the listener. " I'll be hanged if I will! I'll leave it on his writing-table! ")

" —that it was probably not her own doing altogether, and I wanted to tell her I'd say no more about it—and—and I'd overlook her share in it."

" Very good of you, sir," said Jimmy, respectfully (while he thought " The boot's rather on the other foot in the matter of overlooking! ").

" But that dam' feller Lester'd better look out for himself! " Sir Ingram went on, feeling himself here on firm ground. " A dairyman that I have out there told me that he found the body of a sheep in the covert, as full of poison as an egg is of meat! That's what he said! I met him on the road. He said he found the vixen lying dead beside it, and only God knew how many more had taken it as well as herself! That's what he told me! He's the man who stops for me, he knows what he's talking about! "

" Perhaps it was no harm to get the hounds out of it in a hurry? " ventured Jimmy.

This was a step farther in the matter of clemency than the Master was prepared to go, but he was so far pacified that he began upon his luncheon, and between mouthfuls soothed himself by sketching roughly the course his interview with the elder Lester (" that psalm-singing scoundrel ") would take.

(Why the qualification of psalm-singing should imply a very special form of hypocritical turpitude it is difficult to say. Very respectable people sing psalms, also hymns, with great and entirely innocent enjoyment, even though this may be to themselves rather than to their neighbours.)

" I'll write to Maud to-night," Sir Ingram went on; I've missed the first post. I don't understand this bolting out of the house of Patsey's, without a word to anyone—I don't approve of it—what's more, I won't have it!" He glared at Jimmy, challenging a contradiction that he was in no danger of receiving. "I don't know what girls are coming to nowadays! I should like to have seen one of *my* sisters ordering a horse and trap and man out of the stables as if the place belonged to them! My poor father would have had a word to say to them, I can tell you! Why, not even I myself would have done it—and I was the eldest son, mind you—not till he had a stroke and lost the power of speech!" Sir Ingram took a long pull at his whisky and soda. Then he laughed reminiscently. "The poor old governor! He couldn't talk, but if things weren't going as he liked, he used to lay about him with his stick as he lay in bed, and let 'em know he wasn't pleased! *He* had the Kirwen temper right enough! *He* made the feathers fly, and the maids, and my poor mother too! *I* kept out of his way, and let the women handle him the best way they could! I tell you what, Jimmy, it's no bad thing to be your own father—as you are! I had the devil of a time to wait before I came in!"

To this proposition Jimmy (whose father had been killed in a point-to-point when he was a year old) assented without difficulty, as, indeed, he would have agreed with anything his host chose to say, being prudently determined on keeping the peace at any price. "But," he thought, "I don't think I can stick it here much longer, now. I think I shall have to send myself a telegram——"

It was queer, he said to himself later, knocking the billiard balls about for want of other occupation, what a difference a woman made in the house. Cousin Maud, for instance; it wasn't as if he saw such a lot of her, but somehow one felt she was there, rum little thing as she was, she was always friendly and pleasant. And Patsey . . . yes, Patsey . . . Hadn't he been entirely an ass about the way he had "handled," as Sir Ingram said, Patsey? . . . He thought of the rides they had had together, "schooling" all over the country, with Pat racing to be first over the jumps . . . and what fun it was strumming duets with her, when she'd hustle him along faster than he could go, and would slap his hand —a good hearty slap—when he came in in the wrong place! . . . And then he lived again that moment when he had sat so close to her on the tool-bench in the Old Playroom, and had held her hand in his. . . . Why had he let her go? . . . He saw her face when she had looked up at him and tried to thank him. . . . Oh, why hadn't he kissed her there and then . . . held on to her, told her that he wouldn't let her stir till she had promised to give up that rot of going to Paris, and to stay at home, and—yes! it had come to that—marry him? He knew now that nothing less would content him. What an unspeakable fool he had been to absolutely grease the wheels for her! To have done it with his own dirty money! To have simply chucked it at her to help her to get away! . . . Oh, what a fool! . . . He hit the ball with which he was playing a smack that drove it flying round the table from cushion to cushion, till some mysterious impulse that had been latent in the smack lifted it off the cloth and sent it spinning to the floor, along which it sped until it ran under the immense leather-covered seat at the end of the long room. Jimmy had to lie down and rake under the seat for it with a cue-rest. The bottom of the seat was no more than six inches off the ground, and it was impossible to see where the ball had rolled to. He had raked out a good dustpanful of dust and fluff before at last he touched the ball and compelled it to break cover.

He put it back on the table and, finding the clothes-brush devoted to the toilet of the green cloth, brushed himself down.

"Yes! Here I go again! I'm a damned fool!" he repeated, brushing violently. "Everything's all my own fault! What the deuce did I knock the beastly thing off the table for?"

And why, oh why—the thought kept grinding on—why had he drawn that idiotic enabling cheque?

CHAPTER XVIII

DIEPPE at four a.m. on a dark and dripping morning in mid-September can be a depressing introduction to the pleasant land of France. But Patricia's spirits were proof against depression. George had been ready at the place of tryst, and together they had fought their way ashore through the mob of resolute, shoving fellow passengers, all inspired by the same fixed and dog-like determination to be the first to leave the boat.

With the clatter of strange voices and wooden shoes in their ears, their eyes bewildered by the dazzle of the gas flares with their blinding reflections in the puddles of the rough pier and upon the wet railway-lines that intervened between steamer and station, Patricia and George joined the procession of laden passengers and still more laden porters, splashing onward in semi-darkness to the *Douane*. To George, the resonant, nasal clank of the French official voice conveyed no more of human meaning than had the sounds of strange wild creatures that he had listened to in the Dublin Zoo. But the Mademoiselles, First and Second, had not been entirely worthless, and, before thay had perfected their English, Patsey had learnt something of their French. Now, enforced by the fact of having a companion, helpful and yet helpless, she faced the ordeal of the *Douane* with an undaunted front and a silent prayer for Dooley's immobility. Frankly unbosoming her hat-box, she then, in the halo of honesty thus acquired, boldly presented the green carpet-bag, plump with

Dooley, with the assurance that there was nothing in it to be declared. A moment of supreme tension ensued. But Dooley lay still as the dead, and the official, being unacquainted with the lines—

> " *Judas had eyes like thine,*
> *Of candid blue!* "

gazed affectionately at the charming young English Miss, and, without so much as a glance at the green bag, made, unhesitatingly, the sign of the cross in white chalk on the swelling for which its occupant's ribs were responsible.

The wild night had discouraged travellers, and it was easy to find an empty carriage.

" But that's a First, I'm going Second! " Patsey said, proud of her economy.

George said to himself that his luck was turning. She climbed up the steep steps, and took his burdens, that were hers, from him, and looking down on him from the open door, thanked him for his help.

" They'll do the other things in Paris—they told me so at Victoria——"

George, having no " other thing," heard this with composure. He picked up his little portmanteau.

" Is there anything else I could do for you? "

His upturned face was very pale. Few people can look their best after a rough crossing, but his recent afflictions had only added a becoming touch of tragedy to George's good looks.

Patsey thought: " He looks wretched! Poor thing, he's been very useful to me. I'll give him some of Mother's brandy——" Aloud, she said, " Won't you come with me in this carriage? "

* * * * *

Few apartments could be more aridly unsympathetic than that into which the First Mademoiselle conducted Patricia, with trumpets that flourished at full blast, from the *rez-de-chaussée* to the *belle petite chambre au troisième* destined for the guest.

So small, so hard, so shining was its every aspect, that Patsey stood with her feet close together on one of the tiny mats on its frozen floor, feeling several sizes larger than she ought to be, fearing that movement might involve her in collision with the dolls' furniture by which she was surrounded. Moreover, the attitude of the First Mademoiselle—whose name, it may be well to mention, was Leroux—with regard to Dooley, filled her with anxiety. Dooley, with less than her usual *savoir faire*, had opened relations by growling offensively at the Lady of the House; had then dashed upstairs in advance of her owner, making a hurried inspection of any room of which the door chanced to be open, in more than one instance shrieks of alarm, and invocations of the Deity, indicating the presence of an occupant, and when Mademoiselle Leroux, with a last laudatory blast, flung open the door of the room dedicated to her late pupil and future *pensionnaire*, Dooley raced in tempestuously, and leaping immediately upon the bed, proceeded to trample circle-wise in the centre of a pink satin-covered *duvet*, even, with small angry groans, to bite at it, in the effort to arrange it to her liking.

Mademoiselle Leroux regarded this performance with a bitter eye. It was obvious that Dooley's dislike was reciprocated.

"Ah, this dog, he wishes to make himself comfortable!" she said, with a laugh in which she was unable to repress the acidity.

She had grown a grizzled beard and moustache in the ten years that had elapsed since Patsey had been her pupil. Patsey had not trembled before her then, having despised personal chastisement, and been skilled in escape—trees, haylofts, and stables offering the needed facilities—but how much more terrible might she not now prove, when escape was impossible, and so vulnerable a point as Dooley offered itself for attack? She felt suddenly beaten and discouraged. The deadly conviction of having made a mess of everything, that can be the revenge of a tired body on a sensitive mind, again fell upon her. Could she stand it? Was it all going to be beastly like this?

She plucked Dooley from the bed and held her in her arms.

" I will teach her—she will soon learn—please pardon——"

Mademoiselle was effusive in indulgence, even though Dooley's owner felt that a steel wire of animosity threaded the froth of forgiveness. A flood of affectionate enquiries for all whom she had known in Ireland followed, and Elijah could not have welcomed his ministering ravens more warmly than did Patricia the stout maid, whose arrival with food and drink interrupted the catechism. Ireland being disposed of, Mademoiselle Leroux entered upon biographies of her *pensionnaires*, to which Pauline, the stout maid, supplied, as it were, elucidating footnotes, while the steam from the coffee and the hot milk grew less and less; but at length mistress and maid talked themselves out of the room together; their voices faded gradually down the well of the winding staircase, and were still.

" *Enfin seul!* " quoted the most recent of the *pensionnaires*, hurling her hat and gloves on to the floor and sitting down to coffee, less hot than it had been, and to about half as much bread and butter as she and Dooley were ready to eat.

* * * * *

It was eleven o'clock, and Sunday morning. Patricia had unpacked her trunk, had arranged for the disgruntled Dooley a bed in its depths, and seated in a narrow, serious armchair with upright back, and rounded padding of iron covered with red velvet, was smoking one of Jimmy's cigarettes and trying to compose her mind.

There came a light tap on the door. Pat, controlling, not without difficulty, the temper she had inherited from the Kirwen side of the house, threw her cigarette out of the window (because, in the then social conditions, such a sacrifice was practically compulsory for a self-respecting young lady) and said " *Entrez!* " in a voice hostile with its loss.

The door was opened for a few inches.

" May I intrude upon you? " said, in English, a very gentle, almost melancholy voice.

Pat thought, " What's the good of asking, when you've done it? " Then, since there was nothing else to be said, " Please come in."

" Oh, but why did you put out your pipe? " continued, from just without the doorway, the gentle voice, with its mournful sweetness of tone.

The sacrifice had been in vain. Pat went to the door. A small, dark-haired, dark-eyed girl, very smartly clad in outdoor attire, was standing, smiling and hesitating, on the threshold.

" I smoke too," said the visitor, " Virginians, same as you do—I'm Virginian myself."

She looked up at Pat, from under long dark lashes.

"I like Virginians," said Pat, awkwardly, feeling not only too tall, but also badly dressed.

"But how sweet of you to say so?" cooed the little Virginian. "I heard you were Irish, and now I know it! English people don't pay compliments!"

She laughed, a low seductive laugh that made Patsey think of warm cream. "Now, please let me tell you why I've pushed in like this. I saw your little dog coming upstairs—I'm just crazy about dogs—and I want to warn you that there's a great big dog here, Hector, who'd swallow that little fellow of yours whole——"

"She'll take care of herself!" said Pat, feeling more friendly.

"Oh, *she*," said the visitor, with understanding. "Hector's a real Frenchman, always civil to the ladies—except at night. He'd eat his own mother if he met her after dark!"

"It's very kind of you to tell me—I've only just come——"

"Why! of course we all know that! And that your father's an Irish nobleman, and that you've a *vrai talent pour la peinture!* Why! We've talked only of you for the last three days! The *pensionnaires* think you're going to be more interestin' than a dog-fight!"

Another soft and creamy laugh followed the statement.

Patricia looked at the visitor with horror, tempered by incredulity.

"Not really?"

"Why yes." The visitor nodded her head, smiling; her smile was as attractive as her voice. "They're all just only trying to live till they see you! But *you* needn't mind! You know what that song says—'She was far too lovely to care!'"

"But, I *do* care! I won't go down!"

The little Virginian put her head on one side, putting the first finger of a small hand, sparkling with rings, to her forehead, and affected to think deeply.

(Pat thought "How pretty she is!")

"Well . . . Say, this is Sunday morning, our *jour de repos*—you come out just now, in one half-hour, and have lunch with me and my friend. Give the *déjeuner* here a miss! That'll give them all a jolt, and it'll give you time to make up your mind to face them like a little Christian soldier!"

Patsey began to laugh, and the little Virginian's face sparkled like her rings.

"That's all right! Then you'll come—but, oh my! what manners I've got! *None*, *I* think—I've never made myself known to you! My name's Mercy Le Mont."

"Mine's Patricia Kirwen, and my father isn't a nobleman!"

"You don't think we don't all know your name!" exclaimed Miss Mercy Le Mont, almost with pity. "Why," she went on, meditatively, "it is my sure belief that if you cut any of our boarders open, you'd find it written across their hearts!—like that old queen of yours and Calais." She got up from the small gilt chair on which she had perched. "And specially *chez* the Princess!" she added.

"A Princess?" Patsey echoed.

"Well, just a darkie princess—she don't amount to much—from Java—I'm a true-born American, I don't bow the knee to Royalty—or not the coloured sort. Well, *au revoir*. I'll call for you. It's a real nice day; let's improve the shining hour."

CHAPTER XIX

MADEMOISELLE LEROUX'S Pension was situated within the bounds of that region that is, theoretically at least, devoted to " The Four Arts "; and is known as the Quartier Latin. It was the end house of two small and quiet streets midway between the Luxembourg Gardens and the Boulevard St. Germain, the latter being the point to which prominence was given in Mademoiselle Leroux's prospectus. The house was tall, narrow, and dark; a small, impregnable courtyard lay between its front and the street, surrounded by high walls, with a huge *porte-cochère*, in which was a lesser entrance, like a rabbit-hole in the face of a cliff. There was no *concierge*, and the more favoured of the *pensionnaires* (who were all of what has been called " the more plentiful sex ") were given latchkeys, thus lightening, to some extent, the labours of Pauline in answering the summons of the bell that jangled on the wall outside the kitchen window.

In the courtyard, whose gloom was such that it discouraged even weeds from growing, Miss Mercy Le Mont, and her friend, awaited Patricia.

" This is my friend, Miss Henriette von Kappf, German by birth, American by adoption and grace! " warbled Miss Le Mont, in the voice that suggested the musical whine with which a glass bowl responds to a moistened travelling finger. " Which means that I've adopted her, and now I'm imparting grace. Hans, *fais le beau!* "

"Very pleased to meet you," said Miss Henriette von Kappf, gruffly, on the note G below the line, and in a tone that combined the accents of the lands of both birth and adoption.

"Give a paw, Hans!" continued the adopter.

Miss von Kappf put forth a large hand, red and damp from recent washing.

"Oh, Hans! Look at your nails!"

Hans withdrew the hand she had proffered, and turned indignantly on her friend.

"Well, if you had washed your broshes yourself, instead of——" she began.

"Hans, honey, don't hang out the family washing in public quite so soon——" Miss Le Mont had begun, when Patsey broke in, impulsively.

"Oh! were you painting? Have you a studio?"

"We work at Pianelli's place," said Hans, eyeing her up and down with what seemed to Pat to be disapproval. "It iss not clean. English ladies do not often stay there. Zey come, and zen zay go. It is *l'académie* for all day there. It is too serious for zem." She paused; then, with a more cheerful inflection in her solemn voice, "Is zat your dog?" She indicated Dooley, who had been minutely investigating the courtyard, taking special note of a large dog-kennel that stood in one corner, and had now joined herself to the party. "He iss a pretty sing! Do you see, Hector has observed him?"

"*Her*," put in Patsey, who was sensitive on the subject of Dooley's sex.

"It is well he is a lady, or Hector would eat him whole!" The slow solemnity of Hans's voice gave weight to her slightest utterance. "See him now! He watches!"

At one of the lower windows the stern, blue-grey face of a Great Dane had appeared.

" He should be introduced," Hans went on. " He is a friend to me—I will bring him."

Hans was a solid, strongly built young woman of about three-and-twenty, with a uniform complexion of deep pink, and very fair, almost white, hair that was cut short and parted at one side. Her eyebrows and eyelashes were of the same pale gold hue; she had a short nose and a large mouth. She wore a shirt and a collar and tie, a " Tyrolean " man's hat, and a Norfolk jacket. If, as it seemed, her intention was to be taken for an English schoolboy, only her pettitcoats frustrated it.

" But," thought Patricia, watching her striding across the courtyard to the house, " she's nice about Dooley—I think she's all right."

Miss Le Mont followed the direction of Patsey's eyes.

" I do think you'll take to old Hans," she said, pensively. " She's one of the singed cat sort—better than she looks—and she's a dandy painter."

" And do you paint? " Pat asked, thrilling at the thought of having found so instantly the friends she wanted.

" Face or canvas? asked Miss Le Mont, with an upward glance at Patsey's ardent face. " Whiles I powder my nose. But that doesn't count, does it? "

" Don't pretend you don't know what I mean! And, of course, powder counts! "

Patsey was fast becoming enamoured of this little, unexpected, exotic being. She thought " She's a darling! The very idea of that perfect complexion wanting paint! " It was delightful to be chaffed by her.

" Oh! " she continued, gazing entreatingly at her new friend. " Do you really work at Pianelli's with Miss von Kappf? Do you think I could go there too? "

" Why, sure! " Miss Le Mont laughed at her. " You don't think old Pie and Jelly keeps his *atelier* going for Hans and me? We'll bring you along to-morrow morning. It's just as good as any other—better than some—cheaper than any of them—and, dirtier! It's knee-deep in charcoal and bread-crumbs, but you won't mind that! "

" No, oh no! " panted Pat.

" And it's real serious. The *Professeurs* skin you regularly twice a week; never miss it; and the models have got to behave. Pianelli was one himself. He's up to their tricks! "

Here the hall door opened, and Hector burst out, towing after him, on a lead, the stalwart Hans, who, stalwart though she might be, was obviously being led rather than leading. The big dog, with cropped ears pricked and stern erect, advanced across the courtyard to interview Dooley, who, at first alarmed, soon recovered her self-possession, and presently, with a shriek of coquettish annoyance, sprang at his enormous head and affected to bite his lip.

" Zat is all right now," said Hans, who had studied the proceedings with profound gravity. " Komm! I am as hongry for my *déjeuner* as a wolf! "

Patricia squeezed herself out through the rabbit-hole in the *porte-cochère* in a mental condition bordering on delirium. The sun shone for her as it had never shone before. This was Paris at last! The wonderful reward of rebellion, and of secret prayers; of mutiny where obedience was owed, but also, yes, of fidelity to an ideal! She followed the enchantresses, who were putting the gilded roof on it all, feeling as though she were walking in the streets of the New Jerusalem, whereas the humble Rue Vavin, through which she was being led, narrow, rough, and unclean, as in those days it was, cherished no pretensions about itself, and would never have suggested that it was made of pure gold, or even of transparent glass.

The sour, vinous smells of the frequent *cabarets*, the whiffs of rankly luscious cookery that issued from the open doors of small restaurants, the mingled odours, all-pervading as the ether, of garlic and strange tobacco, were, to this entranced enthusiast, airs of Paradise. Everything she saw, and heard, and smelt went to her head like champagne. Even the sight of blue-bloused masons, hard at work, on the white walls of a house, regardless of the fact that it was the day of rest, gave her a pang of pleasure in its assurance that she was no longer in Ireland.

Dooley, pulling hard on the lead, shared Patsey's emotions. Never before had scents so rare and so various ravished her little black nose. Never before had cats so monstrous, so oblivious of her proximity, aroused her futile indignation. Dooley was accustomed to cats that fled at her rebuke; these offensive creatures remained immovable, plunged in malign meditation.

" As well, perhaps," thought Dooley, sententiously (for little important dogs, like Dooley, are apt to be sententious), hurrying, perforce, along after Patsey, " as well, in fact, that I am on the lead and cannot wait. These are super-cats, and their tactics incalculable."

They had walked by tortuous by-streets, led, at a round pace, by Hans, for some twenty minutes, before a final turning brought them out on the wide Boulevard of Mont Parnasse.

" We're taking you to the *Crémerie* in the Rue Bréa, where most of the studio crowd go," said Miss Le Mont. " You won't mind if it's not quite Meurice——"

" Or even a Duval," put in Hans on a bass note.

" *Mind!* " gasped Patsey. " If you only knew how I'm enjoying every minute."

They had arrived at the top of the Rue Bréa, and Miss Mercy Le Mont stood still and looked up at Pat's glowing face, laughing.

(" What a delightful laugh she has! " thought Pat.)

" Well," said Miss Le Mont, slowly and devoutly. " O all ye Green Things upon the Earth, bless ye the Lord! I never thought I should see that happen! You just wait a minute, Hans, and give this Green Thing time to bless the Lord for the Rue Bréa! "

" There will be nossing left to eat if we wait! " rejoined the practical Hans, trudging steadily on.

In a few moments she stopped at a half-glazed door, with the word *Crémerie* on the glass.

" Miss Kirwen, this is *le Père Fusco's Ménagerie*," Hans announced. " Look in, and see ze animals feed, wissout paying ze extra sixpence! "

" Don't be silly, Hans; go in quick and grab a table! "

Miss Le Mont pushed her friend up the two steps that led to the door. " If Hans can lay her tongue to any little old English wheeze, she's just as pleased——!" Hans's friend went on, in mellifluous complaint to Patricia. " If you have any Irish funny jokes, for the sake of pity don't pass them on to her—if you do, you'll regret it for ever *and* ever——"

The two stood inside the door while the process of grabbing a table was being accomplished, and the hot, unfamiliar odours of foreign foods wrapped Patsey about as with a garment, while she gazed, fascinated, telling herself that this was really she, Patricia Kirwen, and that Patricia Kirwen was really and truly here, in Paris!

Before her was a long narrow room, with bare sanded floor, and rows of small tables up either wall, leaving a very limited central passage. Seated at the tables, combining the rapacious consumption of food with loud and incessant conversation, were those who had been described to Patsey as the studio crowd.

Young girls, middle-aged girls, women of all ages, English and Americans, Germans and Scandinavians, only the Southern nations, and France herself, were unrepresented, among the clients of *le Père Fusco*. Three or four tables, only, were occupied by young men, but these, comparatively few though they were, contributed effectively to the general uproar. A hurried and harried waiting-maid darted to and fro, between the clients and the hidden source of supplies at the end of the room, chaffed, scolded, reproached, cajoled, her short full skirts snatched at as she flew by, while protests in every accent save that of her native land assailed her.

"*Voyons, Jeanne!*" An English voice, in aggrieved tones. "*Vous ne m'avez donné que trois pruneaux, et j'ai le droit de six!*"

"*De jus et mon droit!*" mocks another voice.

"*Hé! Jeanne! J'attends ce café il y a une heure!*"

"*Deux heures! Trois heures! Quatre heures!*" from the next table, sympathetically.

Then, from a distant table, a rhythmic chant, oft repeated, gathered steadily in volume:

"*Jeanne, Jeanne, l'addition! Jeanne, Jeanne, s'il vous plait!*"

"*Allons, Jeanne! Vous marchez comme une poule mouillée! Dépêchez vous un peu, n'est ce pas?*"

This, when Jeanne, in arrowy flight from the kitchen, had collided in mid-channel with a departing client, causing the mollient egg that she was carrying to leap from its *plat* and squander itself on the floor.

The sombre voice of Hans sounded above the din from the back of the room.

" *Komm!* A table is here! "

A momentary hush fell on the assembly, as Patsey preceded Miss Le Mont up the narrow gangway between the tables. Every eye was directed at the stranger, so tall, so good-looking, so startlingly clean and well dressed.

" Say, Mercy Le Mont, dear "—a compatriot youth sprang from his seat, intercepting Miss Le Mont in her passage—" make me known to Blue Eyes, won't you? "

" You lie down and keep quiet, Willie Jefferson! " returned Miss Le Mont, with more severity in her voice than in her face. " I'm not going to give her the shock of her life the first day she comes to Paris! "

" 'The quality of Mercy is not '——" began Mr. Jefferson, loudly, with a dramatic gesture.

" Oh, for the Lord's sake, give that old chestnut a rest—I'll see about it "—she nodded at Pat's light figure—" s'mother day! "

Patricia, seated at the small table, with its coarse table-cloth (quite clean for Sunday), its twin glass dish of pepper and gravel-like salt, its wineglass of wooden toothpicks, and its tall *carafe* of *ordinaire*, waited in silence the skilled decisions of her introducers as to the selections from the *menu*.

" *Pain* anyhow," began Miss Mercy, " *et beurre*, and, Hans, what about *tête de veau?* It's only eighty."

" Wait! " said Hans, magisterially. " Soldan has eaten it—I will ask her how it is——"

She rose and went to a table at a little distance, at which a big fair Finlander was sucking an orange, with placid disregard of the fact that her mouth, though large, was not large enough to master the superabundant juice.

" She says it was quite good—all but the eye of the calf. She said it look so blue through ze sauce," Hans reported seriously. " Miss Kirwen," she went on, " I took it from her for your dog. Here it is."

" Now, isn't that just Hans? " exclaimed Hans's friend. " She'd bring it home and make soup of it if she thought I shouldn't catch her out!—Real old *Deutsch Haus-frau*—gather-up-the-bits-that-nothing-be-lost! That's what you are, Hans! "

Hans took no notice of the reproaches. She put down a plate before Patsey, and Patsey, anxious though she was to comport herself as became a genuine student of the Quartier Latin, was unable to repress a cry of horror.

" Oh, *don't* give her that awful thing! "

" But why not? " expostulated Hans. " Poor little sing, she would loff it! "

" Well, give it to her quickly," said Patsey, shutting her eyes.

CHAPTER XX

IT was Monday, September 22nd, not much after 7.30 a.m., and Patricia was bound for Monsieur Pianelli's *Atelier des Dames*. On Sunday afternoon, instructed by her new friends, she had invested in the necessary instruments of her coming toil—a large *carton*, a dozen sheets of white Michallet paper, a bundle of sticks of charcoal, a lump of bread, and a box of *punaises*. (Had Patsey been a little older she might have been touched, instead of faintly bored, by the innocent pleasure Miss von Kappf derived from speaking of these as " bugs.")

Now, laden with these, and palpitating with excitement, she was hurrying, in company with Hans, to " inscribe " herself as a student in the Atelier Pianelli. She had scarcely slept during the night that preceded this memorable day. She had sat up till late, writing a long letter to her mother, in which a glowing description of her two godmothers in Art occupied several sheets, and it had seemed to her that when, after she had abandoned all hope of sleep, it had at last crept upon her, it had been immediately routed by the thumps of Pauline upon the door, heralding her entry with the meagre meal with which Mademoiselle Leroux's clients were invited to break their fast.

The dinner of the previous evening had seemed to the new *pensionnaire* of insupportable length, and its quality of an indifference that went far towards reconciling her healthy young appetite to its lack of quantity.

Her neighbours had been, on the one hand, an elderly German lady, stone deaf, with an elderly daughter, both practically speechless, and, on the other, the little fat coffee-coloured Javanese princess, of whom Miss Le Mont had spoken, who, erring on the other extreme, of excessive conversation, had made instant and passionate overtures of friendship, and had then proceeded to embarrassing and prolonged disparagement of their hostess, and their companion guests, together with bitter complaints " *à cause de la nourriture*," all hissed in a hot whisper in Patsey's reluctant ear. Patsey had attempted to stem the confidences by an enquiry as to the reason of the absence of Miss Le Mont and Miss von Kappf, but this had but served to divert the stream of disparagement into another channel. " *Ces dames*," did not mix with Mademoiselle Leroux's *pensionnaires; ces dames* made their *ménage* for themselves; they were entirely isolated; their *appartement* (" of two little rooms only ") was *au quatrième*, there was nothing above them but *le bon Dieu*, they did not care to associate with *nous autres en bas!*

Patsey thought the dinner would never end. She longed to take up the gage of battle for *ces dames*, but felt that she was as yet scarcely privileged to do so. There had followed a quarter of an hour of social distraction, in response to an invitation from Mademoiselle Leroux to join their " little circle " in " *le petit salon vert* "; when, at length, the newcomer had escaped to solitude and Dooley, she told herself that she felt like a squeezed lemon, sour and flat, and decided that, in writing to her mother, whatever else she might tell her, it would not be advisable to quote the Princess's remarks *à cause de la nourriture*.

The Pianelli Studios, for there were three, one of

them for women, and two for men, formed three sides of a paved courtyard, to which life and interest were imparted by a few anæmic plane-trees, two yellow cats, and a good many weeds. An ancient wrought-iron gate closed the courtyard to the world without, and was guarded by a small porter's lodge. There, shepherded by Hans, and received into the fold by Madame Marthe, the *concierge*, Patricia Maud Kirwen inscribed herself, and paid her fifty *francs* for the coming month of work in both classes, morning and afternoon. It seemed little to pay for admission to Paradise.

She felt as if she were walking in a dream as she followed Hans along a dark passage, jostling her way among equally early birds (for it was but just eight o'clock), into the Studio. The first impression she received was one of light and space. Then she absorbed in detail the more salient features. An immense window, high up in the high wall, facing to the north; a huge room, with a forest of tall wooden easels, and lesser groves of rush-bottomed stools of varying height, all ranged in serried half-circles, whose formation was determined, as far as the new student could judge, by a high wooden stand in conjunction with an immense stove, placed against the centre of the wall that faced the window. The walls were coloured a non-committal drab. A heavy curtain, that might once have been green, but was now in complete dusty accord with the walls, draped the farther end of the room. Near the door a zinc-lined trough, with taps above it, and a roller towel beside it, indicated the possibility of ablutions, but to the dispassionate observer the general impression produced by the Atelier Pianelli and its occupants was that the trough, unpretentious though it might be, was as much for ornament as for use.

From behind the curtain a few young women were dragging *cartons;* others were clothing themselves in dingy calico overalls; a few others stood with their backs against the wall under the window, talking, and giving an idle attention to the movements of a fat, dark, elderly man, who was mounted on the stand beside the stove. He had his back to the room, and though it was apparent that he was arranging something, his very stout person hid what he was handling. There was a petulance in his gestures which suggested that this, whatever it might be, was of an intractable nature; he was talking loudly in Italian, and the big *Finlandaise* (she who had rejected the eye of the calf) was standing near, and was talking simultaneously and equally loudly to him in French. Suddenly the fat man descended from the stand, and moving on one side, shouted:

"*Elle est bien comme ça, Mesdames? Hein?*"

In the year eighteen hundred and eighty-four Queen Victoria had ruled her realm for nearly fifty years, and Monsieur Pianelli's latest *élève* had been born just midway through that period of protracted and intensive decorum. Moreover, Ireland, wherein her twenty years of life had hitherto been spent, was a country that, at that time, prided itself upon its extreme delicacy of feeling and regard for the conventions. And even though Patricia's mamma was considered—by her step-daughters—to be "lax" in some respects, her papa was a prime and perfect product of the Victorian era, and it was even told of his mother, the late dowager, that she threw a shawl over her mirror before she took a bath.

Taking these facts and the general influence of environment into consideration, it will be better understood why Patsey turned crimson, and wished that the studio floor, grimy though it indubitably was, might swallow her up, when the portly M. Pianelli moved to one side, and it became apparent to her that he had been arranging the pose of an entirely naked female model.

Immediately, in response to the challenge of the *Patron*, a chorus of indignant voices answered, in accents for which England, America, and Germany shared responsibility, that the pose was identical with that of "the woman of last week," that it was boring and intolerable, with much more to the same effect; but before their joint vocabulary of complaint had run dry, M. Pianelli, flinging up both arms, and shrieking a brief appeal to his God for support and patience in these trials, sprang, with surprising agility, upon the model stand, and addressed himself impetuously to a fresh disposition of the model, a small and exceedingly plain Italian. At length, a show of hands having been called for, a pose was decided upon by vote, and the *Patron*, remarking in a tone of relief, "*Maintenant, pour les hommes!*" departed at full speed.

"Does he always do this?" said Patsey, in an indignant whisper to Hans. "I think it's horrible!"

"Bot why?" returned Hans, in her slow voice. "He was himself a model. He can do it very well. Do you find ze pose not *sympathique?*"

"I suppose I've got to stand it," muttered Pat, the scarlet of shock reinforced by indignation; "but I call it barbaric!"

"So? Is it *l'Académie* that you find, yes, shocking? Or zat ze old Pie and Jelly should pose her?"

"Both!"

Hans began to laugh, and produced the particular phrase of her large *répertoire* of English that she felt to be the most brilliantly idiomatic.

"My child, do not flooster your keedneys for a small sing like zis! Wait for ze monthly *Parade Marsch*, when six or eight are here to be chosen!"

Before the inwardness of the threat could be revealed an English girl approached.

"Hullo, von Kappf, have you taken your place? I'm going to get next you—old Bouvier's always a bit sweeter after he's done you!"

"Bouvier's not coming this week," put in another Englishwoman. "Pie and Jelly's just told me. I met him outside. He says he'll have to do the corrections himself."

"What a swindle!" said the first English girl. "I don't believe in old Pie! Von Kappf, you'll give me a 'crit' some time, won't you?"

"Why, sure!" said Hans, amiably, in her best American accent. "Bot I find a help of ze old Pie is very goot! Ha-ha! you see the choke?" She appealed to Patsey. "A help of pie! Yes! *Komm*, you shall sit by me, and Mercy next to you——"

Splendid Hans! She had refused the Englishwoman, and was exalting the humble and meek! Patsey grinned at her own definition of herself. Such had not been her reputation at home! It just showed, she told herself, how Paris was improving her!

Work began. Patsey watched Hans' operations with the rapt attention of an eager dog, whose master is investigating a rabbit-hole on its account.

"Here you shall be——" Hans established the new *carton* on the easel next to her own, and chalked the floor with Pat's initials, marking the position of the easel. "And here, beyond you, is for Mercy."

"But are you sure she's coming?" Patsey tried not to appear too anxious.

" Oh, she will come at nine o'clock, after the first *repos*. She slept too long."

" Slep' it out! " murmured Patsey, automatically. The well-known phrase brought home back to her, with Kate bringing her breakfast up on a tray, and charging her reproachfully with having " slep' it out "! It felt a thousand years ago, ten thousand miles away. Then, she had been an idle amateur, now, she had a career!

" Why do you not pin up on your *carton* your paper, and begin? "

Patricia's soul returned from Kirwenscourt. This was not careering. She pinned up her paper, but to begin was a matter less simple. With a pencil she was a quick sketcher on a small scale, but this vast expanse of roughish white paper, and the unfamiliar stick of charcoal, so coarse, and wanting in sympathy and neatness of touch, was alien to all her methods. She began, following her usual practice, to dash in the model's head, emphasising salient points, exaggerating frankly wherever exaggeration seemed effective. Then she began on the figure. She perceived that the scale on which she had started was less than half that which she could see was the rule in neighbouring drawings.

" I prefer this size," she thought, with decision. " It suits me best."

She worked on; the ugly little figure was nearly blocked in.

" If you do not fill ze paper," said the heavy voice beside her, " you will find Bouvier will wipe ze floor wiss you! "

Patricia swept away (not without some violence) all that she had drawn, and made a fresh start on a larger scale. She was resolved to show that she was not merely a beginner. . . . All the same, she did not find herself moving with the ease that had, at home, attended her many successes in caricature. Movement seemed to be the privilege of the model. Surely the pose had changed? . . . She was too diffident to make a public protest. . . . Never mind! . . . She worked on, confident in the accuracy of her eye. . . . She had again blocked nearly the whole figure in. . . . It didn't look too bad. . . .

"Haf you a *fil-à-plomb?*"

Patsey felt menace in the question. She began to wish she wasn't sitting next Hans.

"No? Well, I will make one for you——"

Hans drew forth a pocket-knife and a piece of string from the pocket of her Norfolk jacket. She made a loop on the end of the string and closed the blade of the knife on it. Then, quietly, she pushed Patsey off her *tabouret*, and seated herself upon it.

The knife dangled, fateful as the sword of Damocles, between Hans and the model, then she surveyed Patsey's drawing. "Now you see," she said equably, "it is nearly all quite wrong. You haf lost ze movement—you gif her eight heads and she has hardly six——" She demonstrated the faults, one by one, implacably, unanswerably.

"How can I keep the movement when every bit of her is going like—like a clock, all the time!"

"No, no!" Hans shook her cropped head. "I do not find zat. And her hands, at least, are quite still. Zat is not like a clock! No!"

In spite of the improving influence of Paris, Pat was beginning to feel that the Kirwen temper might slip its moorings. Hans was certainly a swell, but even swells can exasperate, expecially when they talk so slowly, and make such very dull jokes, and are so inevitably in the right.

" Well, what do you want me to do? "

" I would turn ze paper and begin again on ze other side after *le repos*," said Hans, placidly, returning to her own stool. She looked at the studio clock. "*Modèle!* " she called, " *il est l'heure!* "

CHAPTER XXI

It was near the end of Patricia's second week in the Studio. Ten o'clock had struck, and the ten minutes of rest had begun. The model, a haggard young Frenchman, had seated himself on the edge of the stand, as near the stove as was possible, and, with his coat thrown over his bare bony shoulders, was eating something disgusting out of a piece of newspaper. At least it seemed disgusting to Patsey. But so did most things at this juncture of her career. The Pension Leroux dinners had been as tedious, the Javanese Princess as pushing, and the "*réunions dans le petit salon vert*" (so vaunted by the First Mademoiselle in her letters to Lady Kirwen) as stupefyingly dull as on her introduction to these amenities.

And her work. . . . By the end of that first Black Monday she had almost come to the conclusion that she had made the mistake of her life in believing that Art was her vocation. Hateful, from all points of view, as she had found the rotatory model of the morning, the afternoon study, a very ugly old man, attired in a loin-cloth and a long white beard, had revolted her.

"He's a nightmare!" she had said to Mercy Le Mont, and Miss Le Mont had replied that she wished he'd sleep it off, and she begged Patsey to go and shake him awake before he began to snore, and Patsey had replied that she wouldn't touch him with the tongs—"not even for you, Mercy!"

Miss Le Mont was, for Patsey, so far, the brightest

feature of the case; but even a growing passion—which can be as occupying as a profession—hardly consoled her. She had escaped early on the night before from the flow of soul in the little *salon*, and had spent the evening, with Dooley on her lap, in moodily writing to her mother.

The thought of Jimmy Corran, who had, for that throbbing moment in the Old Playroom, seemed to come between her and her Career, now only interposed itself at intervals. He had been William of Deloraine, good at need (and it was certainly he who had made Paris possible), but, on the whole, she preferred to forget all that episode. What was more to the point was her work at the Studio. She seemed to be going from bad to worse. . . . And on this Friday, as ever was, the dreaded " Old Bouvier " was coming to correct.

During the *repos* she wandered round from easel to easel, noting and appraising to the best of her knowledge, and, finally, sitting down before Hans's drawing, and studying its many excellences, fell into silent depression.

" *Mesdames!* " the voice of Pie and Jelly called to his flock. " *Voici Monsieur Bouvier*——"

The model leaped into position. The strife of tongues, that had, as usual, arisen during the ten minutes' pause, ceased abruptly. *Les élèves*, hurrying back to their places, began work again upon their studies, with breathless anxiety, with hopeless effort, with the calm of despair, according to their varying temperaments. Monsieur Bouvier, elderly, short, thick-set, with a long white moustache and close-shorn white hair, blew in like a storm, and tackled the study nearest the door before its perpetrator had realised his arrival. Dead silence reigned, as the *Professeur* banged his way from easel to easel, silence that was broken only by his brief comments, harsh and sharp as the barks of an angry dog, or by the crashing fall of a *tabouret*, as someone, in trying to yield her place with obsequious promptitude to Monsieur Bouvier, found that the more haste she made the worse speed was achieved.

" *Mal!* " " *Pas assez bien construit!* " Then a squeal of rage. " How is it possible that you can see it like that? "

Biff! The angry little man's coat-sleeves had smudged out the offending drawing, and in the next instant he had ground, with vindictive violence, a set of heavy black lines of correction into the paper, the charcoal splintering and snapping under the stress, until at length a fragment not an inch long remained between his blackened finger and thumb.

He had stormed round to Hans now, and suddenly there was a lull. He looked at the model, and at the drawing, and at the model again. Then he turned on the stool and looked at Hans, who had stood back, yielding her place to him.

" *Ah, c'est vous, Mademoiselle*——" The voice had changed.

(" He loves old Hans! " whispered Mercy to Pat.)

" *Eh bien, votre étude a beaucoup qui est très bien—mais très bien, je vous dis! Continuez!* "

He wagged his head at her in affirmation. Then he jumped up, looked at his watch, gave a cry of horror, and started at a run for the door.

" *Monsieur!* " wailed Mercy Le Mont. " *Vous m'avez oublié!* "

" *Impossible, Mademoiselle! Je suis trop pressé*——"

The Professor had turned on the words in mid flight, and, in thus turning, his eye fell on Pat, standing beside

Miss Le Mont, tall and slim and clean, her blue eyes bright with the excitement of the moment.

Monsieur Bouvier looked again at his watch. It seemed he had, after all, a minute to spare. He took half a dozen quick steps back, and sat down on Patsey's *tabouret*.

" *Mademoiselle vient de commencer, n'est ce pas? 'Ein?* " He twisted round and stared up at Pat's face. Then he put his head on one side and surveyed her drawing. " *Voyons! C'est pas mal! Pas mal du tout——* " He made a few life-giving strokes on her study. " *V'la! vous pouvez marcher la dessus! Allez!* "

He rose and looked at her again. The white moustache spread like a seagull's wings across his rosy face in a smile that flashed with gold-set teeth. It was evident that he was pleased with what he saw. Then, once more, he flew to the door—" *Bonjour, Mesdames!* "—and was gone.

" Now, look at that! Isn't that a man all over? " protested Mercy Le Mont. " Sugar and spice and all that's nice for Hans and Pat, and nothing at all for poor little Mercy Le Mont! " She shook her small fist at Patsey. " To think I warmed you in my bosom for this! "

The colour of life had changed for Patricia. All was rosy as were Monsieur Bouvier's cheeks. Hadn't he said " *Pas mal!* " even " *Pas mal du tout!* "? All was well with the world—she was going to be a great artist! The occasion must be celebrated.

" Come on! It's just the hour. We'll drink his health in black coffee. My show! "

In the little *conciergerie* Madame Marthe dispensed coffee, black and white, and, if specially demanded, she provided a colourless liquid, quite devoid of taste, which she described as *Le thé Anglais;* it cost three sous more than a *café noir*, and was therefore considered very *chic*, and was seldom asked for by her customers.

Patricia and her two guests seated themselves in a corner of Madame Marthe's dark little inner room. Sketches in every medium known to art decorated the walls.

" There's a new *croquis*, Hans," Mercy said. " Quite good, isn't it?—in a sort of caricature way——? Sort of Forain touch about it? Eh, Hans? "

Mercy was four years older than her friend, but she deferred to her opinion in artistic matters. She was looking at a rough drawing in charcoal on grey paper, touched up with coloured chalks. It showed two naked men fighting, their weapons gigantic paint brushes, with palettes borne as shields. From one of the shields dripped Indian red, from the other Prussian blue; the combatants were daubed, each with one of these colours.

" It's really very smart—*très mouvementé*——" Mercy continued, in the slang of the Studio, where a piebald mixture of English and French was fashionable. " I wonder who did it?—One of the men, of course."

" And why not one of the girls? " Patricia demanded. " Mercy! You're a regular man's woman! "

" Well, look at the subject," retorted Miss Le Mont. " Why, goodness! I bet you a *crème de menthe* that thing happened in one of the men's *ateliers*—the Beaux Arts for choice. That's the kind of fool-monkey trick they play there! I know their ways! Yes, sir! What do *you* know about such things? You're only a new-born babe! "

She looked up at Patsey, a dark, delightful glance, in which was wisdom, and chaff, and an affection that had in it a protecting, maternal quality.

Pat gazed back at her, adoringly, and forgot to argue. She was blissfully happy. The *Professeur!* Mercy! Life! Everything! . . .

Madame Marthe ran in with the coffee. She was a thin, black little woman, reputed to be a great judge of art, and to be the recipient of valuable confidences from *les Professeurs*. She was, moreover, generous in trusting her customers, who, impecunious though most of them were, always paid her in the end, and she was, for all these reasons, held in high honour.

" *Dites*, *Madame*," said Mercy, " who has given you this beautiful drawing of a duel? " She pointed to the sketch.

" *Ma foi*, *Mademoiselle Merci!* " replied Madame Marthe, crashing down on the table the tray with three thick glasses, with their attendant plates and squares of sugar, and the *petits fours* that so great an occasion had demanded. " I do not know the young man's name. He is a *nouveau*. He has himself been one of *les combattants*. *Enfin*, *c'est bien fait!* "

Another customer had come into the outer room. Madame Marthe swirled into each glass its portion of inky liquid from a giant coffee-pot, and hurried away. The three coffee-drinkers heard a man's voice say, in very slow, careful French: " Give me a cup of tea, if you please."

" *Finlandais!* " said Mercy.

" *English!* " said Hans.

" George Lester! " said Patsey, jumping up impulsively, and, in a few swift strides, confronting her late travelling companion in the outer room.

" I've been wondering what had become of you all this time! " she said, beaming upon him.

She felt in a state of elated friendship with all the

world. She longed to tell even George Lester that the *Professeur* had said to her " *Pas mal du tout!* "

" You had my address," she went on, " why didn't you tell me where you were? "

George began to mutter apologies. Then he said, shyly, " I've been working in the Studio here since Monday."

How extraordinary! So was Pat! Why had he come to Pianelli's?

" Because I was told it was the—the least expensive ——" George stammered, ashamed of the confession of economy, feeling that he was obtruding his private affairs on Miss Kirwen.

" Well, it's awfully good! " announced Miss Kirwen, proudly, and went on to ask if the men had the same *Professeur* that they had, *chez les dames?* Monsieur Bouvier? He had just been in our " place." Pure ecstasy for Pat to talk of " our place," to talk down, as an old hand, to George Lester. The great pronouncement of Monsieur Bouvier had very nearly escaped from custody. She forced it back.

" Won't you come and drink your tea with us—' back in the room,' as they say at home? My friends and I are having coffee—Madame will bring it in there for you——"

George followed her into the little " back in the room." He had to stoop his tall head to go through the doorway, and the long wing of black hair fell over his eyes. He stood erect, and shook it back; the light from the window in which Miss Le Mont was sitting was full on him. In a lightning glance she had taken stock of him. She said to herself that if he and Patsey were average specimens of what Ireland could do in the line of boys and girls, the Irish were some people.

George, apprehensive and stiff, was introduced to the two strange ladies, and sat down to drink his tea at their table, thinking that high though was the privilege of being admitted to such company, he would have had more enjoyment and less anxiety out of meeting Miss Kirwen when she was alone, and when he was not embarrassed by a cup of tea.

It is, it may be allowed, difficult to dispose of refreshment of any kind without the assistance of the hands. One cannot lap tea—especially when it is very hot—like a dog. Yet George was particularly anxious not to display his hands, and it was obvious that lapping his tea was out of the question. Therefore he sat with his hands on his knees under the table, edging his chair sideways, in order to avoid, as far as was possible, the light of the window, and wished that he hadn't ordered tea, and asked himself angrily why he hadn't a pair of gloves.

"Mr. Lester, won't you have one of our *petits fours?*" Patricia said, pushing a plate towards him. "They're really quite nice—Dooley adores them! Don't you, Dooley?"

The lady addressed was now a regular frequenter of the Studio, in spite of having, on her first introduction there, imperilled her right of *entrée* by a furious attack upon the model, whose lack of costume had scandalised her Irish sense of decency. She now stood on her hind legs, in honour of the *petits fours*, and twirled round twice. George longed to be able to do the same, and, having twirled once, to fly from the room. But this was impracticable. He hesitated, frowning nervously, then, unable to think of a reason for refusal, drew from concealment a hand, stained in patches of a deep blue colour, picked up a cake, and withdrawing his hand with excess of speed, upset his cup of tea.

If he could, at that instant, have died, it would—as he, long afterwards, confessed to Miss Le Mont—have been a comfort to him. In the anguish of the moment he forgot that his left hand was no more presentable than his right. Even the pocket-handkerchief, with which he tried to wipe the table, was stained with blue.

Through sympathies and apologies Hans's voice clove its way, in invincible determination to be funny in English.

" It wass a blue look-out for ze tea! "

Mercy Le Mont turned on her friend and smacked her hand. " Hans! Manners! "

Patsey began to laugh, so also did Miss Le Mont and the chidden Hans. George had turned scarlet.

" It's Prussian blue," he murmured, incoherently. " I know it's awful—it wouldn't wash out——"

" Prussian blue? " repeated Patsey, staring at him. " But how in the world—— Oh! and you've a great smear on your forehead too! "

George's back was, metaphorically speaking, to the wall, but before he could reply Mercy Le Mont exclaimed:

" But, of course! Look at that *croquis!* He's one of the duellists! "

Gradually it was brought home to George's agonised consciousness that, in the eyes of these ladies, and even especially in the eyes of Miss Kirwen, the disgraceful incident of the duel, fought in savage nudity, had, so far from horrifying them, absolutely raised him in their estimation. They gave him no quarter, every detail was exacted.

" Yes," George had to admit, " they—that is the other chaps—said the other *nouveau*—that's what they seem to call new fellows—and me must fight. It was the custom of the Studio. He was a Yank——" George checked himself, in confusion, and said he meant an American—" a very nice chap——"

(" All right," cooed Miss Le Mont, " I've quite a liking for Yankees myself! ")

" And—and—they—well, they stripped us, and they gave him the Blue, and me the Red, and——"

" Who won? " broke in Pat.

" They said I did," said George, modestly, " because I got him one in the mouth, a good one, with a brushful! " He began to laugh at the remembrance, and forgot, for a moment, to be shy. " He was spitting for a quarter of an hour! "

George pulled himself up in horror. This wasn't the way to talk to ladies.

But the ladies only seemed delighted, and laughed far more than he did, and wanted to hear all that he could tell them.

" And who did the sketch? "

" Oh, it's only a rotten thing—I don't know who brought it in here——"

" Did *you* do it? " demanded Hans, with flattering surprise (or was it unflattering?). " I call it cholly goot! "

CHAPTER XXII

UPON the two mothers had fallen, as is not unusual, the weight of paternal indignation, but Lady Kirwen had, undoubtedly, the least to bear. Never before had she regarded her dentist as the shadow of a great rock in a thirsty land (nor is this a point of view very generally held). Yet thus, in this emergency, did that usually dreaded being appear to her. She said to herself, comfortably and with conviction, that Ingram would never leave the hounds just as he had begun the cubbing, and on her return from London she went to ground in Finnegan's Private Hotel, confident that no attempt would be made to bolt her.

Letters, of course, had to be faced, but, as has been seen, Sir Ingram was one of those men of action in whose hands any weapon is mightier than the pen, and his wife, knowing her lord, felt that the sweet influences of Johnny Ryan and the young entry would soothe his troubled spirit, if not to forgiveness, to forgetfulness. To supplement these, Lady Kirwen wrote cheerful and tactful letters. She mentioned the unexceptionable chaperonage of the First Mademoiselle, and she touched on the fact that the child would miss her hunting—but one can't have everything, and she seemed very happy where she was, and her mare might come in usefully. Hard experience had taught Lady Kirwen wife-craft, and she had earned success.

Sir Ingram simmered down to his normal temperature with comparative speed. After all, he thought, as

Maud suggested (with more sense, begad, than he thought she had!), not having to mount Pat was certainly a consideration, it left him a horse to spare in case of accidents. . . . Lady Kirwen had no need to call out her reserves, and to hint—in the event of there being any difficulty about Patsey's allowance—that in the month of November Pat would have attained to the age of twenty-one, and to the unrestrained disposal of Mamma's forty pounds.

By the time Lady Kirwen's dentist had dismissed her, and she had met Gilbert and forwarded him to school, and had been lunched by Jimmy Corran at the Shelbourne, and heard that he had changed his mind about hunting with Sir Ingram (from which she drew her own deductions) and was going to hunt from Gurtinure—which was his ancestral and neglected home in the County Brandon—by the time, in fact, that she had reached home, and found Patsey's third weekly letter awaiting her there, peace was in full blast at Kirwenscourt. (Which might seem to be an unsuitable form of expression, but meets the case in connection with the moods of its Master.)

For Mrs. Lester the situation was more complicated. She had known that the tempers of both her Georges were in an inflammable condition, entailing on her the functions of a sand-bag, or, at more critical moments, of a safety-curtain to be dropped between father and son, and she had seen that the younger George was what she defined to herself as " queer-like—not himself at all "; but she had contented herself with the assurance that once he was ordained—and that should be next year, she thought with a pang of pride—all would be well.

George had departed decorously, if sulkily, on the

day appointed for the resumption of his studies in Dublin. If his farewells to his mother had been more affectionate than usual, those to his father had been more chilly, which preserved the average, and neither parent objected to the proportion of filial devotion allotted to them. Holy George had given no credence to that outburst on his son's part, which had suggested to him the mutiny of Balaam's ass. There had been nothing in that, he knew, worthy of consideration. As for having slapped young George's face, Mr. Lester felt that *he* bore no malice in the matter, and why should George do so?

George wrote to his mother from Paris. Even the postman, who delivered the letter, was bewildered by the French stamp and the postmark, and would have liked to linger and hear the mystery explained. But Mrs. Lester did not open the envelope at once, as Billy the Post had hoped. She had been making a cake, and her hands were floury, so she took the letter from Billy in her finger and thumb through the corner of her apron, and went back into the scullery, and washed her hands before she opened it.

But while she was washing her hands in the scullery sink, she was gazing at the letter, and, guileless optimist though she was, she could feel herself going cold with formless panic, as her brown eyes, that were so like Georgie's, dwelt on the mystery of her boy's writing and the Paris postmark. She dried her hands, and then she picked up the letter and went out through the kitchen and down the passage to the sitting-room.

She felt glad—she hardly knew why—that Minnie had gone to school, and George was out on the farm. Whatever the mystery was, it would be best to face it alone—to resolve it in the alembic of her soul before others should intervene to share it. She took her scissors out of her work-basket, and sat down on the sofa, and very carefully, with the help of the scissors, opened the envelope. It might easily be, she thought, that it was all a mistake, that—yes! now she had it!—it must be that Georgie had given it to a friend to post for him, and it had been forgotten by the friend till he got to Paris—that French master he had, of course! Well, she'd soon see the explanation. She had been wondering why he hadn't written before, he was usually such a good boy about writing to her—it was near a fortnight since he left home—the French master, to be sure, there was the reason of it! Yet her hand shook as she drew out the letter, and fear snatched with a physical grip at her heart as she unfolded the thin foreign note-paper. . . . What did it mean? . . . There was " Paris " in Georgie's own writing, at the top of the sheet, and the address of a post-office! What *could* it mean? . . .

She read:

" *Dear Mother, this will surprise you, I expect. I could not write sooner, being travelling, etc. I have known for some time I was not suited for the Church. I told my Father this some time back, the day*——" (Here a sentence was scratched out)—" *you may remember I cycled to the Hunt.*" (Mrs. Lester groaned, and muttered, " Indeed and I *do* remember—wasn't it me that sent him, God help me?) " The letter went on: " *My Father told me I should be no loss to the Ministry, and I agree with him. I am determined on being an artist, and I have joined an Art School here.*" (" Merciful God! the child is mad! " moaned the mother, her hands shaking so that she laid the letter on the table in front of the sofa, and bent over it to read it.) " *I will be no expense to you and my Father after this term. I have a promise of a job to teach English and that will keep me till I can earn otherwise* " (" ' earn otherwise '! God help us! "). " *There is a matter that I am very sorry about, but I had no alternative. I will make it good later on. Do not think my education is wasted. I will always be thankful for it. Please, dear Mother, do not be upset about this. I would have made a bad clergyman, and I mean to be a good artist. Your loving son, G. W. Lester.*

Please write me to the address I have given. Kisses to you and Minnie."

Two circles endorsed the message.

Mrs. Lester put her head down on the letter, and kissed the circles, moaning like a creature in bitter physical pain. Her boy, her handsome Georgie, gone from her, lost to her! He whom she had so often, in blissful vision, seen in the white robes of the Church, or in the refined black suit and clerical collar (for which she had been secretly sequestrating all the egg money that she dared, so that the best broadcloth should be his!). She had seen herself walking with him to the Parish Church in Templenoe. He would be taking the service. All the parish would see how beautiful he was, how clever, how good!

* * * * *

When Holy George came in by the back-door from the farm, to the eleven o'clock cup of tea that broke the morning for him between eight o'clock breakfast and two o'clock dinner, he was surprised not to find his wife in the kitchen, preparing the tray, as was her custom.

" Where's the Mistress? " he asked " the girl."

" She's within, sir, I think. I didn't see her since the post came in."

"Here, give me the tray. I'll take it in——"

He carried the tray into the sitting-room with the anxious care of a big man unaccustomed to so light and perilous a burden, and set it down on the table before he took his eyes from it. Then he saw his wife sitting on the sofa facing him. She was sitting erect, her hands in her lap, doing nothing. That alone would have startled her husband, but when he saw her face, white and wet with tears, that was usually so pink and cheerful, his heart gave a sickening leap, and he cried out:

"In God's name, Annie, what's the matter?"

"Read that!" said Mrs. Lester, with a sob, pushing the letter towards him.

"What's this? What's this?" He caught the letter up, and held it away from him, trying to focus the writing for eyes that did not see as well as once they did. "Who's it from?—Where are my specs?—Annie! For mercy's sake tell me——"

"Give it to me!" said Mrs. Lester, hysterically. "It's from Georgie!" she cried, wildly. "He's left us! He's given up the Ministry! He's gone to Paris—to be an artist—that's what he says! He says you"—she sobbed—"you told him he'd be no loss to the Church! Oh, George! And you slapped him——!"

"Paris!" said George Lester, in a shaken voice, "Paris! Good God! That Sink of Iniquity!" He paid no attention to his wife's reproach. Horror, that was perfectly genuine, was on his face and in his voice. "The boy is lost!" he said, thickly. "My God! I'd sooner have heard he was dead!"

He dragged a chair from the centre table, and sat down heavily, facing his wife.

"What is it you say he's gone there for?"

The letter had fallen from his hand. Mrs. Lester

picked it up. " He says he's joined an Art School——" she said between sobs.

" To be yoked with unbelievers in that City of Belial! " said Holy George, with grim despair, yet not without a subconscious sensation of gratitude to St. Paul for a helpful phrase. " I won't say ' unequally yoked,' " he continued, gathering wrath as he went on, " because no man having put his hand to the plough—the Gospel Plough, mind you!—is fit for the Kingdom of God! George has gone, like Judas, to his own place! "

There are, happily for sons, few mothers who will listen acquiescently to the abuse of a son, and specially an only son. Least of all will a mother, however indignant she may be, fail to defend her son from his father. Had Mrs. Lester found beneath her feet that useful magic carpet that was once such a simplifier of the troubles of travel, and had it then transported her to her Georgie's attic in the City of Belial, she would undoubtedly have given him a very faithful and penetrating scolding. But to acquiesce in her husband's relentless condemnation of the sinner was quite another affair.

" I'm surprised at you, George, to be comparing my poor Georgie with Judas! If he's gone to Paris itself, who was it drove him there? I'd like to know that! What young man would stand the treatment he got from you! The height of abuse and slapping his face, and him nearly a clergy—clergy—clergyman! " Sobs broke down Mrs. Lester's defence of her boy.

The accuser was silent. He rooted in all his pockets until at last his spectacles yielded themselves. Then he stretched across the little table and took the letter out of his wife's unresisting hand. He read it through, slowly and carefully, murmuring the words to himself.

Then he began to read it again, silently this time. Presently he put it down, open, on the table.

" Annie! What d'ye make of this that he says? " His great hand nearly covered the sheet; his thick forefinger was on that sentence touching a matter about which young George had written that he was very sorry, but he would make it good later on.

" There's something about that I wouldn't like at all! " said young George's father, darkly.

Young George's mother wept on.

CHAPTER XXIII

MR. LESTER'S opinion that the city of Paris was a Sink of Iniquity was one that was not peculiar to himself. At intervals, such as those succeeding a blank day, or during a visitation of chill on the liver, Sir Ingram Kirwen was prone to take a similar view; and although he did not go so far as Holy George in suggesting a comparison between his offspring and Judas Iscariot, he, like the other afflicted father, found consolation in passing on his apprehensions to his wife.

" What's she living on, I want to know? I want to know that! Frogs and dandelions, I suppose! She'll lose her looks and come back half-starved, and no man'll look at her twice! Millie tells me it's a damned indecent unhealthy life for a young girl—and what's she going to get out of her daubing and scribbling? You know, Maud, as well as I do, that if she don't marry she'll starve! *I* can't leave her enough to live on! There's little enough for Gilbert as it is——"

Lady Kirwen had not argued the point, because the violent language ascribed to a lady of so eminent propriety and refinement as her step-daughter had appealed to her unfortunate sense of humour, and for the moment she found reply impossible. She slurred over the questions as to Patsey's finances with generalities as to her allowance, and " some little pennies I had put by," and thus composed, temporarily, Sir Ingram's not very acute anxieties. She did not think it necessary to make mention to him of that little transaction in Dublin in connection with her Aunt Austin's pearls. Such as it was, it had eased her mind as to that loan which was providing for Patricia's present necessities. Rum little thing (as Jimmy Corran considered her) though she was, she was aware that for a young gentleman to finance a young lady, and in Paris (that Sink of Iniquity), was unconventional and open to comment, if not to misconstruction. A cheque representing some more of Aunt Austin's pearls had gone to Jimmy, and Jimmy had immediately returned it to his Cousin Maud, assuring her that he didn't want it in the least (which was quite true), and asserting that he intended to take it out in a portrait of himself, as soon as Patsey would undertake the commission (which was problematical). Cousin Maud had, however, informed him, with unusual firmness, that he could then make a fresh bargain with Patsey, and the cheque, with Jimmy's signature on the back of it, went, ultimately, to Jimmy's bank.

This possibly complicating matter disposed of, Lady Kirwen felt that she could lift her hand serenely in the sunlight as before, and went for so long a walk with the remnant of the dogs, that she was late for dinner, and as it was a special dinner, and one of the nature of a post-bridal feast to Millie and her Colonel, with twelve guests and champagne, this was a serious matter, and Lady Kirwen's face was only saved by Kate, who flew to the drawing-room and the hall, and put back both the clocks, as the first carriage drove up to the door, which occurred not two minutes after the guilty rush of the lady of the house to her bedroom.

In domestic crashes, such as those in which Patricia and young George had involved their respective families, it is not the sinners who suffer. While their blameless relatives at Kirwenscourt and Corran Farm were exhausting their powers of invention in proffering creditable and credible reasons for the taking of what may, not inappropriately, be termed French Leave, by daughter and son, the two runaways, living in an ecstasy of effort, feeling as if they had come out of darkness into a growing glory of light, were happier than they had ever been. The weeks, for them, swept on, changelessly, and yet full of change. The outer world faded. For a time Patricia read the newspapers that her mother sent her, but soon the politics of the Studio rose like a mist round her, intimate and obliterating. She found she hadn't time to think about Mr. Gladstone or Mr. Parnell, with so many more important matters to attend to—a composition to do for dear old Bouvier, or a canvas to stretch, since De Brémont—he was the afternoon Professor—was going, as a great favour, to let her paint, just for once. Or there was the row on the subject of the morning model's head. The Studio had split into halves over it. Miss Wilson was the leader of the British-American contingent, and Fröken Hellquist headed the Northlanders, and between them—for it chanced that week that the rival parties had been massed at opposite sides of the Studio—they kept the model spinning like a top. Patricia and her allies, Mercy and Hans, kept clear of the battle, being precisely midway between the two factions. Pat's neutrality was, indeed, so perfect, that she bestowed on her study of the model two heads, one of them scowling towards a sufficiently recognisable, if unflattering, caricature of "Old Wilson," the plain and elderly English leader, the other smiling upon an equally unflattering portrait of "Hell's Delight," the title bestowed by the Studio upon the grim champion of *les Scandinaves*. For this impudent frivolity she was taken seriously to task by M. Bouvier, who left her humbled and penitent, but she noticed that he had no sooner left the Studio than M. Pianelli strolled in, and came casually, yet directly, to her easel, and stood behind her, and when she turned and met his eye, though he waggled a fat forefinger reprovingly, he did not even try to suppress the grin that spread like oil all over his brown, jolly, pudding-face—a fact not unnoted by the Studio, in whose estimation Patsey immediately rose.

Apart from the life of the Studio, existence for Patricia was less ecstatic. Daily she found the *ménage* of the First Mademoiselle less tolerable. Punctuality at meal times was rigidly enforced on all save the cook (who appeared to fall into trance between each course), so that for Pat to escape from the confidences of the little Princess in less than an hour was seldom possible. Dooley was forbidden the dining-room, while the privileged Hector roamed round the table unchecked, often stooping his great head over a *pensionnaire's* shoulder, and with a single swing of his tongue clearing her plate of its contents. By the end of the second month, Patricia found that she could no longer endure the conditions imposed by Mlle. Leroux on her subjects, and, while composing Lady Kirwen's anxieties by remaining in the house as a *locataire*, she escaped from more direct bondage to an eyrie on the fourth floor, beside that of *ces dames* (who, it may be remembered, had over them only *le bon Dieu*), where freedom reigned combined with indefinite meal times and amateur cooking.

Following on this emancipation, housekeeping became for Pat and the dwellers in the neighbouring eyrie an eager competition in economies, a competition of which the details, had they been revealed to Lady

Kirwen, would have caused her, despite her Bohemian sympathies, to feel it was her duty to hurry to Paris to rescue her child from the food and the fate so graphically described and anticipated by Sir Ingram. Mercy Le Mont was, in the eyes of her comrades, a lady of means, who paid all the bills for herself and Hans, and mocked at the frugalities practised by her German friend; but Hans was an economist, skilled and subtle, and Patricia learned in her school to shop in *sous*, and to keep account of her weekly expenditure for food (which, it may not be out of place to say, came, all told, to little over three francs a day) with a precision that would have shocked Jimmy Corran, with the thought that his fifty pounds (or rather their successors) were being treated with such respect.

Patsey had written to him occasionally, in recognition of his share in having given reality to a dream, and a dream in which he had no part. But as the weeks went by her letters had grown ever more short, and Jimmy's replies, treating of his horses and his hunting, seemed to her to come from a more and more remote existence, and, now that he had gone to another and, for her, an unknown country, were not very much more interesting than the "Hunting Notes," with their careful geographical particulars, that she used to scan in the weekly sporting papers. Poor Jimmy was not a letter writer, and the hopes, and fears, and sighs that went between the lines were written in invisible ink, and in Paris was no fire that would warm them to life, rather a determined flinging of cold water on such embers as still smouldered and might have sufficed to give them life. Pat had driven from her mind the remembrance of the last time that she had seen him; when, in the old playroom, they had sat side by side, and the air had felt charged with electricity, with portent, with the conviction that this moment was the first of a new era. She had remembered, and at first the remembrance had shaken her, the look in his eyes when his arm had been round her; she had been so tired, so bruised and hurt, and Jimmy had seemed—but, she assured herself, only for that moment—so safe, and—yes, she did not deny it—so dear. When, sometimes, at first, his face had come back to her, she wondered if she had made a mistake. . . . No! Moloney had saved her! She had done the right thing! There was to be no more looking back!

And since Patsey was young, and her work grew ever more absorbing, she found the resolution easy to keep.

Nothing more remote from the hectic existence that is usually credited to art students in Paris could be imagined than the manner of the two *ménages* on the fourth floor of the Pension Leroux. The Studio held their occupants fast from eight in the morning till midday, and again from one till five, and, as the autumn evenings grew dark, scant time was left for aught save housekeeping, and its attendant marketings. On most Sunday mornings a little party, conscious, almost to agony, of godliness and best clothes, would proceed, decorously, to the American Church, where Patsey, as an ex-organist, would criticise professionally the mellifluous quartet who formed its choir. Or, seriously (and still in Sunday clothes), they would, after an extravagant Sunday lunch, at something under a franc a head, at the *Crémerie* in the Rue Bréa, proceed to the Luxembourg and critically inspect the pictures, while the Studio still lisped out in all they uttered, and if they didn't smell of bread and butter, it was only because *alcool à brûler* and paraffin possess more pungent perfumes.

Patsey and Hans used to go shopping together on their way home from the Studio, buying for the pot at the little shops of the quarter.

" For nine *sous*," Hans would say, " I will make you so goot a dinner as would sicken a dog! " A statement that might have been regarded as a threat, but Patsey knew it for a boast, and was moved to invest in a stove with whose help she might rival Hans's triumphs. This was a serious outlay, representing the best part of one of Aunt Austin's pearls, although its appearance did not suggest such an origin. For two days it belched its smoke in any direction save up the chimney. On the third day Pauline was seduced from her lawful sphere below, as a consultant. In what way she intimidated the stove was never known, but after an encounter that lasted twenty minutes she summoned Patsey and Hans—the rival and baffled expert—and pointed to the now submissive stove.

" *Vous voyez! Il marche comme un loup! Mais!* " She shook a menacing finger. " *C'est comme une vierge! Faut pas la toucher!* "

Patsey, filled with an awed gratitude, placed her saucepan of milk to boil on the sensitive combination of wolf and virgin, and straightway became absorbed in the details of the next composition (an abstruse subject, set by M. Bouvier, involving deep study of the Apocryfa). The door opened, and a shriek from Mercy Le Mont tore the student of *Le retour de Tobie* from her researches. The stove's wolf-like ferocity had caused the milk to boil over, and an enveloping veil of virgin white now justified Pauline's definition.

Excitements such as this were not lacking to Patricia's *ménage;* she found everything delightful. To sample a new *Crémerie*, and there to receive six stewed prunes for the same price that *Le Père* Fusco charged for four; to buy a small gobbet of raw meat, and with it to wing her way home, like a hawk to its nest, and to devour it, burnt to a cinder, for her dinner, completing the repast with what was known as a resurrection omelette, in which old forgotten things found their last home; to join with *ces dames* in a dinner to a studio friend, when Hans would give a demonstration of her *hauslich* skill in a series of masterpieces, produced for the sum of fifteen *sous* a head: these were among the minor joys of an existence that Pat found wholly ideal.

Yet sometimes, almost reluctantly, she found herself noting the day of the week, and looking at the cards of the Meets that her mother and Jimmy Corran had each sent her; or thinking of a "mountainy fox," and the wind on the heath, and wondering who was riding Miss Keating, and if the men had succeeded yet in absolutely spoiling her mouth. At such times the Studio would feel rather stale and stuffy; her *académie* would look all wrong, badly drawn, rotten; and the greasy black-and-tan Italian model would remind her of a Kerry Beagle ("only it's an insult to dear Faithful and Fiddler to say so!"); and she would have to crush down the thought of going home for Christmas (as Mother had hinted at more than once) and having a hunt on "Stephens's Day." "*Johnny Ryan is longing for you to come home*," Mother had said, "*and I think Jimmy would come to us for a bit, and bring a horse down. He suggested it himself*."

Jimmy's letters to Pat had, since November the first, been enlivened a little by occasional mention of "neighbours"—"*at least they live eight miles away*." "*Nice people, I played some of our old duets there yesterday, with Mrs. Ridley*."

Pat had been conscious of a slight pang of disapproval on receiving this information. " *She is much kinder to me than you were. She hasn't hit me over the knuckles once.*" This was stated in a later letter. Still later had followed further information. " *We had a topping hunt yesterday—thirty minutes without a check, going hell for leather all the time. Mrs. Ridley showed me a wall that she had jumped when she was a girl. She said it had been measured and was six feet two inches then. It looks all that. She goes awfully well, and so does her daughter. I was wishing you were out.*" Patsey thought, " He seems to be doing very well without me! "

George Lester had, for a time, sunk below her horizon. He was a negligible quantity; such portion of her soul as was not given to the Studio was devoted to Mercy Le Mont. An idle thought of him recurred sometimes, when, at Madame Marthe's, she and her comrades drank the three *sous'* worth of black coffee that gave the true Parisian flavour to their mornings, and her eyes fell on that sketch of George's initiation into artist life. Mercy would say that he had talent, and was quite a *joli garçon*, and why wouldn't Patsey ask him to come and see them, and be nice to him? It was impossible to make Mercy understand that if anything could disimprove for Pat her position with her father it would be to make a friend of Holy George's son.

" But why should you tell the old folks? I'm sure that poor boy is real lonely."

" He might write home," Patricia had replied, and added gloomily, " You don't know the Master!—or Holy George either! Lucky for you! "

" Besides," Hans struck in, sagely, " ze old Leroux would raise Cain, and Abel too, if a male were brought in this pure house! "

"Oh, you're nothing but an old maid yourself, Hans!" Mercy declared. "I think George Lester's a nice thing, and I believe old Leroux would think so too! I saw him this afternoon," she went on. "He was just leaving the *Atelier* and he didn't see me. I thought he looked real sick and lonesome, right under the weather—poor boy!"

Mercy's tuneful, wistful voice had—as it seemed to Pat—a note of compassion so divine that her soul melted within her. "Well, we'll have a tea-party for him at Madame Marthe's, and you shall be nice to him, and I'm sure he'll forget to be lonesome!"

"He don't want *me* to be nice to him!" replied Mercy, nodding her pretty dark head at Patsey.

This was near the end of November, and George, as Miss Le Mont had guessed, had been going through deep waters. The efforts of M. Dupin's colleague had procured for him a couple of English tuitions at night-classes that sufficed to pay for his lodging, an attic, *au sixième*, in the same street as the Studio, simply furnished with a bed, a table, a basin-stand, and some nails in the walls on which to hang his clothes. His food seldom cost him as much as two francs a day, and he had calculated that he could exist on his store of money for nearly a year. It was not, therefore, financial anxieties that had made him look sick and lonesome. It was a letter from his mother that had hit him hard.

"Lesterre? 'ein?" they had said at the Post Office, and George had been flattered by so elegant a version of his name, and had decided, when he sent his first picture to the *Salon*, or drawing to *Le Rire*, that he would sign himself L'Esterre.

Then he took the letter into the Luxembourg Gardens, and found a quiet place before he began to read it. It was well for him that the place he had chosen was a quiet one, for he had not read far before tears were standing in his eyes and slowly following one another down his pale face.

" *Georgie, my darling, I couldn't believe it, not till your Father showed me the check and proved to me what you did. If you might have trusted me. I feel that so hard that you could do such a thing and go away from me letting on it was to college you were going. Your father will never forgive you. He has forbid me mention your name. It was Mr. Day at the bank thought there was something wrong in the check. Your father told him no that it was alright. He said to me he never thought to have to tell a lie to clear his son from being called a forger. Oh, Georgie, if you might have told me*——"

" How could I tell her? " said George, with a groan; " and what good would it have been? Only for her to let it out to him, and then, I suppose, for him to take the stick to me! Slapping my face wouldn't be enough for him! "

CHAPTER XXIV

JIMMY CORRAN, having, as has been mentioned, met and fed his Cousin Maud, suitably, as became a recent guest with a kind hostess, had stayed in Dublin no longer than was necessary to buy a couple of horses—to supplement the two local crocks and the County Cork mare that, his agent informed him, were awaiting his arrival at Gurtinure—and he had then betaken himself to England, to see his mother and his tailor.

Lady Corran, early in her widowhood, had abandoned the West of Ireland, and, during her son's long minority, had only visited Gurtinure as a matter of conscience, occasionally spending Jimmy's summer holidays there, and, when he came of age, filling the house temporarily, giving a ball to "the quality" and a dinner to the tenants, and then, when Jimmy went back to Oxford, feeling that all her duties had been worthily accomplished, thankfully returning to the very comfortable home that she had made for herself in one of those faultless villa-residences of the Home Counties, which would seem to have been specially created for comfortably widowed ladies with a turn for gardening.

Lady Corran was undoubtedly comfortably, it might almost be said fortunately, widowed, because the late Lord Corran, charming and good-looking as he was, had been what his sporting friends in the County Brandon indulgently called "a lad," and it is equally certain that the point-to-point in which, after but two years of matrimony, he met his death, might have proved less fatal had the preliminary stirrup-cup been less potent.

Jimmy had not suggested to his mother that she should bear him company at Gurtinure, not wishing to provoke the attack of rheumatism that such a suggestion would involve. Lady Corran was very fond of her son, but not quite fond enough (as he was aware) to abandon the faultless villa in Surrey, in the month of October, for winter quarters in Gurtinure House, in the wet west of her native country.

Gurtinure was very far from being faultless. It was a large, long, low, yellow building, with very big rooms, and very long passages, and successions of dreary and rather damp bedrooms, that went round three sides of the brightest feature of the place, from the late Lord Corran's point of view, if not from that of his widow. This was a great square stable-yard, which could boast of the best stabling that could be found, even in a county so sporting as the County Brandon, wherein hunting-horses receive a consideration even exceeding that which is always extended to human hunters. Six hundred acres of level grass surrounded the house, with fir plantations and dense laurel coverts lying like islands about its wide expanse, and with four drives, radiating from the hall-door to four entrance-gates. Tennis-lawns and a formal garden lay in front of the windows, and beyond these and their protecting white railings went, as far as could be seen, the long stretches of pasture, dotted with grazing bullocks. From upstairs it was possible to look along a straight half-mile of avenue to one of the entrance-gates, and, on a clear day, a low, pale-blue, wavy line gave an assurance that the county was not wholly devoid of the dignity of hills.

Despite popular belief, it may be confidently asserted that it does not always rain in the County Brandon. The first fortnight after Jimmy's arrival was as beautiful as a Western Irish end of October can be when it applies itself to the effort. There were light frosts at night, but the sun in that far west country still shone in power. Jimmy, shaving at his bedroom window, could see the frosty mist moving like smoke as the sunshine gathered force. The leaves of the beech trees in the wood behind the stables were like little flecks of flame; in the garden the scarlet double dahlias and the clear yellow single ones, and the fierce orange balls of the African marigolds, still made a gorgeous chord of colour. Virginian creeper hung in trails of all the hues of sunset over the great archway that led into the stable-yard. The yellow walls of the house were a warm background for the mantle of gold and crimson leaves; not even the faultless villa-residence in Surrey held a tighter grasp of the garments of departing summer than did Gurtinure.

In that wide country of distances the word neighbour is a misnomer in its implication of nearness. The railway station, the post office, the church, the doctor, and, most important of all, the hunt kennels, were all gathered together in the little town of Rossmult, five miles away from everywhere and six from Gurtinure. The nearest settlements of what may, for the sake of convenience, be called those of white men, were spaced out, each in its demesne, at distances often to be counted in double figures. None the less, during his first fortnight, Jimmy could not complain of loneliness. Gurtinure held a strong position near the middle of the Hunt country, and the owner of its reliable coverts was not a person to be neglected. In the words of the song,

" *From the Minister down, to the Clerk of the Crown, all were coortin'* " the young Lord Corran.

Jimmy was a sociable youth, and he took his visitors to his bosom with a warmth that surprised and delighted them.

" He's good for a whacking subscription! " said the Hon. Sec. of the Hunt.

" He says we can have the Hunt Ball at Gurtinure! " said the Hon. Sec.'s wife.

" He's promised to come to the bazaar next week! " said the Parson.

" I may put him down for all my raffles! " said the Parson's wife.

" I've fixed it up with him to have the opening meet on the First at Gurtinure, and he'll have a breakfast—grub and drinks for the crowd! " announced the M.F.H., who, as is not unusual in Ireland, was an Englishman, young, rich, and unmarried, cutting his hunting teeth on an Irish country, and, being about to start his first season, well pleased at the prospect of a good send-off.

He and Jimmy discovered that they had been at Oxford together, and they spent an enjoyable afternoon inspecting Jimmy's coverts and horses, and discovering mutual acquaintances, and similar tastes, even to a turn for music; and when he had gone, and Jimmy sat down to his solitary dinner, he found himself very solitary indeed, and wished that he had kept little Cox-Munro to share it with him. Cox-Munro might look like a hot pink baby, but his little bullet head was screwed on quite the right way.

It was six weeks now since Jimmy had seen Patsey drive away, with Dooley and Denis, and the black horse, and he had been hopeful that the very distressing emotions that had then perturbed his breast would have been subdued by time, and dispelled by the rival interests of Gurtinure and buying horses, and hunting in his own country where he had never hunted before. He assured himself that he was doing the right thing, and that Patsey was no more than a *migraine*, a temporary indisposition that would pass off with the treatment—Duty and Sport in equal parts—which he had prescribed for himself. He had had a fortnight now of exhibiting (in the medical sense) these remedies. He practised assiduously—as has been seen—those duties towards his neighbours enjoined by the catechism; he submitted, unmurmuring, to penitential mornings over accounts with his agent, old Mr. Bolger, and to reviews of his farm-stock with his farm-bailiff, which he found even more arduous, since old Bolger didn't expect him to know arithmetic, while the farm-bailiff was confident that his Lordship knew a Shorthorn from a Polled Angus, and was scandalised when, on pointing out to his Lordship a bunch of bullocks as being Herefords, his Lordship had replied airily, " Oh, are they? I thought they were mine! "

The other restorative of his peace of mind was more efficacious as a sedative. He was asked to shoots, and, being a good shot, he did a creditable share in the destruction of his neighbours' pheasants and rabbits; and he tuned up his horses, getting them fit, compelling those that he had bought in Dublin to realise that they must forget all that they had ever learnt, and must remodel their style on that of the indigenous crocks who had had their education in the straitest school of East Brandon.

Therefore his days were well filled; but the evenings, the long, long evenings, after horses and gun-dogs had been tucked up and put to bed, and visitors, murmuring their annual discovery that the days were closing in very fast, had driven away, and Jimmy was left with no more to do than to strum a little on the piano, trying over again the basses of the duets he had played with Patsey; or to read a few pages of a detective story; or fight for the centre of the hearth-rug with a demoralised, fat old cocker spaniel, thoroughly spoilt, and thankfully cast out by Lady Corran (who had given her a home since Jimmy left Oxford), and to smoke unnumbered cigarettes, while one insistent thought battered at his heart behind all the barricades that he had built to keep it out.

October the thirty-first had come. The night before the opening meet. All Hallowe'en night. He was reminded of it by the dishes of hazel-nuts and apples that Blake, his man, had placed before him at dessert. He thought of the last All Hallowe'en night that he had spent at Gurtinure, twenty years before, when he was six years old. There had been revelry in the kitchen in which he had taken part. He had " dipped " for apples with the servants, in all amity and a basin of cold water common to all competitors; he had jumped at a spinning device, baited with an apple and a tallow candle, and had caught the candle in his mouth—he remembered the horrible taste quite well—and Robert, the footman, had thrillingly applied a red hot poker to his tongue, where it sizzled for a second, but did no damage; and then his nursery maid had placed a couple of hazel-nuts on a bar of the huge open fireplace, that must have burnt quite an acre of turf every day, and told him that he was one of the nuts, and " his own young lady " was the other, and he was to watch would they burn together, but, " Oh! " the nursery maid had exclaimed, " look at the lep she threw away from him! "

He had been bewildered, but deeply interested. Now, he said to himself, it was seen that Nora the nursery maid had been a seer, and was justified of her incantations. Why hadn't he remembered that lep before he supplied his young lady with the requisite jumping-powder? He lay back in his big armchair, and stretched his legs along the hearthrug, seriously annoying old Sarah the spaniel in doing so. Then, suddenly, he jumped up and went back to the dining-room and took from the dish a couple of hazel-nuts, and returned to the study where he had been sitting. There was a good clear fire in the grate, and he put the two nuts, side by side, on the top bar of the old-fashioned grate that was trimmed with the brass " Nelson-rope," and sat down again to watch them, mocking at his own folly, pretending that he was only playing the game for the sake of old times. . . . If Patsey were only there, playing the game with him. . . . Patsey was such a good playboy, always ready to play any game that might turn up. . . . Yes! If she were there, sitting opposite to him, " his own young lady," his, to have and to hold till death them did part—wasn't that how it went? He ought to know, he had been best man often enough! . . . What fun it would be! . . . He thought of the look in her face when she had tried to thank him for that miserable cheque that he had absolutely forced on her, fool that he was! How wonderful she had looked! He had known her in many moods, but never till then had he seen her blue eyes softened to tenderness.

* * * * *

He had forgotten the nuts; a tiny sound made him open his eyes and look at them. The one he had nominated as his representative had caught fire, a little fairy spire of smoke was rising from it. But the other, the Patsey-nut, had hopped from its place on the bar, and had thrown a lep into the cinders under the fire.

CHAPTER XXV

EVEN for a young man who is admitting to himself that though he has not been precisely crossed in love his affairs of the heart are not prospering, even, in fact, for Jimmy Corran, there was undoubted, if superficial, consolation in the almost sacrificial rite of attiring himself for hunting in a completely new outfit, and, after critical survey in a long glass, feeling confident that the absolute had been attained.

He was going to ride the younger of the two Dublin horses, the best looking and the smartest of his five hunters (smartness, at that time of history, being imparted by a mane hogged to the bone, and a tail no longer, and rather less fledged, than the average clothes-brush). This, also, for a youth attempting from Love's fever to fly, was of the nature of a palliative, and when, a few minutes before the orthodox eleven o'clock, he was summoned from the stable-yard (where horses sent on early, and second horsemen, were gathering fast), with the intelligence that the hounds were "in it," the flight had been at least temporarily successful, and Patsey was, for the moment, left far behind in the unsatisfactory past.

The day was all that could be wished for, sweet and soft and sunny. How exhilarating to find the hounds at his door! To see them glittering there, in their snowy white, and golden tan, and jetty black attire, gathered in a tidy circle, staring about them with eager eyes and waving sterns, listening with aristocratic composure to the raucous threats that old Sarah (a mere cur-dog) was hurling at them from the security of the dining-room window! How gay and jolly the new scarlet coats and white breeches of Cox-Munro and his men, with their shining horses, iron-greys all of them, their spurs and bits and buttons sparkling in the sunshine, all grouped as if for a photograph, all beautiful and—which is better than being beautiful—correct, to the last buckle and button of their equipment. Cox-Munro, young though he was, revered and followed the tradition of the elders in its most minute particular, and had he shown the faintest indication of straying from that strait and narrow path, there is little doubt but that his perfect English huntsman, bred and nurtured in the bosom of a perfect English Hunt establishment, would, with a crack of his whip, and a shout of " 'Ware Riot! ", have rated him back into the way in which he should go.

Converging on the house by the various avenues came the Field, between forty and fifty riders, with a train of outside-cars and dog-carts following in their wake. Men of all classes, county gentlemen, mostly, and their young, two or three soldiers from the Barracks fifteen Irish miles away, professional men from the nearer towns, a couple of sporting priests, a few farmers, with a leavening of a dozen or more of the hard-riding ladies of East Brandon, a number which was, in those days, considered a large proportion of the sex whose place in the hunting-field was still, by many conservative husbands and fathers, considered to be a four-wheeled pony-carriage on the road; while, even there, the presence of " the ladies " was only legitimated by intelligent anticipation on their part of the moment when time and place and loved one should coincide, and the luncheon basket might with advantage be produced.

Jimmy Corran was one of those happily uncritical human beings who are primarily well disposed towards everyone, and towards whom, consequently, most people are well disposed. Already the seal of approval had been set on him by old Mr. O'Reilly, the senior member of the Hunt, who, in the formula employed also by Sir Ingram, and consecrated to the use, in such case, of elderly gentlemen, had stated that he was a dam' nice young feller, and had added that he was the very cut of his father, poor Tony.

One of the priests, a venerable sportsman of the old school, said that the young lord was a hardy young splinter, and would be a credit to the County. Old Mrs. O'Reilly, driving herself in a low phaeton nearly as old as she was, whipped her pair of ponies up to the hall-door, with her shrewd old eyes appraising the new Corran, and tossed off the glass of cherry-brandy that he brought her, and wished him good luck and good sport.

" A very pretty boy, and nice-mannered! " she said to her ancient ally, Sir Thomas Ferrers, who, seated near-by on a seventeen-hand old white horse, was drinking something less frivolous than cherry-brandy. " And," she went on, her eyes still on Jimmy, " upon my honour, he has a smaller waist than any of my granddaughters! "

" Ah, Arabella! " says Sir Thomas, with a loving roll of a rather bloodshot eye, " time was when my arm went round a smaller waist than any of them have! "

" Get away with you, Tom! You and me are too old to be talking nonsense! " returned Mrs. O'Reilly, well pleased. " I'll complain you to Helena if you don't take care! "

(" Helena " was Lady Helena Ferrers, Sir Thomas's wife, and when it is said that her name in the country was " Lady Hyæna," it will be understood that the threat was not an idle one.)

The hall and the dining-room were full of jovial people, drinking, gobbling, talking at the tops of their voices, as happy and in as high spirits as befitted a lovely morning and the opening meet of the season. A more gratified host than Jimmy Corran never viewed the demolition of a hunt-breakfast; even the farmers, clustered shyly near the open hall-door, ventured, under the thawing influence of his manner, as far as the side-table where Blake was dispensing drinks, and there forgot their hesitations. It was Jimmy's special gift to be able to show the good fellowship that other people may feel but are too self-conscious to display. He personally superintended the administration of refreshment to Mr. Will Mason, the Huntsman, and to his subordinates, Harry and Tim, without resenting the greetings of the hounds—who were as facilely affectionate as the lady-pack is wont to be—even though Science and Wilful's demonstrations imperilled the flawless beauty of his breeches. He beamed upon his guests with a satisfaction that was so obviously genuine that the Hunt beamed back upon him, and there and then took him to its joint bosom as a man and a brother, a position that is not always easily attained, even by well-off young men who are the owners of trustworthy coverts.

Fifteen minutes " law " is enough for any right-thinking Master to allow, the opening meet and a hunt-breakfast notwithstanding. Little Cox-Munro stood for tradition and the rigour of the game, and at precisely a quarter-past eleven he put his knee into the hand of the helper who held his horse, and was shot up into the saddle as neatly as a ball into its attendant cup. With the little look across the crowd for which Mr. Mason was waiting, he set the pack in motion. The gathering of horses and traps opened and parted, making way for Tim, the Second Whip, to canter away through the crowd to take up his appointed position; he was followed at a steady trot by the Huntsman, with the hounds rippling in prim propriety round his horse, and with Harry bringing up the rear.

The Master, on his dancing iron-grey mare, looked round for Jimmy.

" Corran, do you mind——? "

Jimmy minded nothing. He put spurs to the young Dublin horse, and galloped away over the grass to watch the end of the covert.

" All you people," Cox-Munro addressed his Field, " please stay outside the covert. If he breaks the far side, I won't go away without you. Sir Thomas," he appealed, in a lower voice, " keep 'em quiet if you can! "

" If one of 'em opens his damned mouth, I'll open mine," replied Sir Thomas. " I venture to say he won't do it twice! "

Sir Thomas had himself Mastered the County pack at some prehistoric period, and might be relied on in an emergency to say the right thing.

The younger Dublin horse was a gentleman and a good mover. He permitted himself but one modified buck, and then settled down to gallop, sweetly and steadily, over the yellow stretches of coarse grass. Away to the left, on the western avenue, Jimmy saw the little speckled group that was the hounds suddenly detach tself from its guardians and flow into the laurel covert that stretched wide, across the avenue, between the far-away house and the western gate. The two hunt-servants and the Master followed, and Sir Thomas, unmistakable on his white horse, instantly stationed himself across the avenue, guarding the covert, as it were the angel at the gate of Eden, but with a flaming tongue for a sword. The Field stood, submissive, spreading out on the grass on either side of the drive; the string of laden cars waited behind them, extending back nearly to the house.

Jimmy galloped on. His point was at the far east end of the laurel island, where it extended almost to the demesne wall, at a place where a farm gate made a way of escape into the open country. There was a little hill, hardly in any other country to be called a hill, grown over with heather, with great blue limestone boulders scattered over it, their crowns only showing above the heather. An old, old thorn-tree grew a little way up the hill and a holy well was beside it. Jimmy took his stand beside the well. He looked at the rags, hanging on the lower twigs of the thorn, propitiatory offerings whose purpose was to beguile the guardian saint of the well to grant the petitions of those who came to pray and drink the water. He remembered how, as a small schoolboy, trying to shoot rabbits, he had come to the well and taken a sip of the water, and torn the hem off his pocket-handkerchief, with a wish to be helped to shoot straight. And thereupon he had slain three rabbits, who had not, presumably, taken the precaution of counter-sips, praying for immunity from danger.

The minutes, that go by so slowly to the watcher of a covert, passed and passed. Could it be that the keeper who had so faithfully sworn to the presence of "a dose of foxes" in the western covert had been lying or mistaken? The cold dread that assails the owner in such case began to creep over Jimmy. Cox-Munro, and all that gang of people, brought here on false pretences! It was a horror unthinkable!

"If Pat were here I'd ask her to run a drag for me!" he thought. "If it weren't too sore a subject! . . . Why wasn't she here? . . . On the other Dublin horse . . . or even on Dairymaid? . . . The crocks weren't smart enough for her. . . . There! wasn't that a hound speaking? . . . No, confound it! I believe there isn't a blooming fox in the whole blooming place! . . . Wasting her time mucking in Paris. . . . Losing the whole season, by Jove! How on earth can she stick it? . . . If she were here——" He lost himself in formless wishing.

The young Dublin horse advanced a step and stretched his head down, nosing towards the water. "You want a wish, do you?" said Jimmy to him. "Hold on! I think I'll have one myself first—just for the sake of old times. Let's see, what shall it be? A fox in five minutes, or——" The alternative needed no words.

He swung his right leg over the Dublin horse's outstretched neck, and slipped to the ground. He pulled off his gloves.

"Oh, by Jove, a rag? Well, hang it, I suppose I must sacrifice something!"

A new silk handkerchief with a deep hem defied him. He drove the rowel of a spur through it and tore it asunder and tied a strip to the thorn-tree. Then he scooped up a handful of the clear well water. He looked down at it, pondering, half in contemptuous amusement at his own folly, half in earnest, while he tried to decide what his wish should be. And, as he looked at the tiny shining pool in his hollowed palm, Patsey's face looked back at him.

For the fraction of a second he stared at it. Then it vanished, and he saw only the lines of his hand, and the twinkle of gold of his ring. He stood bewildered, still staring at the water that was beginning to ooze through his fingers. "Well! if that doesn't beat——" He put his face down into his hand and drank the water. "Give her to me!" he murmured to the Saint, all in earnest now.

The young Dublin horse snatched his head free from restraint and sucked a big mouthful out of the well.

"That's enough for a wish!" Jimmy said to him, feeling rather dazed. "I hope you wished for a fox—because I didn't!" He tugged the horse's head up, and backed him a step down the hill and mounted.

Had he really seen her? . . . Funny what imagination will do for one! . . . Well, his last wish here came off all right. . . . If only the Saint would play up again! . . . Then he said, very positively, to the young horse's ears, "I saw her as plain as I see you!"

The young horse did not reply. He was looking hard at the end of the covert where the fox (for whom he must certainly have wished) was standing on the grass, uncertain whether to go away or to dodge back over the wall into the laurels. Jimmy saw him too. In a moment every other thought was swept from his mind. Patsey, and the Saint, and the Vision, and the Wish! With a jerk, every nerve was screwed up to concert-pitch, he and the Dublin horse vibrating together, absurdly, uncontrollably, at the sight of little Dan Russel the Fox, making up his mind whether to flee into the sun-lighted country or to slip back into the green silence.

But it wasn't silence now. The wood suddenly was

wild with the cry of ecstasy, of discovery, of glory, as the hounds " found "—that pregnant past participle that contains in itself all that a fox-hunter most needs to know!

Dan Russel made no delay. He put back his ears, and straightened his brush, and went away through the open farm-gate into the open country. In less than a minute Jimmy was beside the gateway, uttering screams that set the Dublin horse dancing and brought the pack crashing through the covert in a gorgeous flood of mad music. Back in the wood, he heard the responding shouts of the Hunt servants, yelling at stragglers:

" Forrad, forrad, forrad! Get to cry! Gerr' away forrad to cry there! "

Then the bitches, like a mountain torrent, foaming out over the wall of the wood, whirling through the gateway, hurling themselves over the thin wall on the opposite side of the farm-road.

Next Mason bursting through the laurels—" Come up, 'oss! "

With a clatter of stones he was away after his hounds.

Jimmy waited to let a couple of hounds, who had followed their huntsman, through the gateway and over the wall, now considerably reduced in height. Then he heard the following thunder of the Field, coming galloping up the grass parallel with the covert, and he waited no longer. He let his quivering horse go, and was across the road in a flash, and into the field over what was left of the wall. The next instant Cox-Munro, his round baby face blazing, came galloping up beside him, yelling, " Come along! They're well away! We've got a good start, and we'll keep it! " Two or three more hounds were with him. Harry, the First Whip, was materialised, mysteriously, on the spot, as is the way with good First Whips.

"They're all on now, Master!" he shouted, with a crack of his whip to stimulate the three ladies, streaking away after their leaders.

The Field were now hustling through the gateway, but before the first of them had crossed the lane Jimmy and the Master and Harry were charging the ensuing wall, all three abreast. The strange, yellow-green, empty country, with neither houses nor trees to break its monotony, stretched away in long levels to the horizon. Great square fields, intersected by grey stone walls, all alike dry-built of rough round stones, few stopping short of four feet in height, many exceeding that very sufficient altitude by a foot or more. The pace was tremendous; the bitches swept on, flicking over the walls, racing across the big fields; it was all the horses could do to keep with them, even though galloping their best, swinging over the lower walls out of their stride, checking just a little to buck over the tall ones, some old veterans shamelessly banging away the topmost stones with their knees, knowing that the loose-built walls would yield to violence, caring nothing for the resulting big knees. Jimmy Corran found himself in better company than he had often known before; seeing, right and left of him, men and women all going hard, charging the walls unfalteringly, not turning from their own line unless when a wall, hit hard by a leader, showed an attractive round gap, like a bite out of a slice of bread and butter. There was nothing to stop a fox; no rocky hills with helpful crevices or deep badgers' earths; no plantations netted with undergrowth and perforated with rabbit-holes, to give him a chance to check and dodge, no drains or culverts, nothing but a main earth somewhere, if by luck he had set his mask for a place that was out of the " stop."

The Dublin horse didn't like it. To gallop across the wide flat fields was all very well; there was something County Meath-like and reasonable about that, but to be obliged to buck, like a Ward Union stag, over walls, all day, was not *his* idea of hunting—nothing to change feet on, and not so much as an open ditch in the whole country! He felt thoroughly upset and exasperated.

One brief check there was, when the fox ran through a small and compact fir-wood, heading for the home of certain of his relatives with whom he hoped to spend the rest of an agitating morning. But the earth-stopper had been before him, and, to his annoyance, he had to decide on a haven of refuge considerably farther away. The young horse, not being, after thirty minutes of hard going, as fresh as he might be, was also annoyed; he had taken a dislike to two chestnut cobs who had come up during the check, and, when he had to start again, these accompanied him, one on either side, bouncing like india-rubber balls over the walls, with an ease and enjoyment that he was far from sharing. But he had no intention of giving in, and, at the end of another fifteen minutes, he and Jimmy were up in time to see—even if from some way back—a speck, that was the fox, cross a road, a tired speck, that, making a final effort, ran, cat-like, up the rough face of a high demesne wall, and squeezed itself through a happily remembered hole, half-way up in its height.

In less than a minute the hounds came storming up, too late to see the white tag of Dan Russel's brush vanish through the opening, but near enough to know that but for the hole in the wall his minutes had been numbered. By the time Jimmy had got up, the Master and a few others were in the road, the hounds were yelling and leaping at the wall, the hole that had served the fox so well being just low enough for them to reach with futile clawings. Cox-Munro was yelling almost as loudly as they, for someone to tell him which was the nearest adjectived way to the nearest adjectived gate. The Hunt servants, on foot among the hounds, were trying to lift some of them high enough to enable them to scramble over the wall, and were almost, yet not quite, succeeding in the attempt. Each successive member of the Field, as he arrived, shouted some unintelligible suggestion, shoving his way as near the centre of excitement as those who had preceded him would permit. Jimmy, as a newcomer, remained at a respectful distance. The two chestnut cobs came up soon after he did. They were ridden by two ladies, and at sight of their riders the Master cursed and crushed his way through the crowd, back-firing bad language like a motor-car in frenzy, and roared an enquiry to the ladies as to whether the earths in the Park were——

"No, they're not stopped!" screamed back the elder lady. "We had no orders—I'm afraid it's no good trying——"

Little Cox-Munro, purple with passion, did not wait for the end of the sentence. He whirled his mare round, and began to blow his horn furiously, while he trotted fast down the road away from the fatal hole.

The younger of the two ladies began to laugh.

"Look at his cross old back!"

The elder said, "Poor little Archie! But it wasn't my fault—I should have had them stopped if I'd been told——" Then she turned her horse and looked hard at Jimmy.

"Lord Corran, I'm going to introduce myself. I'm

Mrs. Ridley. I used to know your father so well—and of course your mother too—and I was at your coming-of-age ball—and that's not so *very* long ago, is it? But I don't expect you to remember me!" She put her head on one side, and looked up at Jimmy with a little laugh that assured him of forgiveness. She had pretty blue eyes, and the laugh had revealed the existence of a dimple.

"And this is my daughter Joan," Mrs. Ridley went on, "but you needn't feel obliged to remember *her*, as she was still in the schoolroom when you were last at Gurtinure!"

Jimmy raised his hat as gracefully as his hat-guard would permit.

Miss Joan was small, like her mother, but was dark, with very bright dark eyes, and a sharp, neat little nose. She reminded Jimmy of a blackbird. He thought, with the swift inconsecutive thought of such a moment, "Dashed if I remember either of 'em! . . . The girl's not as good-looking as the mother. . . . This horse won't go another yard. He's cooked. . . . I don't believe I ever met this woman . . . I never heard mother talk of her——" Aloud he said, "Of course I remember you, Mrs. Ridley! It's awfully nice of you to remember me!"

And Mrs. Ridley said to herself, "Of course he does nothing of the sort! But he's a very nice-looking boy, and the very image of poor Tony!"

Cox-Munro and the hounds had departed in storm. The Field straggled after them, Jimmy and the two Ridley ladies last in the procession.

"He told me at the Meet he'd had Moneymeen stopped," Miss Joan announced. ("He" at such times is always either the Fox or the Master.) "I told him we all hated Moneymeen—it's no fun bucketing round and round those plantations. He said he didn't care! I shall pay him out somehow next time he comes to Peterstown!"

"Quite right!" said Jimmy.

"Please don't encourage her to be naughty!" Miss Joan's mamma begged him.

Jimmy defended himself. "I'm only speaking for the Field! I've got to go home. This horse has had enough. He's rather green still——"

"Oh, why go home?" exclaimed Mrs. Ridley, impulsively. "Come back with us to Peterstown and have some lunch. I'm sure our ponies, also, have had as much as they want. You provided us with such a good fox! My husband will be so glad to meet you—you were out when he went to see you. And your horse shall have lunch too, with the ponies! He's such a handsome fellow! We've been admiring him! Haven't we, Joan?"

It was generally assumed that Mrs. Ridley was older than her daughter, but no one quite believed it.

CHAPTER XXVI

THERE may be hunting countries where members of the Hunt never criticise the Master or the Huntsman, never disparage their fellow-members' horses, and never permit themselves the indulgence of gossip about each other. But if such a millennium exists, innocent of insinuations as to the friendship of the lion and the lamb, incredulous of good feeling between the weanéd child and the cockatrice, it cannot be claimed that these praiseworthy restrictions obtained in the country in which Jimmy Corran now found himself. And even in a millennium there must be limitations to indulgence. That two rich and entirely eligible young men should be swept in, appropriated, absorbed, or cannibalised (as Mrs. O'Reilly, who had herself been a cannibal in her day, and ought to know, put it) by one house, and that a house with but one legitimate man-eater, was, in the opinion of many other competitors in disinterested hospitality, not cricket.

Mrs. Ridley, however, who was the cannibal alluded to, having obeyed the sound precept that advises the combatant, no matter how just his quarrel, to " get his blow in fust," was able to ignore her neighbours' views in the matter. The jaws of Peterstown House were said to have closed on Jimmy Corran and Archie Cox-Munro, as they had, before now, closed on other ingenuous youths, and it was further asserted that Goodness knew she might have been content with the father, without getting her claws into the son. Goodness, being no doubt aware that there are generally two sides to a flirtation, no less than to a quarrel, was probably not unmindful of the fact that the late Lord Corran had been (in the opinion of his friends) a lad, and might have pointed this out when invoked in condemnation of Mrs. Ridley; but no authority, however impartial, could deny that she had a dimple.

Peterstown was eight miles by road from Gurtinure, and the roads of East Brandon were no better than they should be (though without the excuse of a dimple). But though motors had not, in that dark age, arrived on the scene, a distance of eight miles, even of Irish miles, was not an insuperable difficulty. Jimmy's head groom, Mr. John Griffen, imported from Dublin with the horses, had, early in his incumbency, discovered that in the Gurtinure Home Farm was concealed a pony whose merits entitled her to a higher station than that of the farm bailiff's maid-of-all-work, and Ahab was not more determined on the possession of the vineyard of Naboth than was Mr. Griffen on absorbing the farm pony into his stables.

The farm bailiff, in indignation that, though deep, was far from being too deep for words, appealed for support to old Mr. Bolger, the agent, asserting that if the pony was taken away from him he might as well go under the sod for all he'd be able to do on the Farm. Old Mr. Bolger sympathised with the farm bailiff, but, being old and wise, he recognised the power of Ahab, and decided that Jezebel's example had better be followed. So, in what was unconsciously scriptural language, he told the farm bailiff that the pony was " the Lord's " (for thus was Jimmy referred to by his retainers), and there was no use in talking, and he had better look out for another. Upon which the farm bailiff bought a pony from his wife's sister's husband, which, as being a family job, was something of a solace, and the ex-farm pony, now full of oats and impudence, trotted (shying at pigs and donkeys) from Gurtinure to Peterstown, with "the Lord," in a little over forty-five minutes about three times a week (on an average), since the hounds only went out Mondays, Wednesdays and Fridays, and playing duets with Mrs. Ridley wasn't bad fun. Mrs. Ridley wasn't as severe as Patsey (and Jimmy would tell Patsey so), and she let him have a shot at the treble sometimes, which Pat never would submit to (but, after all, he preferred the bass, he was more used to it, and it wasn't so tricky as the treble).

He had fallen into the habit of joining company with Mrs. Ridley and Joan out hunting. When hounds were jogging on from one covert to another, Jimmy found the jog less tedious when Mrs. Ridley was jogging with him. His horses and the chestnut cobs might have been stable companions, so devoted were they to each others' society. Jimmy had even to suppress a childish inclination in the younger Dublin horse to whinny when he saw in the distance Mrs. Ridley's little mare approaching.

And Mrs. Ridley was sympathetic and helpful. When his cook fought with the senior housemaid it was Mrs. Ridley who divined that both of them were in love with Blake, the butler, and advised him as to which of them to sack. She used to know the Kirwens too, Sir Ingram and Cousin Maud—not Patsey; "the elder girls" were more her contemporaries, she said. Rather queer-tempered, Mrs. Ridley had found them. "That Kirwen temper, you know—they all inherited it. But I expect this nice second little Lady Kirwen has neutralised it, hasn't she? She was one of the younger ones at my school—I didn't know her very well——"

Jimmy felt a little uncomfortable about the reference to the Kirwen temper; he couldn't deny that Pat *was* a bit hot sometimes. Mrs. Ridley changed the subject.

Jimmy liked Mr. Ridley too—a very good old sort (centuries older than Mrs. Ridley, of course)—keen about archæology, prehistorics—harmless maggots that worried no one except himself. He knew nothing at all about horses or hunting, but there was always a fox when the hounds came, and he had sense enough to let Mrs. Ridley run the stables and see about the coverts. There were three sons, two in the Army, and one in the Navy. Miss Joan was the youngest. Cox-Munro told Jimmy that he had met the sons and liked them. His opinion with regard to Miss Joan was sufficiently apparent. He and she talked to each other incessantly, squabbling, snarling, making it up, and beginning to wrangle again, like two puppies. " Silly little things, aren't they? " Mrs. Ridley would say, confidentially and indulgently, to Jimmy, the dimple deepening, and the pretty blue eyes smiling into his. (" Mother *must* be mistaken in saying that she can't be a day under fifty-five! " Jimmy would think.)

Lady Corran had read her son's accounts of the lady of Peterstown House with suspicion, and wondered if she had better go over to Ireland and keep an eye on things in general.

" It doesn't seem to be the girl," she said to her sister. " The very idea of that Nancy Ridley at her tricks still! And I had thought he was so taken with Maud's Patsey! "

The sister had replied that of course there was nothing really in it with a woman of that age——

" Eleanor! I don't trust her! " Lady Corran had answered very emphatically. " And I detest and distrust these maternal flirtations! I can so well imagine the way she is petting and spoiling Jimmy, giving him wrong ideas and keeping him in her pocket! So bad for a young man! I should go over to Gurtinure at once, if it were not for my rheumatism and the awful damp. And he *ought* to marry—I should be *quite* satisfied with Maud's girl——"

" I thought we had heard that she had run away to Paris?" objected Lady Corran's sister.

" Oh, my dear, she can very easily be made to run back again!" replied Lady Corran, with some impatience. Eleanor was always in opposition.

The ex-farm pony was getting very sick of the road to Peterstown. Twice a week, nearly always, and invariably on Sunday afternoons, it was her portion, and even the glories of the stables, being clipped down to the ground, and wearing a warm rug, and having as many oats as she could eat, scarcely indemnified her for the tedium of trotting eight miles on a stony flat road, without so much as a hill to give a little variety, and her new master kept her going so hard, he gave her no time to shy even at a wandering sow, no matter how offensive. Jimmy had fallen into the Peterstown habit almost imperceptibly. When he wasn't shooting or hunting, or if he wanted to escape from being talked to about the tenants by Old Bolger (which was the next thing to eternity), it was almost inevitable that he should order round the pony-cart and turn up at Peterstown for a " cup of tea " (which generally meant three, with proportionate hot cakes) and cigarettes afterwards. He and kind Mrs. Ridley used then to sit and talk over the drawing-room fire, in the winter twilight, while Joan and Archie went off, talking hard all the time, to play billiards, or battledore and shuttlecock, or some such silly game, in the hall. Old Ralph Ridley was kind, too, and friendly. He would take Jimmy into his study, and show him photographs of Stone Circles and Dolmens. One dark December afternoon Jimmy told him all about the Nine Stony Girls, and felt that he had gone up several pegs in old Ralph's estimation. He went back to the warm, fire-lighted drawing-room, thinking, like Patsey, of the wind on the heath, and of old Flora and Pat stalking that poacher chap, and finding that he was only a painter. How Patsey had buttered the fellow up about his beastly drawings! While he and Gilbert were longing for lunch!

Mrs. Ridley was always game to talk about the Kirwens, and Patsey in particular. Jimmy was confident that he had concealed his sentiments concerning Pat, and that he discussed her with complete detachment.

" And what studio is she working at? " Mrs. Ridley asked.

Jimmy had seated himself on the fender-stool, and had gone into the story of the Stony Girls and the poacher.

" Some chap they call ' Pie and Jelly,' " Jimmy said. " I forget his proper name——"

" Isn't that extraordinary? " exclaimed his hostess. " I actually know a woman who is working there too!—it's Pianelli's, of course—she was here, in the year One, to give the children painting lessons!—and she still insists on writing to me occasionally. She's a teacher in a school somewhere, and she goes to Paris every now and then to have a wash and brush-up. Wilson's her name. I shall probably have one of her usual Christmas reminders of her existence soon."

" Oh, do ask her how Patsey's getting on! " Jimmy usually spoke of Pat as " my cousin " (which implied detachment), but the thought of that afternoon on the hill had made him, for the moment, forget to be detached.

" Are you very anxious that she should do well? " (Why should she ask him that? Had she spotted the position? Should he explain things a little?) He hesitated. " You see, her people loathe it, and if she didn't make much of a hand at it she'd be more likely to come home——"

Yes, Mrs. Ridley saw.

" And what do you think about it? "

" I—well, I——" he twisted round on the fender-stool and stared into the heart of the red turf fire, with his back to Mrs. Ridley. " Well," he spoke slowly, " I think she's wasted out there. I want her to come home."

" Poor boy! "

Jimmy felt a hand on his shoulder, and, turning, met Mrs. Ridley's eyes, full of sympathy; a kind maternal smile, emphasised by the dimple, told him that his secret sorrow had been discovered. How agreeable it was that it should be discovered, and that he could now say what he liked! How soothing and consoling was Mrs. Ridley! Overwhelmed by all these circumstances, combined with his sorrow, now, so happily, no longer secret, Jimmy put his forehead down on Mrs. Ridley's knee, and a soft hand stroked his hair.

Lady Corran's surmise as to Nancy Ridley's pocket had not been amiss. Any young man might be glad to be kept in so kind and warm a pocket.

CHAPTER XXVII

CHRISTMAS, far off as it had seemed when Patricia had made her break for freedom, nevertheless advanced, as it habitually does, steadily and stealthily, arriving at last, quite suddenly, when experts in the calendar ask their friends if they are aware that it will be Christmas that day week, and the friends, if merely human, and more than twenty-one years of age, utter loud cries of horror.

Patricia, although more than twenty-one, having attained her majority during the month of November, nevertheless contemplated the arrival of the coming festival with calm, until an enquiry into the state of her finances gave her a shock for which she was quite unprepared.

How had the money gone? When had it gone? Where had it gone? She knew she had had fifty pounds to credit at the bank when she left London on September the twentieth, and her mother had given her her ticket to Paris. Very well then. These were the primary facts of the case. She studied her account-book—the first that she had ever kept; begun with minute accuracy of detail, degenerating rapidly into approximations, generally incorrect, always, when incorrect, under estimated. But her bank-book was disastrously reliable. Its cold statements could not be disputed. Out of the twelve hundred francs with which she had begun the Career, there remained but some three hundred and fifty with which to continue careering. " Not much better than a month, or six weeks at the outside," thought the accountant, despairingly, " without allowing for Christmas boxes—and even Hans couldn't do it for less."

Everything had been so much cheaper on paper. The fifty pounds was to have held out for six months at least, and then " Grandmamma's forty " would have come into play; in fact, Pat believed herself to have budgeted for a year " or thereabouts "—a period of time that is practically endless when one is twenty. Now, it seemed, horribly, as though—— She refused to contemplate the future. There was, at all events, Grandmamma's forty. The first quarter of that would be due in February. Even including Christmas she could hold out till then. But ten pounds would only last her for a month. Oh, how disgusting was money—or the want of it! Such a miserable thing to have power to spoil a life!

She wrote to her mother, a passionate letter, stating her financial position, saying that surely the Master could spare *something*, just to keep her going (" he can't want it *all* for himself, and Gilbert! ")—she would be most excruciatingly careful—would spend only on the most utter and abject necessities. " I don't want to brag," she wrote, " but I *am* getting on. Even old Bouvier says so, and all the people in the Studio think I am *forte*, but three months' work is simply nothing at all! " Then came an outburst: " It's too brutally unfair! Oh, Mother, why do men make the world such a *beastly* place for women? "

And Lady Kirwen, with tears (of which she said nothing) in her eyes, wrote back that she had talked to Papa about it, and Papa had been afraid that just now . . . (What Sir Ingram had actually said was that he wouldn't give Patsey " a bloody mag "—whatever that singular and unpleasant entity might amount to—until she chose to come to her senses, and come home and live like a young lady!) " But, darling " (this was not Sir Ingram, but Lady Kirwen speaking for herself), " I dare say five pounds won't come amiss and will help you over Christmas. I only wish I could give you more."

What made it worse still was that this same week she had asked old Bouvier to be allowed to paint. She had showed him, with some trepidation, a study of a head that de Brémont had permitted her to paint in the afternoon. (It was well known that M. Bouvier didn't think much of M. de Brémont, whom he held to be *pas serieux* and coercible by his female pupils.) Old Bouvier had looked at the head, which was that of a young girl, with a surprise that he could not quite conceal. He said, "*Tiens, c'est pas mal touchée!* " and then, grudgingly, that it was an " *assez jolie tâche de couleur*," and he even went so far as to mutter, almost to himself, that Pat had " *du talent* "; but he then recollected himself, and went on to criticise and condemn the study as being " *mal construit*," and he had proceeded to embark on a lecture to Patricia on the folly of trying to run before she could walk, ending by assuring her that if after two years—" but two good years *je vous l'dis* "—in the Studio she began to paint, it would be soon enough. "But," he continued, nodding his cropped white head and eyeing Pat's discouraged face with all-perceiving eyes, " it is always the same with the English young ladies—you come for a time—two months, three months—*et puis, vous disparez!* "

Patsey had assured him that she wasn't English, and didn't want to disappear. It was useless to try and explain that in Ireland, no less than in the rest of the world, if there wasn't enough money to educate both brothers and sisters, the sisters did without. This would be for old Bouvier beside the point, which had nothing to say to sex or money, and was concerned only with the irrefutable fact that omelettes involve broken eggs.

The prospects of the other runaway, young George Lester, though necessarily cloudy, held, none the less, a brighter promise for the future than Patricia could look forward to. George was already regarded among his fellows with respect, even with some apprehension, as a caricaturist of quality. He had sent a set of drawings to *The London Descriptive*, and *The Descriptive's* editor had paid for them quite a respectable sum (for in those days illustrated papers did not regard the photographer as their sole contributor), and had asked for more of the same vintage.

George had sent the cheque intact to his mother, to be put into her Post Office Savings bank-book. Time and remoteness were having their inevitable effect, and were healing the wound in his conscience that had been kept open by remorse. He was coming to look upon that five-and-twenty pounds as a loan from his father; an involuntary loan, no doubt, but one that should and would be paid off to the uttermost farthing. He spent some of the *Descriptive's* next cheque on such a slouch black felt hat, and flowing black necktie, as were considered thoroughly *chic* in the *Quartier*, and, meeting Miss Le Mont in the *cour* of the Studio, felt himself so supported by the hat and tie that he asked her " and her friends " to do him the honour of lunching with him on the following Sunday.

" Why, we shall be proud! " responded Mercy, thinking that the title *Le Beau Lesterre*, conferred on him by the Studio, and revealed to her by Madame Marthe, was very well bestowed; " that will be just perfect! Where is it to be? "

" I thought of the *Paradis des bons Cochers*," George said, nervously. " The fellows in the *Atelier* tell me it's a good place, though it sounds rather——"

" Rather one-horse? " suggested Mercy, laughing up in his anxious face. " *I* think it sounds like a coach-and-four! Much too grand for poor painters like us! "

George fell under her spell. How pretty she was! How gay and yet sympathetic! He pulled out of his pocket the copy of *The Descriptive*, and showed her his drawings. He apologised to himself for " showing off " —it was only because she looked as if she would be interested. And so she was, so that was all right.

The lunch was a great success. George had taken a private room, and had brought with him a supporter, who was that Willie Jefferson whose desire to be made known to Blue Eyes was now gratified. Mr. Jefferson told stories, and justified his position as a supporting guest, observing the obligation (of conscientious guests) of " keeping the table in a roar "; and even though the roar was contributed mainly by himself, it strengthened George, imparting an atmosphere of brilliant worldliness, besides serving as a shelter beneath which he could murmur, diffidently, comments on affairs of the Studio to the sympathetic Miss Le Mont, Miss Kirwen, and Miss von Kappf, being, as it were, swept away from him in the flood of Mr. Jefferson's conversation.

But it was easier, and pleasanter too, to talk about Miss Kirwen than to compete with Willie Jefferson for her attention. George told Mercy of the Meet at Drumgoole, and dwelt upon Miss Kirwen's courage and horsemanship. He spoke of their meeting on the hill, at the Druid Circle, and how Miss Kirwen had encouraged him, and given him the notion to come here to Paris.

" And now you're here and making good! " cooed Mercy, her soft dark eyes encouraging him.

George enjoyed his party. Monsieur, the *Chef* of the *Paradis*, had done him well, and the student appetites of the guests responded to his skill. Willie Jefferson had selected the wine with ability, and was playing up, George felt, like a little man; the ladies were all charming, and looked as if they were enjoying themselves as much as he was himself. Miss Le Mont made him bring forth the page of *The Descriptive* with his drawings. " I know you have it there, next your heart! " she accused him.

The now historic duel was the centre-piece of the page. Mr. Jefferson, with dramatic indignation, pointed out other Studio celebrities whom George had first libelled and then given to the world.

" He's a dangerous man! " Miss Le Mont agreed. " He'll be making laughing-stocks of us next! "

George, looking shy, handsome, and happy, fumbled repudiation of such irreverence. Success and wine, to both of which he was but little accustomed, had gone to his head. They gave him courage. He looked at Patricia, and said he was afraid beauty was out of his line.

" Well, don't you dare to make fun of us! " said Mercy. " We've got a caricaturist too, *chez les dames*, who could make you men sit up! Haven't we, Hans? "

" Do not ask me! Go to ze old Wilson, and to Hell's Delight, for such information! " replied Hans, darkly. " '*Alle Schuld rächt sich auf Erden!*' Zey will avenge zeir wrongs, and will yet drink Patsey's blood! "

* * * * *

Even though the Studio shut its doors for Christmas Day only, George's party was not the only dissipation proper to the season. On Christmas Eve a return hospitality was offered to him and Willie Jefferson by the young ladies; this took the form of a light supper, at which Hans's skill as a cook was called into fullest action, and after it had run its course the two young men were invited to escort their hostesses to St. Sulpice, to attend the midnight Mass, and to hear the usual Christmas anthem, the "*Noel*" of Adam.

The immense church was very dark, and was crammed with a moving, whispering crowd. Patricia and her company slowly and gradually made their way forward until they were able to see, behind the altar, the recessed piece of sculpture that represents the Holy Family, and that was, on this night of nights, softly lighted; it was as though, by a miracle, its whiteness had become translucent, and was permitting some inner radiance to shine through. As the final stroke of midnight sounded, a very delicate and gentle tenor voice began to breathe forth upon the darkness the sugar-sweet melody.

"*Minuit! Chrétiens! C'est l'heure solennel-le!*"

The stealing music swelled and strengthened. The odour of incense filled the great church. The crowded people knelt, listening and gazing, their whispering stilled; the mysterious composite impulse of a common devotion was like a cloud, overwhelming them, bowing their heads in a common humility.

The three girls and their escorting youths went home soberly, still silenced by the service. At the *porte-cochère* of the *Pension* Hans unlocked the little door.

"Let me make sure Hector is well chained in ze kennel," she said. "If not, he will eat you all wissout salt! But me not, for he loffs me!" Then she called, "Hector! Hector!"

A burst of deep barking replied from the kennel.

"All is well! You do not, zis time, provide ze ros bif and blum budding for his *Weihnachtsfest!*" She pushed Patricia and Mercy through the rabbit-hole. "Happy Christmas to you, Messieurs!" she called out, following them and slamming the little door in the face of the escort.

CHAPTER XXVIII

BETWEEN Christmas and the New Year work at the Studio slackened and tea-parties broke forth; some, very select, held in the bedroom of the hostesses (there were generally two involved), where most of the furniture contrived a double debt to pay, nothing, from the bed to the bath, being quite what it appeared to be. Other entertainments, wider in range, were given by the owners of private studios. At these would be found a varied assortment of guests, drawn at large from the maps of both hemispheres, but all alike following " the Foolish Flame " of Art, the will-o'-the-wisp which for one that it leads to high ground, leaves a crowd of others, inveterately hopeful, unalterably helpless, up to their middles in the mire of mediocrity.

Among these victims of a pleasant delusion may be found a proportion of elderly philosophers of both sexes, who possess just enough income to exist, humbly yet comfortably, in the *Quartier*; and if, as in some fortunate cases, they can afford themselves the privilege of an *appartement* of which a studio forms part, they ask nothing more of life than to potter intermittently among their juniors at one of the public studios, with interludes of indulging in a model at home, an extravagance that, although it may have no very appreciable result, can, at least, imply the distinction of being an independent artist.

L'Atelier Pianelli was blessed with an American widow, a perfect exponent of the foregoing type, hospitable, good-natured, and reputed among her fellow students to be a lady of great wealth, since she had been known to buy the sketches of others, and at the entertainments which she occasionally gave, cakes and cigarettes were unstinted and of high quality. In honour of the last night of the year, as well as of a recent move into a large and very superior studio, Mrs. Gapes held an evening reception to which she invited not only her especial friends, among whom Patsey, Mercy and Hans were allotted high place, but also all those, male and female, who owed allegiance to the communion of "Pie and Jelly."

Mrs. Gapes' studio in the Boissonade, hung with Chinese lanterns, and with every possible jet of gas doing its best, made an impressive effect. Mrs. Gapes herself, gorgeous in a red velvet mantle (that she had bought at a *Mont de Piété* wherewith to garb a model) and wearing a very large "picture-hat," received her guests with a manner so stately as to suggest to the more observant that the picture-hat sat lightly on its throne; a suspicion that was confirmed when, later, in a less restrained moment, it rocked over one eye, and Mrs. Gapes, declaring that if she wore it any longer she would yell with "nyurves," hurled it behind a curtain into a dark retreat, believed to harbour her bed.

"Why, Mrs. Gapes, dear," Mercy, the consoler, assured her, "I like you best without it!" She appealed to Patricia. "Mrs. Gapes should give us a chance to admire her lovely Titian hair! Shouldn't she, Patsey?"

"*Méchante!*" exclaimed Mrs. Gapes, much gratified, snatching a glance at her greying red locks in a neighbouring mirror. "If you'll excuse me, gyurls, *oon pitty momong*, I will just leave this glad scene and make a little *bout de toylette*. I've got a real cunning little bang-comb, all covered up with pearl bugs, that'll keep my Titian hair settin' down good and tidy." She followed the discarded hat into obscurity.

Mercy and Pat did not await the success of the bang-comb. The room had filled, and it was amusing to see the Studio no longer engrossed in work and clad in paint-stained overalls, but dressed in its best, and determined on enjoying itself. Patsey found herself elbowing " Old Wilson " in the throng, and spoke to her. It had become known that Miss Wilson and Fröken Hellquist had, no one knew how (but " Pie and Jelly " was accused), heard of the audacity of Pat, a new-comer, in caricaturing offensively two of the oldest of the pupils, and it was believed that they had satisfied themselves as to the extent of the crime by secretly examining the contents of Pat's *carton*. The sharp point of Pat's pencil had gone home. " Hell's Delight " had not attempted to conceal her hostility, but Miss Wilson had been either more forgiving or less candid. She now responded politely, and, after the requisite exchange of seasonable bromides, she remarked that she had just heard from " a friend, who was seeing a good deal of a friend of yours, Miss Kirwen—Lord Corran—a very nice young man, I believe," Miss Wilson added, with condescension.

Patsey was conscious of resentment that Old Wilson should bestow her second-hand approval upon Jimmy Corran.

" He's my cousin," she said, lightly, beginning to move away; " but he really is quite nice, in spite of that! "

Miss Wilson thought, not for the first time, that (quite apart from that preposterous caricature) there was something about that girl that she had always disliked—spoilt; thought too much of herself; had had too much attention. And what was her father, after all? Nothing but an Irish baronet! Miss Wilson wondered why dear Mrs. Ridley should be interested in her.

Someone had begun to thump a waltz on a very old, very long-tailed grand piano, which had been utilised, as indeed were most things in Mrs. Gapes' *ménage*, in being that which it was not, and was now, dressed in a lace tablecloth, pretending to be, a sideboard. The cups and saucers danced and clinked. One of the young men drew forth a violin and began to improvise an obligato. Willie Jefferson and George Lester approached Patricia simultaneously.

"May I?" said Mr. Jefferson, with a profound bow, cutting in in front of the more diffident George.

But before the young American raised his head to receive Patricia's answer, George, looking her full in the face, with eyes that implored, mutely offered himself to her. He knew he could dance. Dublin girls had often given him assurance on that point. He had the poise and balance, the speed and lightness of a runner and a jumper, and, as is so often found with painters, music and rhythm were in his blood.

Other couples were already spinning in a cleared space in the centre of the long room. Patricia put her hand on George's shoulder, and with the first step knew that he was an artist, even as she was, a dancer to whom she could resign herself with confidence. A waltz, as it was then danced, could be a very beautiful and graceful thing. Patsey and young George Lester were much of a height, slender and long-limbed; each in his and her own contrasting way—as Mercy had thought when first she saw them together—fair, and dark, very good to look at. In both of them was the same delicate sense of rhythm, and sensitive response to the dictates of the music.

The fiddler lad felt in an instant that in this couple he had exponents worthy of the best of his art. With his eyes on them, he played for them alone. They were borne on his music; sometimes, like sea-birds, gliding and sliding, rising and sinking, floating on the heaving breast of a slow in-coming tide; sometimes like swift swallows, that stoop and swing in long delicious curves to tunes that they alone can hear.

The spinning and whirling of the other dancers ceased ; couple by couple they stood to watch these two.

" Don't stop! " George muttered.

" I could go on for ever! " Patsey answered impulsively, hardly knowing what she said, lost in the dream-like enchantment of measured movement.

Willie Jefferson stood by Mercy Le Mont. When Patsey had been reft from him he had appealed to Mercy, but after a turn or two they also, like the other dancers, had ceased, and they stood, staring, connoisseurs, both of them, silenced and stilled by the ecstasy that a perfect thing can inspire.

" She's a thoroughbred! " said Willie Jefferson in Mercy's ear. " Why can't we paint that? "

Mercy murmured assent, but her eyes were on young George Lester.

When, at last, the fiddler's music drooped and faded to a close, and the two dancers loosed their hold of one another, and drew back into the watching ring of the guests, Mrs. Gapes gave the lead, and the room applauded, with clapping hands, and demands in most of the languages of Europe for another exposition of the poetry of motion.

" Will you? " George whispered, his heart beating. He thought: " Shall I hold her in my arms again? " His eyes told Patsey more than he knew.

She shook her head. " I'd rather not—I never thought they'd all have stopped just to watch us! It was absurd, wasn't it? "

Mrs. Gapes had followed them to press for an *encore*, but Patsey refused; she was wondering if the dance had been a mistake; thinking that she would have done better to have taken Willie Jefferson.

" I want to play the next dance."

She disregarded the reproaches of her hostess, and pressed her way across the room to the piano.

" I'll not allow it for more than one dance! " protested Mrs. Gapes. " I wonder at you, George Lester, giving in to her like this! "

Patsey had attacked a polka with the energy that she brought to most things; the emulous violin joined in, out-screaming the crashing of the piano. In a moment the room was full of prancing, hopping, swooping couples, talking at the tops of their voices, vieing with each other in agility, chasing each other from end to end of the long studio, boys and girls wild with sound and speed, letting loose the mad spirit of youth, pent during long effortful days.

As the hour grew later the revels became more uncontrolled. A " punch " was drunk at midnight, and Mrs. Gapes, standing precariously on a *tabouret*, holding high a steaming tumbler, and only retaining her position by a grasp of a satellite youth's coat-collar, called for cheers for the New Year. Then descending, she hustled her now uproarious guests into a circle, and, seconded by the English-speaking section of the company, she led the singing of " Auld Lang Syne."

" And now I've a dandy surprise for you all!" she cried in triumph. " We'll begin the *Nouvelle Année* with a *cotillon*! Bring out the presents, Howard Judd!"

The satellite youth dragged from behind a curtain a basket filled with the *Bon Marché's* most flagrant fantasies. Mrs. Gapes fought her way through the riotous crowd, calling at the full strength of her strident voice for Willie Jefferson.

Mercy turned to Patricia.

" Patsey! I *must* go home—I promised old Hans I'd go early. She went hours ago—she'll think I've run away with a soldier! One of these boys will fetch you home——" George was beside her. " Here's George Lester, he'll do it—won't you, Mr. Lester?"

" I'll go with you——" Patricia had begun.

Willie Jefferson, shouldering his fellows aside, stood before her.

" Mrs. Gapes requests you and me to lead the *cotillon!* Please don't say no, Miss Kirwen! Mercy, you mustn't be so mean, taking Miss Kirwen away! I'll call Mrs. Gapes! I guess she'll be real mad——"

" *I* don't want to take her away!" Mercy interrupted him; " but I'm looking after her, ain't I, Patsey dear? I'll leave you here now, and then you come home like a good little girl, with George Lester, when this thing is over.—No, no, Willie Jefferson, not you! You'd be dancing a *can-can* with her up the Grands Boulevards likely as not! But I trust George Lester!"

CHAPTER XXIX

THE night was very cold. A hard frost held the town in its grip, and the sound of the voices and the foot-steps of Mrs. Gapes' departing guests echoed in the narrow, quiet streets, and probably earned for them from awakened sleepers the reverse of New Year good wishes.

It was past three o'clock when Patricia and her com-panion, young George Lester, arrived at the *Porte Cochère* of the *Pension Leroux*. Patsey was tired and spoke little; George, living in the memory of the waltz with her, was silent as she. It was not till she had handed him the latchkey of the rabbit-hole in the great door that George summoned resolution to utter some-thing of his thoughts.

" Miss Kirwen, I wish I could express to you," he began, formally, with the unconscious pedantry of his class that suggests the faithful study of books of " etiquette," " how grateful I am for the—the privi-lege of dancing with you——"

Patsey interrupted him, pulling herself together, anxious to avoid solemnities.

" Oh, please don't try! I enjoyed it—your step and mine went quite well together, didn't they? It's awfully late——" she hurried on, " I mustn't wake Mademoi-selle Leroux or I shall get into a row! How cold it is! I shan't be sorry to get in! "

George abandoned his acknowledgments. He struck a match, and found the keyhole, and turned the key and pushed the door in. No sooner had he done so than a resounding roar from the dark courtyard told that the great boarhound, Hector, was on guard.

" He's chained, thank goodness——" Patricia had begun, when, with a sound of rushing feet, the roar was nearly upon them.

George slammed the little door; it was shut but just in time before the big dog flung himself against it. The thunder of his barking filled the frosty silence.

Patricia and George looked at each other aghast.

" He'd have made short work of us! " said George. " I didn't see him but the one time I had tea above with those ladies."

" He's a fiend," said Patsey, " and especially at night—they must have thought we were all in and unchained him."

" If I even had a stick——" George began, feeling himself a failure as a protector.

" You mustn't think of going in! " Patsey exclaimed in horror. " I'll ring the bell."

Through the roars of Hector the jangling of the bell by the kitchen window could be faintly heard, but there was no response. They waited, while the loud snuffings of Hector under the door told that he was there, waiting his opportunity. She rang again.

" The worst of it is that Pauline sleeps up in the roof somewhere, like a bat! " Pat began to laugh. " What on earth am I to do? "

" I'll ring again," George said, with determination. He attacked the bell handle, and at his third pull the bell-wire broke, and he staggered backwards with the handle, followed by a long length of wire, pulled out by the roots.

" Now you've done it! " said Patsey, with the grim triumph that is accorded to a thorough-going disaster.

Hector replied with a volley of sonorous barks.

"What about going round the corner and shying a stone at a window?"

"But our rooms don't look out on that side," Pat objected.

"Well, anyone's window!" George answered, firmly, walking away from the door. "You can't stop out in the cold here——"

The house, as has been said, was a corner one. Patricia followed him round the corner and into the next street, on to which its other windows gave. A half-moon shone on them.

George picked up two or three stones. "Now, which window shall I have a go at?"

As in the first enterprise in which with her he shared the perils, his shyness and his fear of her were forgotten. He thought of nights of adventure in Dublin, and laughed aloud. "Let you be praying the bobbies aren't around!"

And Patsey's spirit, as ever, responded gleefully to the stimulant of risk.

"I'm only praying that you don't break Mademoiselle's window! She'd be worse than any number of bobbies! And I don't know which it is!" she added, with a fearful joy.

George moved out into the road.

"I'll go for the moon in the middle window and chance it!"

There are not many Irish lads who are not what they would describe as being middling handy with a stone. George let fly at the moon in the middle window, and the stone flew into the house like a bird to its nest.

"That ought to fetch someone!" said George, contentedly.

Patsey palpitated, enjoying the excitement of trepidation. A few tense seconds passed. Then the violated window was flung open. A large white form stood at it, and a flood of furious German followed, of which all that the listeners could distinguish was the word *Engländerinn* (" That's me! " whispered Patsey, shaking with laughter), and then that the guardians of the peace were being summoned with a vigour that could hardly fail of success.

" It's old Frau Puttkamer! She's stone-deaf—she's no good to us—we'd better fly! "

" It's a pity she isn't dumb too! " George muttered. " I'll have a shot at another window! "

The suggestion was daring enough to appeal to Pat, but the sound of heavy running footsteps warned them that Frau Puttkamer's cries for help were being responded to.

Lightfoot lad and lass that they were, it was easy for them to take to their heels and to speed through the dark empty streets at a pace no *gardien* could achieve. They passed the *porte-cochère*, where Hector bayed anew at the sound of their flying feet, and fled, without consideration of where their flight was taking them, until they found themselves at the end of the street in which was the *Atelier Pianelli*. If the *gardien* had attempted pursuit, they had easily outrun him, and they stopped to take breath by a lamp-post at the corner of the street.

Patsey leaned against the corner of the end house, laughing and panting.

" It reminds me of the drag! " She was looking at George, with the moonlight on her face. " You and I seem fated to get into trouble! "

George thought, " She said ' You and I '! She makes no difference between us! "

A deep excitement held him. He had caught her hand as they ran, he had shortened his stride to hers, they had sped together in incredible heart-shaking one-ness! His right hand still tingled with the grasp of her slender fingers.

"I would rather be in trouble with you than in heaven with another!"

He hardly knew what he was saying. It was as though he thought aloud. The barrier of shyness had broken down. He told her that since the day of the wedding the thought of her had been ever in his heart. He said that but for her he would never have gone from slavery to freedom. That it was she who had been his inspiration.

Poor George here lapsed into panegyric whose style was unconsciously and disastrously influenced by some of the lessons he had received on Pulpit Delivery. Their sincerity might have saved them had the listener been old enough to feel their pathos rather than their absurdity.

But at one-and-twenty things are more or less what they seem, and Pat only thought, "This is awful! How can I stop him?"

Yet, latterly, George had begun to take a new place in her mind. His modesty, his talent, his looks, all were engaging, and Mercy had not failed to impress on her of what a beautiful and reverential devotion she was the object. And to-night—how distinguished he had looked!—impossible to believe that he was Holy George's son! And how adorably he danced! She had never had a partner that suited her so ideally! . . .

And then this latest episode—the window-breaking, the flight! Without Patsey's being aware of it, a new feeling about George was undoubtedly beginning to assert itself—and devotion seldom fails of an undermining effect.

But the devotion was now becoming rather too excessive. Pat didn't know how to repress it. They had alike forgotten where they were, the hour, the cold, the problem of a shelter.

" I know I'm not worthy so much as to——" George checked himself on the verge of direct quotation from the prayer-book and fell into his own idiom. " I don't know how I've the cheek to speak to you at all! If you knew——" Agony was in his voice. So acute it was that it checked the protest that Patsey was trying to formulate.

The thought in his mind was that he would lift the load from his conscience and be done with it. He'd feel less of a skunk if she—— He began again:

" When you said you were going to Paris that time on the hill—I knew that whatever way it was, I *should* go too! I thought of you night and day—I felt that the world was changed for me—I couldn't go on in the old way—oh, for God's sake, wait one moment more! " he entreated her. Patricia, looking at his distraught face, feeling that she could bear no more, had made as if she would go.

" Well——" he hesitated. She could see, by the light of the street-lamp, his face working in torture, " I had no money. I took one of my father's cheques and I signed his name to it. That's all! Now! Will you speak to me again? "

Before she could answer he had begun a fresh sentence.

" I'll say just one thing—I'm paying him back. He'll not be a loser by me. I have nearly the half sent him already——" His voice died away.

Patsey heard him out in silence. She was torn by conflicting feelings. Pity, sympathy she felt, yet both were chilled by the repugnance that such a fall from the path of honour as George had confessed must inspire in such a nature as hers, reckless, yielding to impulse, but incapable of deceit.

She felt a sort of resentment that he should drag her into what was an affair between himself and his own people only. It was so horribly uncomfortable—so hard to know what she was to say. She felt, rather than saw in the faint light, his tragic eyes fixed on her. She concentrated herself on the effort to hide from him that his confession had startled her into seeing him from a new and disastrous angle. To her young experience it was incredible that anyone she knew could do the sort of thing that was only " committed " by people in newspapers! . . . But poor George! . . . She couldn't help being moved by his misery. . . . How could she hit a man that was down? . . . After all, it wasn't her affair. . . . But wasn't it, perhaps, her affair a little? She had started him on the path to Paris. " The Downward Path! " as, no doubt, Holy George called it! Such rot! . . . Thought after thought flashing, faster than light, through her mind. . . . " That psalm-singing scoundrel! " as the Master called him. . . . Poor George! Bad as the Master was, he was better as a father than the psalm-singing scoundrel! . . . Yes, poor George (who had said that the thought of her was ever in his heart!). Who was she to come down on him, no matter what he had done? . . . And he said he was paying it back. . . .

She looked straight at George's stricken face, and said, nervously and hurriedly, but with the gentleness of pity in her voice, " I'm sure you'll make it right with your father—please don't say any more about it—I'm —I'm sure it will be all right—it won't make any difference—— "

But in her heart she knew that a difference had come, and for all her sympathy some involuntary shade of difference in her voice told George that if his confession had lifted the load from his conscience, it had but shifted the trouble and laid it on his heart.

At the spot where they were standing there was a window in the wall of the house not far above their heads. Before George could collect his distracted thoughts to reply, a voice fell upon them from the window, that had apparently been open, an indignant English voice that said: " *S'il vous plait, monsieur et madame! On a besoin de dormir!* "

Patsey's back was to the house, but the lamp-light shone on George.

" Oh, it's you, Mr. Lester! I had no idea who it was. The talking disturbed me," went on the voice, abating a little its first ferocity. " I always sleep with my window ajar, however cold the weather, *all* the year round! "

With this announcement, delivered with the self-satisfaction that such a practice (in common with its kindred exploit, a cold bath) can inspire, the window was drawn in to the indefinite point indicated by the word ajar, and the voice ceased.

" That was Old Wilson! " whispered Pat, fatefully. " If it were anyone else I'd ask her to take me in! Let's try the *Pension* again," she went on, talking fast, to keep the conversation in her own hands. " The old Frau may have wakened them up and we may get someone to hear us."

She started at a run. George followed her in silence. Again they attempted the rabbit-hole in the *porte-cochère*, and this time Hector's voice was still. Cautiously they opened the little door.

" He may be asleep," George said. " Wait, I'll shy a stone at the kennel."

A hollow bang told that the shot had found its mark, but no response came.

" Hans must have heard him—I'm all right now—good night! Thank you so much for helping me." She held out her hand.

George took it and held it. She could feel him trembling.

" It's I have to thank you for speaking to me, after what I told you just now. Don't think too badly of me. Don't punish me more than I can bear! "

Before Patsey could speak, he bent down and kissed the hand he held. Without another word he dropped her hand and went out into the street again, shutting the little door after him.

CHAPTER XXX

MRS. RIDLEY had not been mistaken in her expectation of a gesture of remembrance at Christmas from Miss Wilson. Such had arrived, and had been responded to with a rapidity that was as gratifying as it was unusual. Mrs. Ridley's acknowledgments in the past of Miss Wilson's attentions had, more frequently than not, taken the form of second-hand Christmas cards. But this Christmas had brought forth a response that was, as the pleased Miss Wilson said to herself, *quite* a letter. Miss Wilson liked—she may again be quoted—to keep in touch with useful people; Mrs. Ridley, who was good-natured, and had occasionally been useful as a reference, was eminently a person to touch, even to poke, annually, if not more often.

The response to Miss Wilson's Christmas poke had arrived on the last day of the year. Mrs. Ridley mentioned that she had just heard that the daughter of an old friend was working in Pianelli's Studio, Patricia Kirwen. Her cousin, young Lord Corran—here followed a word or two about Jimmy, and then a few sentences about Pat. Mrs. Ridley would like to know how she was getting on. "*A very determined young lady,*" Mrs. Ridley had heard. "*Quite resolved on being an artist, ' whether her mother would let her or no '—like the froggy who would a-wooing go!*" Mrs. Ridley hoped that in *this* case the wooing was confined to the pursuit of *Art!*

Miss Wilson was charmed by this affable letter. On

the day after she had received it (it had arrived, as it happened, on the very day of Mrs. Gapes' epoch-making Reception) she applied herself to answering it. Miss Kirwen was certainly clever, and, if she continued her studies, would probably do very well professionally. Miss Wilson knew her but very slightly. Her friends were Americans and foreigners. She had quite taken to the life of the *Quartier Latin*, which Miss Wilson herself had never cared for. The humour of Mrs. Ridley's letter was then emulated in a description of Mrs. Gapes' party, and of the subsequent disturbance of Miss Wilson's slumbers.

" *The voices*," she wrote, " *went on under my window (which I make a point of keeping open at night, cold though it is here at present) until I could really bear it no longer! I went to the window, and was, I must say, rather surprised to find that Miss Kirwen was one of the tiresome talkers, while a handsome young Irishman, named Lester, from the men's studio, was the other. They had been dancing together half the evening. It seems to be quite a* CASE! *They certainly danced beautifully. Everyone stopped to watch them. People said they were as good as Kate Vaughan and Royce at the Gaiety!* " (Mrs. Ridley had said Patricia was the daughter of a friend; Miss Wilson thought that a little commendation might be no harm. But, remembering the caricature, could not help adding) "*But what brought them under my window at that time of night I cannot imagine! I know I was not sorry when they departed! It was past three o'clock, and everyone else had gone home!* "

It is possible to have too much of a good thing, and over-stimulation has to be guarded against. Young men—even to a lady of experience, such as Mrs. Ridley—were sometimes incalculable. It might be advisable to censor Miss Wilson's despatch (or report), carefully, before publishing it. One never knew. Jimmy might go off like a rocket, and—since the scene would be Paris, where *crimes passionels* were quite the thing—shoot this young Lester on sight! The position was now so peaceful and pleasant it seemed foolish to risk ruffling its calm, and she felt that the longer her young friend remained in her pocket the less he would be likely to wish to leave it. Jimmy was a dear boy and a creditable *attaché*; quite apart from Mrs. Ridley's fancy for dear boys, she felt that she wore him as a species of decoration, a conspicuous good-service medal conferred by Providence, to be seen of all, a token of continued youth and of the undiminished potency of the dimple.

Besides (she reminded herself), she had Joan to consider. That little Archie Cox-Munro was far from being a certainty, and if the Patsey affair was tactfully and not too abruptly shelved, it would not, she thought, be difficult to slide, with equal tact, from the position of sympathetic, motherly friend, to that of no less sympathetic and friendly mother-in-law.

Jimmy had dined and slept at Peterstown, for a meet there on January 3rd. Miss Wilson's letter had arrived that morning, and a few selected preliminary extracts were administered to him after breakfast. It seemed that Patsey was doing *so* well with her painting, and was likely to go on with it quite seriously. . . . Mrs. Ridley might be old-fashioned, but she couldn't help thinking that the best place for girls was their own home. . . . She must say that she had been a little surprised that Maud Kirwen should have consented—— Did Jimmy know anything of a young man named Lester? Said to be a very clever artist—a friend, it seemed, of Miss Patsey's?

"Lester?" Jimmy said, frowning. "That's the poaching chap I told you about. I didn't know he was supposed to be a genius. His father poisons foxes. They're farmers, tenants of Sir Ingram's. Quite absurd to say he was a *friend* of Pat's—of course she *knows* him."

"Oh, I *see*," said Mrs. Ridley, with relief in her voice; "of course in a republican sort of atmosphere like those Paris studios—and Miss Wilson wouldn't know the difference—would she!"

"Can't say," Jimmy had replied, shortly, "not knowing the lady."

There had been a nice little hunt out of Peterstown. Now they were riding on to draw another covert, Cashen's Gorse. This involved a long jog from the place where the hounds had run into their fox, and roads and by-ways, bohireens and short-cuts, all had their useful moments, the last mile of the way being along a narrow road that cut in two a vast turf-bog. It was a mild grey day, following on nearly a week of heavy rain. Flashes of silvery sunlight escaped sometimes through openings in the clouds, and found the response they sought in the shallow flood-water that lay here and there on the level grey-green landscape. A distant, jagged line of hills was pure purple; the scarlet coats of the hunt, moving sedately along the bog-road, were beautifully repeated in trembling patches in the water of the wide drains that bordered the road; wastes of dull yellow sedge, striped with brown bog cuttings, stretched far away on either hand.

The long string of riders went in single file along the narrow road. Jimmy was riding a large sensible brown mare from the County Cork, whose name, plain and sensible like herself, was Dairymaid. She was nine years old, virtuous, self-willed, entirely aware of her own intelligence and competence. Were her soul to be freed from its four-legged envelope and desired to fit itself with human habitation, it would have found its spiritual home in the person of a middle-aged high-school mistress, with the highest certificates from all Government inspectors. Mrs. Ridley, on one of the chestnut cobs, was last in the procession, Jimmy was next in front of her. He let his reins fall on Dairymaid's neck, and pushed his crop under his leg, and lit a cigarette. Then he slewed round, with a hand on the mare's broad back, and said:

" Did your friend say anything more about Patsey? "

Mrs. Ridley hesitated.

" She said they had had high jinks at some awful American woman's studio! Dancing, and so forth. That young Lester seems to be a good dancer."

" Do you mean to say that Pat——? "

Mrs. Ridley cut the question short.

" Oh, my dear Jimmy, I really can't scream all these little facts to you now! Wait till we get on to a decent road again! I assure you the letter will keep! "

Jimmy straightened himself in his saddle. He told himself there was something about all this that he didn't like. He wished Mrs. Ridley would tell him exactly what this Wilson woman had said. " High jinks? " Surely Pat wasn't having high jinks in company with that fellow Lester? And " dancing and so forth "—whatever " so forth " might mean! It couldn't mean that she had danced with *Lester!*—that bounder! . . . No, that was inconceivable. What would Sir Ingram think about it? he wondered. Or even Cousin Maud! By Jove! There'd be the wigs on the green!

Jimmy was still debating the scant but disquieting

information that Mrs. Ridley had permitted to escape her, when, at last, they all emerged from the bog-road; but a more drastic enquiry into the nature of the jinks had to be postponed, as Cox-Munro and the hounds had broken into a trot, and Miss Joan, who, riding at the Master's heels, had been shrieking banalities at him to which he had replied in kind, now fell back upon Jimmy's companionship.

"There's the place we're going to draw." She pointed to a low hill about a quarter of a mile away. "It's a beast of a place. All thick bracken and furze and heather, so that you only see the limestone boulders, that are stuck all over it, when you fall over them! If they go away the far side we shall have to go round."

The hill was a couple of fields away from the road. Abreast of it the hounds were stopped, and Cox-Munro held up his hand. He was still new to his little brief authority, and if he had been Joshua, ordaining that the waters of Jordan should stand in an heap, he could not have been more impressive. "Keep on the road, please, all of you, and *Don't Talk!*" He fixed an awe-inspiring eye, that was more specially directed at Miss Ridley, upon the field. Miss Ridley immediately exhibited the pointed tip of a pink tongue.

Tim, the Second Whip, who was young, saw the tongue, and covered his mouth with his hand. The Master saw it also, and turning his horse sharply, jumped him short over the wall out of the road, the class of jump when the after part of the horse follows that of the gentleman sooner, and more violently, than he expects, with results that are often unfortunate. Mr. Cox-Munro, however, succeeded in keeping within visiting distance of his saddle, and had quite regained the normal position before he and Mason, with the hounds, were, with a rattle of round stones, over the next wall, and galloping for the covert.

The Field had not long to wait. The hounds had hurled themselves with enthusiasm into the green and brown thicket that cloaked the hill. It was evident there was a scent. In a moment nothing of them could be seen save the tips of their sterns, that soon were stained with blood from working the gorse. Presently the watching crowd of riders saw the red tips concentrating near the centre of the hillside, then vanishing in the heavy growth. A hound uttered a deep challenging note. A squeal from another followed hard on it. "*Harrk! Harrk! Harrk!*" came from Mason, sharp and harsh as the bark of a heron.

The hounds seemed to be working upwards towards a great rock, whose grey head rose above the surrounding jungle. Then came one of those irrepressible shouts from every throat, when the field, viewing the fox, lose self-control. For an instant he had flashed into view on the peak of the great rock. In the next, every hound opened. The music, gathering strength, swept upwards. In less than a minute a holloa from Tim, on the farther side of the hill, told that the fox had broken.

"Now then!" Sir Thomas loosed his quivering charges. "Away with ye all! Up the road's your best way."

Up the road they went, horses pulling, riders hustling each other, shouting at each other suggestions that no one listened to, advice that no one meant to take. The road bent right-handed up the hill on which the covert lay. Near the top the leaders saw, with the intense relief that such a sight has power to give, the red coats of the Master, and Harry the First Whip, and heard the doubled notes of Mason's horn just ahead, and the pistol shots of Tim's thong back at the wall that enclosed the covert, as the last of the pack fought their way out over it.

"Here you are! In here!" yelled a young O'Reilly, dragging his horse round and crashing over the wall out of the road.

Jimmy and Dairymaid had the wall neck and neck with him. Half a dozen other thrusting spirits charged it in line. The rest of the riders pressed after them, stones flying right and left, as horses, hastily checked, and crammed at the wall into the gaps left by the leaders, banged their way over it, through it, anyhow, wild as their riders to follow the magical music that each instant was growing fainter, filled as they were with harrowing anxiety lest it should fade from them wholly.

Jimmy Corran, pounding along on big Dairymaid, knew no anxiety. The big mare, catching hold enough to be inspiring, yet not enough to give trouble, had caught up the leaders, and was getting over the ground in a huge, unfaltering gallop, that had in it the ordered strength of a great engine; judging her distance as each successive wall came, shortening her stride to buck over it with a perfect economy of power.

The hounds swept down the long slope of the hill beyond the covert at a tremendous pace. The rough going had ceased soon. Grass field followed grass field, tidy wall after wall, with a perfectness that might have been monotonous had not the racing pack kept excitement at fever pitch. Jimmy, among the first dozen, found Mason beside him. They had left the hilly country behind, and were swinging along a green shallow valley, with a slow stream dividing it from a wilder and less civilised region.

"Looks like he's for making Gurtinure, m'lord,

don't it?" said Mason, at Jimmy's elbow. "That'll come 'andy for you! Runnin' lovely, ain't they?"

Jimmy agreed, while he thought that a bit of a check wouldn't do anyone any harm. But the fox stopped not nor stayed, for the excellent reason that in this clean, relentless country there was not as much as a rabbit-hole in which he could take shelter. So he altered his course a little and crossed the stream and made for the moorland country, where broad, heather-grown banks took the place of walls, and the hard heathery ground held a less undeniable scent, and the inexorable hounds didn't have it all so terribly their own way.

Jimmy saw the banks coming, and his heart gloried. Banks were few in the East Brandon country, and were not popular with its horses or riders; but Dairymaid came from the County Cork, and while she could jump "single" walls with the best of them, the high art of banking was her supreme accomplishment. How intoxicating to feel the send of the great hindquarters, the sure vigour of the spring to the crown of the bank! How composing the brief instant when the balance is being re-established, the forefeet and the hindfeet exchanging responsibility! And how packed with exultation the sailing leap from the height, out into the future that till that moment has been unseen, unknown!

Jimmy, delighting (contrary to the views of the Psalmist) in the strength of his horse, was first over the first bank; Cox-Munro and the hunt-servants were soon after him. The two riders next behind them were immediately involved in a contest with their mounts that showed every sign of becoming a protracted one. The ground was rising gradually; the fox had evidently abandoned the thought of Gurtinure, and was heading for those hills that were just visible from its upper windows. Behind the first few riders the hunt trailed out into invisibility. Two of the ladies, struggling gamely on, and a half-dozen of the men, were coming near the first of the banks, but the chestnut cobs of Mrs. Ridley and Joan were no longer in the picture, and Sir Thomas Ferrers's monster white horse, on the farther side of the valley stream, looked no larger than a hen. Hounds had been running, practically without a check, for an hour and twenty minutes. This was the second hunt of the day, and even though the pace was now less killing, the moment had come when their second horses would have been considered cheap at their weight in gold by the Master, Mason, and Jimmy Corran.

" Of all the damned fools those fellows of mine are the biggest! " Cox-Munro was saying, with an emphasis pardonable at such a moment. " I haven't as much as seen 'em since we left Peterstown! Hold up, horse, will you! This horse is done."

" Scent's failing a bit, thank God! " returned Jimmy, uttering, shamelessly, the thought that many riders of tired horses have known, but few will disclose, while he lugged at Dairymaid's " strong " mouth to reduce her heavy canter to a trot that she might better take stock of the bank that they were nearing.

Slowly, and not without effort, yet faultlessly, the mare heaved herself up on to the bank; beyond it the ground fell, a grassy hill road lay at the foot of the slope, and on the road, an answer less to prayer than to its reverse, were the second horsemen.

" He run the road, sir!—He's not five minutes before you! He's heading for Gurtinure, m'Lord!" Thus the second horsemen in excited chorus.

The hounds had checked at the road, and were

standing, with sterns waving dubiously, refusing to recognise the unauthorised suggestions of the second horsemen, waiting for their huntsman. Mason spurred his tired horse down the slope to the road, in a frenzy of relief.

" 'Ere! Bring up that bloody 'orse! " he roared; then, with the deft spring that looks like a conjuror's trick, he transferred himself from one saddle to the other, and with a blast of his horn galloped off down the road, cheering his hounds, thirsting for the blood of their mutual enemy with all their own passion.

Jimmy's second mount (who was the elder of his Dublin horses) was very far from being as fresh as when he had left his stable (for which he can scarcely be blamed), and his indignation at being denied a hunt in the morning had turned to resentment at having to batter out a finish in the afternoon.

The fox was beginning to run short, dodging and twisting, searching for a place of refuge. The scent was catchy and uncertain, the hounds growing discouraged, with checks coming ever quicker. Suddenly, half a mile ahead, a holloa was heard. A man, standing on a bank, held his hat in the air. Everything revived; the hounds began to hurry; Mason charged the bank in front of him—not a nice bank, high, and hollow-faced, narrow on top, with but one practicable spot in it. His horse, an active little thoroughbred, jumped it like a cat. That there was a heavy drop was obvious from the time that elapsed before he came into view. Cox-Munro followed him, and got over with a scramble. He shouted back, " Heavy drop! "

Twice Jimmy, spurring his horse, essayed to follow, but each time had to pull aside to let a belated hound precede him. At the third attempt his horse, thwarted and provoked, refused. Jimmy, provoked as he, drove him at it again. The horse sprang at it wildly, got his forelegs over its narrow crest, missed with his hindfeet, then, the impetus of his effort taking him, he headered down a drop of near ten feet into the next field. Jimmy was flung out beyond him, and would have escaped unhurt were it not that the horse, on touching ground, turned a somersault, and fell over, partly upon Jimmy, before he had had time to roll himself out of reach of danger.

CHAPTER XXXI

To be torn asunder by wild horses is a punishment beyond (as one would think) the deservings of any crime. And, yet, upon blameless little Lady Kirwen a somewhat similar experience was inflicted, for no crime at all—not even for the crimes of others, rather for their misfortunes, as the letters and the telegram, that she received almost simultaneously, on the morning of January the fourth, will show.

The telegram came first, meeting her on her way down to breakfast. She had felt that morning that a cold was menacing her; she had even thought that it might be advisable to stay in bed. But Ingram hated people being ill, and disliked her not being on duty to pour out his coffee for him; and when the first of the wild horses met her on the staircase, she congratulated herself that she had not yielded to the threat of the cold, and was on foot and ready to take action as required.

The telegram was a very long one. She looked at the office, " Hawthorn Green," and tried, without success, to place it. Who could be sending her this enormous telegram, with a reply-form, presented like a pistol at her head? The signature was on the second sheet, " Georgina."

Georgina? Who in the world——? Oh yes, of course, her first cousin, Georgina Corran. But what was it all about? Lady Kirwen put on her eyeglasses, and, standing still on the stairs, read: " *I implore you go*

Gurtinure immediately agent wires Jimmy has had bad hunting accident am longing to go but am in bed rheumatism rescue him from harpy attentions have wired him was entreating your help so lonely adores you doctor positively forbids journey distracted am writing Georgina."

Lack of the support of punctuation has raised the composition of telegrams to an affair of high art; and since it is conventional, even apart from economic considerations, to omit all words except those only that are, so to speak, visible at high water, the meaning, like the conjunctions, can often remain submerged.

Lady Kirwen read the despatch through three times before its purport fully declared itself. She had always maintained a desultory correspondence with Lady Corran, that had warmed up and had become, like a volcano, more active during the last few months. The telegram was evidently the preliminary of a violent eruption, lava to follow, by post.

" Harpy attentions " Lady Kirwen found at first obscure; then she recalled how, in a letter of a few weeks back, Georgina had mentioned that she feared Jimmy was " falling into the hands of that *harpy*, Nancy Ridley (you remember her, of course? She was at school with us—Miss Critchett's, that expensive place where we learnt nothing!) Nancy Treherne she was then. She made a very good match. Dick Ridley of Peterstown, eight miles from Gurtinure. She wants to *clapperclaw* Jimmy, no doubt! For her daughter, if not for herself! "

A more unworldly, unscheming little mother than Maud Kirwen did not exist, but there is no mother, however unworldly, who can view unmoved the captive of her daughter's bow and spear being " clapperclawed " by another, and that a kidnapper of renown. And the cousins, Maud and Georgina, had arrived at so satisfactory an understanding. Georgina had written, confidently, " as soon as this painting prank has worn out, as, no doubt, soon it will, she must come and pay me a little visit. Jimmy has said nothing *definite* to me, but I very soon saw *the lie of the land!* "

But this was before the harpy attentions had begun. Lady Kirwen told herself that she was very fond of Jimmy, and, *quite* apart from *anything* else (anything else, in this connection, was Patsey), she could not bear to think of his being left to a *stranger*, when his mother's own cousin was within reach. . . . In fact, up to the moment when she began to read the letter with the neat foreign writing, and the Paris post-mark (the other wild horse, in point of fact), the steed that may be taken as representing Jimmy and Gurtinure had had things all his own way.

Mademoiselle Leroux's letter began with suitable civilities, but, these accomplished, the wild horse got into his stride. It pained Mademoiselle Leroux infinitely to have to trouble Lady Kirwen, but it was no more than her duty, Patrice having been confided to her care. . . . Mademoiselle Leroux's elegantly turned periods may be summarised into the bald statement that she would no longer be responsible for Patrice. Patrice had stayed out half the night at the house of an Americaine, unknown to Mademoiselle Leroux, having given no warning of her intention. Patrice had then, in company with a young man, also unknown to Mademoiselle, cast stones at the chamber window of an aged lady, one of Mademoiselle Leroux's most esteemed *pensionnaires*, thereby causing her a *crise des nerfs* of the most grave character. Patrice repudiated the authority of Mademoiselle, who had regarded her as a solemn charge, and had felt herself to represent the Parents, and

Mademoiselle had now but one course, to renounce that charge, and to entreat Lady Kirwen to come herself, immediately, to Paris, to arrange for Patrice elsewhere, with such conditions as would appear to her satisfactory.

With all Lady Kirwen's other-worldliness, she could concentrate upon a problem, and long matrimonial training in diplomatic subservience had taught her to do so in silence, and in the sanctuary of her own mind. A letter from Patsey lay beside her plate. Sir Ingram had noticed it, and had said, idly:

"——you've one there from Pat, haven't you?"

But she had decided that she would not mention *l'affaire* Patsey until she had had time to think (and *who* could the young man, with whom Patsey had thrown stones, be?). It would be easy to turn Ingram's thoughts from Patsey with the news of Jimmy's accident. Therefore Lady Kirwen waited until she had seen her husband tramping down to the kennels before she opened her child's letter.

Patsey and her mother were more nearly of an age, mentally and spiritually, than was usual in Victorian times, and Lady Kirwen, tearing open the envelope with the impatience that she had forced herself to hold in check, could feel confident that whatever had been Pat's iniquities, she would confess them all.

She had not been mistaken. Patsey's letter left nothing untold, save that the particulars of that conversation which had disturbed the maiden slumbers of Old Wilson were withheld.

"What an escape! That awful dog!—But running about the Paris streets at three in the morning, with young George Lester!" thought the reader. "*What* would Ingram say!"

"*The worst of it is,*" said the letter, "*that, even with your fiver, I've only enough money to keep me going here for another month, at the outside, and old Bouvier says*" (old Bouvier was once more quoted fully). "*I believe in him. De Bremont says my eye for colour is* PARFAIT, *but he's rather too good to be true! It's all pretty rotten. It seems to me that I might as well get over the* AGONY" (agony was doubly underlined) "*of leaving the studio, at once, and come home and have a bit of hunting before the season ends. Mercy and Hans will leave Mademoiselle's if I go. She says George Lester is never to enter this house again. Mercy says she's going to have any visitors she likes, and she won't be bullied by the old thing! Those girls like George awfully, and so do I, and Mercy says he has a brilliant future. Of course I've never breathed a syllable to them about Holy George!*" (Lady Kirwen paused in her reading to thank Heaven for Holy George.) "*It's almost worse to have come here and have had these glorious three months, and now to have to chuck it all! Just for want of money! Why didn't you make me a boy, and give me a chance?*"

Lady Kirwen put down the letter. "I wouldn't change you, my darling, for all the boys in the world!"

But this question was not pressing. What had to be decided at once was the nature of the replies to be sent to Georgina, to Mademoiselle Leroux, to Patsey. And there would then remain the delicate matter of presenting her decision, whatever it might be, to Sir Ingram, in such a manner that he should be convinced that he had himself originated the scheme.

She stared at the reply-form, and addressed it "Lady Corran The Nest Hawthorn Green." Was Hawthorn Green two words or one? (Anything to delay this crucial decision.) Then she began to debate each alternative as closely as she could. Patsey had offered to come home—would have to do so, in any case, in a month, or sooner. Then if it were done, 'twere well it were done—et cetera! Let her come at once! (" Poor darling! How terrible to have to disappoint her! . . . If only there were a few more pearls to spare, without spoiling the rope. . . . But I must keep that for her wedding. . . . She's been there nearly four months; with her talent that ought to have done wonders for her! . . . How delightful to have her back again! . . .) That decision was made! There was no need for the First Mademoiselle to renounce her charge. The charge shall renounce her! There was a very disagreeable tone in her letter—making everything as black as possible! " And it was entirely her fault—it was very wrong to keep a dangerous dog like that, and I shall tell her so! *How* cross she'll be! " Lady Kirwen laughed with pleasure at the thought of the crossness of the First Mademoiselle.

And now about Jimmy. . . . It certainly would seem very unkind to Georgina to refuse to go to her boy when she was too ill to go herself. . . . Especially when one thought of the Harpy Attentions! . . . And one might bring him here to convalesce. . . . Patsey would be home . . . (the connection of ideas was almost sub-conscious, but not quite. In Victorian mothers the conviction that a daughter's career was matrimony was ineradicable). " Maud is lax," said her step-daughters, " but even *she* must know that it is her duty to find a good husband for that harum-scarum Patricia! "

And in thus giving their step-mother the benefit of the doubt, the step-daughters were more nearly right than they knew.

CHAPTER XXXII

To Lady Corran, lying at ease in her fluffy nest at Hawthorn Green, yet ill at ease in her mind because of Nancy Ridley, Maud Kirwen's telegram brought a flash of the sunshine that the English climate had neglected to provide.

"Dear, faithful old Maud! She *is* going to Gurtinure!" she said, with enthusiasm. ("Put a little more coal on the fire, Eleanor dearest.) *How* thankful I am to be spared a journey in this bitter weather! (And of course Ireland is so much milder.) You must write to her for me, Eleanor, and tell her how *unspeakably* grateful I am—and say how *quite* unfit I am to travel!"

It was certainly less bitter in the west of Ireland than in Surrey, but that the faithful Maud should have undertaken the journey to Gurtinure, which involved a night on the road and four changes of train with very intermittent foot-warmers, was a high proof of fidelity. She had telegraphed to Gurtinure for news, but had had to start before a reply came. By the time, which was late in the evening of the second day, she had arrived at length at Rossmult, the cold that had threatened the morning before was in full career. It had struck downwards. Her voice had nearly gone and all her bones ached. The six-mile drive from the station, in a decrepit landau of unknown antiquity, which was the only covered vehicle available in Rossmult, was the last but certainly not the least of Lady Kirwen's sufferings.

No carriage had come from Gurtinure to meet her. She had had to wait at the station for a long time before a conveyance could be found. It was raining hard; what may be called the jaws of the landau did not meet overhead, and through the opening a steady flow of water descended upon its occupant, which was augmented by the rain that entered, more legitimately, through one of the windows which could not be shut. The horse was old and slow; the wet wind eddied round the interior of the landau, triumphing over its futile defences. Had Lady Kirwen been sitting on the box beside the driver she might possibly have been wetter, but she could not have been colder.

It was past nine o'clock, and a very dark night, when at last the door of Gurtinure was reached. There were no lights in the windows. The house looked dead. The driver rang the bell in vain. Finally, with an assurance that the horse wouldn't stir at all, he sought the back of the house and the kitchen entrance. The horse, betraying his driver's confidence, roamed about the gravel sweep seeking what he might devour. Lady Kirwen, who was by this time numbed to hopelessness, sat still, feeling that were the landau to overturn, and she to meet death in its ruins, it might be something of a comfort to her.

At length she heard the hall-door open, and saw the driver and a maid, with a lighted candle in her hand, standing in the doorway. The horse was captured and was dragged back to the steps, and Lady Kirwen put her head out of the window and, in a voice that was now no more than a croak, said:

"How is Lord Corran?"

"He's not here at all, ma'am. He was taken to Peterstown——"

"Not here?" croaked Lady Kirwen, feeling as if more cold water had been flung in her face.

"No, ma'am. We heard he was much better to-day."

Lady Kirwen was speechless. All this nightmare journey for nothing! . . . And her cold getting heavier every moment. Then she said:

"I'm Lady Kirwen. Lady Corran telegraphed to me to come. Can I stay here to-night?"

"Oh, my Lady, to be sure you can! The hall's full up of telegrams for you—we were wondering were you coming!"

The maid pushed her candlestick into the driver's hand.

"Wait, Thady, till I call Mrs. Moffat," she hissed at him, and flew.

Thady, the driver, taken by surprise, omitted to shield the flame of the candle; a gust of rain and wind assailed it and it went out.

"Well, may the divil sweep ye for a candle," remarked the driver, without resentment. "It's as good for me to stand in out o' the rain——" He retired into the house.

In darkness and depression, Lady Kirwen, a baffled sister of mercy, bitterly aware of her superfluousness, chilled to the bone, and dog-tired, awaited Mrs. Moffat. She closed her eyes and leaned back against the damp cushions, made callous by fatigue of drips and draughts. After what seemed an endless interval a light reappeared. An austere elderly woman stood in the doorway, and Lady Kirwen heard an English voice desire the driver to open the carriage-door and bring the lady in.

"Sure this door won't open," replied the driver. "It's the other one only."

He appeared at the side of the broken window. In the

dim light of the lamp of the landau, his face, streaming with water, looked ghastly, as it might be that of a drowned man. He opened the door, and the unfortunate sister of mercy, blinded by rain and stiffened by cold, missed the step, and, stumbling, was only saved from falling headlong by the driver, who caught her, and gathering her to his bosom, carried her bodily into the house. It wanted but this to complete her overthrow, and with her head pillowed on the driver's shoulder, the combined odours of tobacco and unclean wet frieze, striking to the roots of her being, the very completeness of her misfortunes tickled her fantastic sense of humour, and in a moment the shattering demon of *fou rire* had her in his clutch.

The driver deposited her, shaking with what appeared to him to be mysterious mirth, on the mat inside the door. Mrs. Moffat regarded her with cold unamused eyes, the driver, with bewildered resentment, believing that she was laughing at him; only the maid, who saw the tears standing in her eyes, said to herself it was crying the poor lady was, and gently shepherded her to a chair.

"We received no warning, m'Lady," said Mrs. Moffat, in a voice that matched the temperature of the stone-paved, fireless hall, "or the brougham would have met you."

Lady Kirwen apologised. She had wired to Lord Corran.

"*We* haven't seen his Lordship since the accident. We understand that he was unconscious at first, and was carried to a cottage until Mrs. Ridley's carriage came and took him to Peterstown. We 'eard this morning that he is going on very well, and the accident is not serious, as was believed at first."

Evidently Mrs. Moffat disapproved of the arrangements made by Mrs. Ridley.

"You can let me stay here to-night, I hope?" Lady Kirwen said, humbly.

"Your Ladyship's room 'as bin ready since yesterday," replied Mrs. Moffat, with severity. "We thought your Ladyship must 'ave changed your plans. Her Ladyship wired us from 'Awthorn Green yesterday, to expect you at once." She turned to the maid. "Delia, go up and light the fire at once; and then tell Mrs. Brady——" Magisterial directions to the cook followed, Lady Kirwen's faint croak, "Oh, just a little tea, please," being ignored. "What a dragon!" the crushed and frustrated sister of mercy thought as she crept upstairs in the dragon's wake. "Georgina might have had more mercy on poor Jimmy! It looks as if she didn't trust him! Oh, shall I ever be warm again?"

The question was answered for her before an hour had passed, though not by reason of the conditions in which she found herself. The bedroom, high and spacious, was gloomy and chill as the night, with massive mahogany furniture round its remote walls, and a catafalquian bed looming large in the darkness. Delia, on her knees on the hearth-rug, was engaged in tense conflict with a refractory fire, whose existence was only deducible from the smell of turf smoke. Mrs. Moffat lighted two candles on the far-away dressing-table, that, like the fire, produced no appreciable effect, and with a farewell salutation that Lady Kirwen felt—as she was intended to feel it—to be a masterly mixture of respect and disapproval, withdrew.

For perhaps half an hour Lady Kirwen lay shivering in the catafalque, coiled like a little dog round an unsympathetic stone foot-warmer. And then, without warning, her temperature shot up. She felt fever rising in her like a tide. " Oh, I'm going to be ill! I'm going to be ill in this awful place! " she moaned to herself. " Why did I come? Oh, why did Georgina send for me for nothing! "

Soon knowledge of where she was forsook her. She was striving in railway stations, rushing along platforms, being for ever just too late to turn the handles of the carriage-doors. Or she was seated in carriages whose sides closed in on her, with horrid faces mocking her through the windows—more and more faces, grinning, triumphing over her, making grimaces that changed and slid from one hateful expression to another. . . . And Patsey was in the train, being swept away from her. . . . She called and called, but no answer came. . . . Patsey was lost . . . if only she could overtake the train . . . she toiled on, and then someone, a porter, she supposed, hit her in the side with the corner of a box. . . . How it hurt! Clumsy brute! He didn't care, and in the course of the whirling eternities through which she was toiling he hit her again and again, and the pain grew worse each time. . . .

In the morning, when Delia came to call her, Lady Kirwen hardly knew where she was. Gradually she mastered her consciousness, and realised that Delia had fetched Mrs. Moffat, and both of them were standing by her bedside, staring at her burning face—she knew it was burning—and the pain in her side was no longer a nightmare, but was a tangible thing, that, when she coughed, and she found herself coughing often, hurt her like the stab of a knife.

Mrs. Moffat put a cold but not unkindly hand on her hot wrist.

"I'm afraid you've got a bad chill, m'Lady. Would you wish me to send for the doctor?"

Poor little Maud Kirwen steadied herself enough to assent. Tea had been brought to her, and she drank a little. Then she said feebly, "I think I'm going to be ill. Will you send some telegrams for me?"

She dictated three messages. One to Lady Corran: "Arrived Gurtinure Jimmy doing well." One to Sir Ingram: "Not returning for a day or two Jimmy doing well." And one to Patsey: "Jimmy had hunting accident not bad I am at Gurtinure advise your coming home soon as you can."

She lay back coughing. "That won't frighten them," she thought, her breath coming short. "Now for the doctor, Mrs. Moffat! What a useful sick nurse I am!" The inveterate tickle of laughter scared her. "Oh, I mustn't laugh!"

"I shouldn't think you'd want to laugh, m'Lady," said Mrs. Moffat, reprovingly. "Now I'm going to get you a poultice, and I'll send for Dr. Moore at once."

Lady Kirwen thought: "She's an old bundle of red tape, but I think she's not a bad fellow." And after that coherent thought ceased, and the dull animal misery of illness possessed her, body and soul.

CHAPTER XXXIII

LADY KIRWEN was not mistaken in thinking that trouble was before her. She was very ill, so ill that for a week she was scarcely aware of her surroundings, or of her attendants, or, indeed, of anything save heat, and pain, and the hatefulness of what Patsey had said the Javanese Princess complained of, "*La nourriture*," only that for poor Lady Kirwen it was excess, rather than deficiency, that troubled her. She was, in a cloudy and distant way, aware that in her limited world there were two supreme beings, the lesser to rule the day, the greater—who (she could just realise it) wore a white cap and apron—to rule the night; but beyond these impressions she knew nothing and cared less. She felt occasionally a faint curiosity as to the identity of the being who ruled the day, but it was too much trouble to ask; it was enough that she was gentle, and skilful with *la nourriture*, and had a voice quite unlike Mrs. Moffat's.

Then, one morning, after the doctor's visit, the ruler of the day having, with her accustomed tact and firmness, administered the ordained variety of that odious form of nourishment which is so unattractively yet appropriately described as "slops," stood smiling at her little patient, so small a spot in the heart of the catafalque, and said, "You know, Maud, the doctor says the lung is clear, and he had such a good opinion of you yesterday that I'm not going to let you cut me any longer! I'm Nancy Ridley!"

Lady Kirwen put out a very weak, pale little paw, and began to remember the dimple, while she tried to express her gratitude (and the thought that she, and not Jimmy, had been the object of the harpy attentions very nearly induced a most untimely attack of laughter). Presently she asked how Jimmy was, and was told that, since he was apparently made of indiarubber, he was now very little the worse for his fall, and his collar-bone was mending well—rather pulled down, but really rather wonderful, considering all things.

"I had to leave him in charge of my girl and Ralph. I thought you wanted a nurse more than he did! Little Archie Cox-Munro—he's our M.F.H. you know—helps Joan to keep him amused. We see a great deal of him. The three young people are great friends!" went on the Harpy, the dimple deepening, as at some hidden thought. "Jimmy talked of driving over to see you to-day, but I won't let you see *him* yet. There might be other visitors—the doctor, perhaps," she added, rather hurriedly. She patted Lady Kirwen's hand. "Now I think you ought to try and take a little nap."

The Harpy, still smiling a dimpling harpy-smile, pulled down the blinds.

Lady Kirwen lay back and obediently endeavoured to embark on the little nap as directed. She felt as if she should never succeed in asking all the questions that had suddenly begun to throng her brain. Her intelligence had been dormant all this time, now her thoughts felt like waves, over-lapping, breaking over each other. Sleep took her unawares, but the restless thoughts wove themselves into complicated dreams, in which Patsey and Nancy Treherne kept alternating, changing identities, she couldn't be sure which of them she was dealing with—so tiring, she thought.

A faint sound woke her, and she knew that the door had been opened.

"Coming to make up the fire," she thought, dully, and closed her eyes again.

A pattering of small feet, crossing the long room, coming towards the catafalque, was bewildering, but before she had time to do more than realise the sound, something flopped softly upon the bed beside her. She opened her eyes and met the ardent gaze of a small white dog, melting with love, beseeching forgiveness for presumption.

"Dooley?" said Lady Kirwen, incredulously. The little dog wriggled up closer, and poked a cold nose into Lady Kirwen's neck.

"Yes!" it replied, rapturously, "it is indeed I!" And it touched Lady Kirwen's ear with a very delicate dry little tongue.

But before the conversation could proceed any further, Patsey had come in, and Dooley's remarks went unheeded.

* * * * *

Mercy and Hans had not failed their comrade when tribulation overtook her. They had stood by her side when the vials of Mlle. Leroux's wrath had been outpoured, Mercy stemming, to some extent, the flood, with counter-denunciation of Hector, declaring that it was shameful that an animal so furious and dangerous should be permitted to imperil the lives of the *pensionnaires*, and that no one less courageous than Mlle. von Kappf would have ventured to secure him and thus enable Mlle. Kirwen to return at last to the house. Had it not been for the cries of the little dog of Mlle. Kirwen, Mercy asserted, no one would have known what had happened, and Mlle. Kirwen might have been kept out all night, a horror incredible!

Mademoiselle Leroux, though staggered by the attack, which was delivered with a velocity and vigour scarcely inferior to her own, and quite unlike the leisured melody of Miss Le Mont's usual utterance, riposted with the outrage of the broken window and the shock to the nerves of the aged lady, Madame Puttkamère. On which Hans, whose supporting indignation had rumbled, like heavy artillery, in the background, came into action, stating that she had visited her compatriot, the Frau Puttkamer, and had explained to her the whole history. Frau Puttkamer was what Hans described as "*tout à fait gomplaisante et chentille*," and, being an old lady of distinguished piety, she had even quoted from the Holy Scriptures, and had congratulated Hans and her friend on having been able to deliver their darling from the power of the dog!

(" I haf not till now thought moche of Saint Paul," Hans, later, remarked to Patsey, referring to this quotation. " He is nasty for women—bot zis was well remembered of *die alte Puttkamer!* " " It was David's idea," Pat corrected her. " But you floored Mademoiselle with it just the same! ")

In the Studio the history of the night's adventures, as circulated by Miss Wilson, had undoubtedly redounded to the fame of its central figure, which was far from being the effect that the historian had meant to produce. But the tale, falling into the hands of " Hell's Delight " and the foreign element, additions to it, inspired partly by admiration of its thrilling situations, partly by envy and all uncharitableness, blew it out like a Louvre *ballon*. Hector, like the dog in the fairy-tale, went from strength to strength. He had eyes like saucers, like mill-wheels; his jaws were those of a lion, of a crocodile. Mees Kirwen had been snatched from those frightful jaws by *le beau Lesterre*. This young man had been so enraged that he had then broken half the windows of the Pension Leroux, and, being pursued by the police, he had caught the young girl in his arms and had rushed with her at an incredible speed to—here the tale was wont to diverge, and to pursue a variety of paths that led anywhere rather than to Mlle. Leroux's unexceptionable *Pensions des Dames*.

The Studio atmosphere had changed, and was not, for Patsey, what it had been, and the further the story departed from the facts, the less to her credit was the impression that it sought to create. Perhaps Pat's success with the professors had been too marked, her drawing had shown too rapid an improvement, her high linen collars too dazzling a standard of cleanliness. (Had not old Bouvier once, in a dissertation upon "values," desired his hearers to observe "something that is absolutely white—that young lady's collar, *par exemple*"?) Whatever might be the reason, a chill had come into the air, the sun had gone in, the glory had gone out of Pat's day.

When Lady Kirwen's telegram came, Patsey was more than half ready to accept its suggestion. Her remaining francs were melting ever faster. Impossible to say how they went; whenever she examined her resources they had mysteriously dwindled; it would, she reflected, be a pretty close thing even to get home on the remnant of what had once seemed inexhaustible riches. What was the use of writing home for more? "Going to the goat's house for wool!" as they used to say at home. . . . Wool enough for Gilbert, of course. . . . Why hadn't she been a boy? . . . Very well!

Soit! Her career was to be cut short. The Fates had turned down their beastly thumbs! She had made her break for freedom and it had failed. She would go home and make the best of a bad job. She would go on painting . . . and painting . . . and, perhaps, some day.——" But oh, Mercy, isn't it all heart-breaking? "

And Mercy had only replied, reproachfully, "Whose heart are you talking about? "

But this was because Pat had been bored by George Lester and had shown it (her temper not being at its most placid these times), and Mercy had noticed it. Mercy had had George to tea, in defiance of Mlle. Leroux's prohibition, and Pat had found his sombre dog's eyes exasperating. She thought they were like brown jelly, and wished he wouldn't plaster them on her. Everything annoyed her. Even Mercy was rather trying, making such a fuss over George Lester. For three enchanted months Patsey had felt herself only second to Hans in Mercy's favour. Now, she said to herself, both she and Hans were taking back-seats, while George was exalted. Darling Mercy was still the nicest person in the world, but Pat, gravely communing with herself, said that she feared Mercy was—what she had once so long ago accused her of being—that base thing—a " man's woman "!

Lady Kirwen's second telegram, sent from Gurtinure, arrived in Paris on January 6th, and brought order into the chaos of Patsey's mind. She decided to wait until her mother was at home again. (Poor Jimmy! Hard luck for him being knocked out half-way through the season!) And then, boot and saddle! Good-bye to Art and the Career!

It was a week later that the summons had come from Mrs. Ridley. A letter, a cheerful letter, that didn't put the case too urgently (the Harpy's heart, as is not unusual with harpies of her type, was a good-natured one—in reason—and had a dimple in it too), "*but I think it would help your mother to get well if she had you with her*," said the letter, and it brought Patsey and Dooley at full speed to Gurtinure.

CHAPTER XXXIV

MARK TWAIN has written an article " Concerning Chambermaids," in which he accuses them of capricious and malevolent rearrangements of the furniture of his room. " So that," he complains, " when in the morning you go forth leaving the rocking-chair by the window, and the slop-pail by the door; in the evening, when you return, you open the door and fall over the rocking-chair, and then you proceed to the window and sit down in that slop-pail. This will annoy you. They like that."

The furniture of Patsey's life had been disarranged with a similar capriciousness. Nothing in it was in order. She had fallen over the rocking-chair. Did the catastrophe by the window await her?

She was summoned from her mother's room by Mrs. Ridley, in order to have what she called " a little talk," the upshot of which was that Mrs. Ridley would now leave Lady Kirwen in charge of Patsey and the nurse, and would return to her " deserted household " that afternoon. And now, after this " joyful excitement," didn't Patsey—" you *will* let me call you Patsey, won't you? I've heard so much of you from Jimmy! " —think her mother ought to be *compelled* to keep quiet? Nurse says the doctor—Mrs. Ridley would just have another little talk with Nurse.

Dismissed by the authorities, Patricia wandered downstairs and began to stray about the house. She had arrived late on the preceding night. All in this big house was strange to her, arid, inhuman, cheerless, in spite of the immense fires of wood and turf that burned, for their own edification only, in all the large unlived-in rooms. Pat thought of the Old Playroom at Kirwenscourt, and reflected, with a pallid and transitory gleam of satisfaction, that no one dared to try to keep *it* tidy—*she* saw to that, anyhow!

The drawing-room was like a mausoleum, the last resting-place of mummied furniture from which all life had long since departed. Old Sarah, the spaniel, on the rug in front of the furnace in the hall, mumbled a growl as Pat and Dooley passed her, but did not move. She evidently had no intention of sharing her rights with strangers. A sleety rain was falling, making the thought of going out of the house, even to the stables, unattractive. A clock struck—twelve heavy bass notes, as slow and boring as the truisms of a dull old man. The hour of *déjeuner!* Mercy and Hans would be hurrying home to cook their picnic-repast. Oh that she were with them! She would write to Mercy and tell her she had arrived, and was alive, but wasn't sure that it mightn't be better to be dead.

At the end of the hall was a door, she knew it was that of the library, she had been taken there when she arrived last night. She might write a letter there. She sauntered over to it with Dooley (who distrusted Sarah, quite without justification) glued to her heels. On one of the tables near the hall-door she saw a man's hat and top-coat. Jimmy's, of course. She wondered why they hadn't been hung up. But it was a relief to see something untidy. She wished Jimmy would come over from these Ridleys—wherever their place was. These Ridleys seemed to have swallowed him up, body and bones! All the same, they might spare him for a moment to come and see her. It would be nice to see him again. Of course there would be no looking back to that last time they met each other—temporary aberration on both their parts. She was rather pleased with the phrase.

Then she opened the library door, and there *was* Jimmy!

It was now nearly four months since Sweep and the dog-cart had, for Pat and Jimmy, fulfilled the rôle of the abhorréd shears, and it happens, not infrequently, after such a period of separation (and especially if temporary aberration has made memorable the farewells), that shyness will develop like a film of ice, and an obsession as of a cold and dumb devil will take control; and this even though nothing may have occurred that can legitimately have caused a fall in the temperature.

Jimmy was sitting by the fire in a long, low armchair. He looked round as Patsey came in, and rose to his feet rather slowly, and with difficulty. He looked unnaturally tall and thin; his right arm was strapped to his side; his face was pale, and his hair had grown long, and even showed a shocking disposition to curl over his ears. Patsey was scandalised. She thought "those Ridley women! . . . " and, as in such a case is not unusual, ascribed Jimmy's demoralisation to female influences.

There was an unfamiliar chill about his greeting of her that dismayed her pleasure at seeing him. He extended a long, thin, yellow hand (where had his big brown fist gone?) and said:

"Sorry I've only a left hand in action. I expect you heard I took a toss ten days ago?"

"Mother said so in her wire. I wrote to ask about you, but of course——"

" Very good of you," said Jimmy, formally. " I'm sorry you should have taken so much trouble."

He remained standing, his left hand on the broad, leather-covered back of the chair, steadying him. (What was the matter with Jimmy? Was he offended because she hadn't written to condole? He wasn't a bit like himself—what with the curls—and talking to her like a very distant shop-walker!)

She didn't know how hard she was staring at him. Jimmy averted his eyes. He said:

" Won't you sit down? "

(As if, she thought, indignantly, he had never met her before!)

He dropped back into the big armchair.

Patsey told herself that perhaps he was still feeling played out after that fall. If she could keep on talking to him for a bit, things might improve. She told him about her painting, and how she was not going to give it up. " I shall go on careering just the same! " she declared. " You started me, you know! I'm going to stick to it! " She looked at him with clear friendly eyes, trying in vain to find response in his.

Then she spoke of her journey, and of how beautifully the little angel Dooley had submitted to the indignity of the carpet-bag. And then, by a sequence of thought, the episode of Hector came into her mind. Jimmy hadn't smiled once. Hector might amuse him. She expanded on Hector's hatefulness. " Dooley and Hans are the only two people who aren't afraid of him! . . . It was a very near thing! We only just banged the gate in time! "

Jimmy's frozen politeness suddenly thawed. He said, with heat that he seemed unable to control, that the imbecility of a woman who could keep such a brute was criminal—she ought to be shot, and the dog too! His face had turned red to the roots of his yellow (and deplorably long) hair. He seemed, Pat thought, as angry as if Mlle. Leroux had set Hector at her on purpose.

Then, with a swift and alarming return to ice, he said, " May I ask who was with you when this happened? "

" Who was with me? " Pat hesitated. She seemed to remember that Jimmy had never fancied George Lester. " Oh, I had been at a dance that was given by Mrs. Gapes—she works at the Studio—Mercy and Hans had gone home. They—Mrs. Gapes—had kept me to dance in a cotillion."

" Quite so. But you said *we* shut the gate just in time. I should be glad to know who was the fool with you who opened it! With a brute like that loose on the other side of it! "

Patsey had seated herself sideways on the fat arm of another monster armchair at the other side of the fire. She twisted round and faced Jimmy. What right had he to heckle her like this? Her temper began to burn.

" I was one of the fools, and George Lester was the other! "

" The Poacher? "

Ice can cut as well as chill; Jimmy's voice did both.

" I said George Lester. If you prefer to call him a poacher, I don't want to prevent you! "

" I beg pardon! I forgot, for the moment, that he was a friend of yours. I found it rather hard to realise."

" Realise what? "

Pat had started to her feet.

" Oh, the position generally." Jimmy tried to keep rage out of his voice, though without much success. " It was, you'll admit, rather unexpected to hear of you dancing with—with Lester's son!" (He thought, not for the first time, "*His arms round her!*")

"Who said I danced with him?" Pat blazed at him, the blue fire of her eyes (which he used to play for—but that was all over now) scorching him. "And if I did—and I *did* dance with him—what is that to you?"

Jimmy heaved himself on to his feet. It was impossible to sit under her and carry on the contest on equal terms.

"Oh, nothing, I allow—only I thought you knew a gentleman from a cad! But," he added, quickly, anger mastering him, "I oughtn't to say this! I believe I have to congratulate you on your engagement to young Mr. George Lester!"

Patsey gasped, as if—which as a matter of fact was precisely what she felt—cold water, or even boiling water, had been flung in her face. If he chose to believe it, well, let him!

"Who told you this?"

"One of your distinguished Parisian friends wrote it to Mrs. Ridley."

The ice had melted. The combatants faced each other, wrapped, both of them, in mantles of flame.

"May I ask if it's true?"

He had propped himself against the big chair. If Pat had been less angry she might have noticed that the left hand, on the back of the chair, was trembling.

"If one of my distinguished friends—who *isn't* my friend—chooses to write lies to *your* distinguished friend, and you and she like to believe them, I don't want to prevent you!"

She was so shaken by anger that she could not keep her voice steady.

"If you have nothing more to enquire about, I've

got letters to write—to *my* distinguished Parisian friends!"

She waited for no reply and strode to the door. She opened it and paused, and looked back for Dooley.

Dooley was seated erect in the warm centre of the fur hearth-rug, her nose held high, her little white waistcoat roasting deliciously. She was saying to herself that this was the first moment of pure enjoyment she had known since she left Kirwenscourt. She turned her head and looked at Patsey serenely and affectionately, but did not move.

"Stay there if you like your company! I don't!" Pat flashed at her, slamming the door.

Jimmy sank back into the big chair. His head swam. This had been his first day at large in the outside world since his accident, and rage is exhausting. But the thought in his mind was:

"She said 'Lies'!"

* * * * *

Lady Kirwen cleared a space in the offal on the carpenter's bench in the Old Playroom and began to write a letter.

"*June 11th*, 1885.

"*Dearest Georgina,*

"*I wish I could persuade you to come and pay us a little visit. Jimmy is here, and we should all enjoy a sight of you so much. He is being* SLAVED *by Patsey to carry her painting-things about for her. They are out all day in this lovely weather. I think they are both very happy. She says she will never give up what she calls her Career—and Jimmy says he hopes she won't—but you and I know more about matrimony than she does!*"

FINIS

TOM STACEY REPRINTS

This series makes available again some of the best books by the best authors of our time, priced at £1.95 each except where stated otherwise. Already published are:

ROMANCE and ADVENTURE

Tarzan's Quest
by Edgar Rice Burroughs

Jungle Girl
by Edgar Rice Burroughs

Monsieur Blackshirt
by David Graeme

The Sword of Monsieur Blackshirt
by David Graeme

The Vengeance of Monsieur Blackshirt
by David Graeme

The Ancient Allan
by H. Rider Haggard

The Ghost Kings
by H. Rider Haggard

Morning Star
by H. Rider Haggard

Pearl-Maiden
by H. Rider Haggard

Red Eve
by H. Rider Haggard

The Wanderer's Necklace
by H. Rider Haggard

The Heart of Princess Osra
by Anthony Hope

Phroso
by Anthony Hope

The King of the Via Veneto
by Ronald Kirkbride

Clementina
by A. E. W. Mason

The Courtship of Morrice Buckler
by A. E. W. Mason (*£2.25*)

Fire Over England
by A. E. W. Mason

Bluefeather
by Laurence Meynell

King of the Khyber Rifles
by Talbot Mundy

The Man in Grey
by Lady Eleanor Smith

Tzigane
by Lady Eleanor Smith

Bosambo of the River
by Edgar Wallace

Lieutenant Bones
by Edgar Wallace

Sanders of the River
by Edgar Wallace

Sandi the King-Maker
by Edgar Wallace

Action and Passion
by P. C. Wren (*£2.25*)

Fort in the Jungle
by P. C. Wren

Spanish Maine
by P. C. Wren

Port O' Missing Men
by P. C. Wren (*£2.50*)

The Siege of Malta
by S. Fowler Wright (*£3.50*)

Blind Corner
by Dornford Yates

She Painted Her Face
by Dornford Yates

MYSTERY and DETECTION

Dead Man's Shoes
by H. C. Bailey

The Sullen Sky Mystery
by H. C. Bailey

The Big Fish
by Francis Beeding

The League of Discontent
by Francis Beeding

Behind That Curtain
by Earl Derr Biggers

Charlie Chan Carries On
by Earl Derr Biggers

The Chinese Parrot
by Earl Derr Biggers

Enter Sir John
by Clemence Dane and Helen Simpson

Below Suspicion
by John Dickson Carr

The Four False Weapons
by John Dickson Carr

The Judas Window
by Carter Dickson

Murder in the Submarine Zone
by Carter Dickson

She Died a Lady
by Carter Dickson

The Ten Teacups
by Carter Dickson

The Unicorn Murders
by Carter Dickson

The Benson Murder Case
by S. S. Van Dine

Bulldog Drummond on Dartmoor
by Gerard Fairlie following Sapper

The Case of the Sulky Girl
by Erle Stanley Gardner

The Case of the Velvet Claws
by Erle Stanley Gardner

Fatal Friday
by Francis Gérard

Secret Sceptre
by Francis Gérard

Murder in the Rue Royale
by Michael Harrison (*£2.00*)

Cork in Bottle
by Macdonald Hastings

Cork in the Doghouse
by Macdonald Hastings

Cork on the Water
by Macdonald Hastings

Phantom Lady
by William Irish

Last Laugh, Mr. Moto
by John P. Marquand

Stopover: Tokyo
by John P. Marquand

Two-Thirds of a Ghost
by Helen McCloy

Here Comes a Chopper
by Gladys Mitchell

The Rising of the Moon
by Gladys Mitchell

St. Peter's Finger
by Gladys Mitchell

The Adventures of Jimmie Dale
by Frank L. Packard (*£2.00*)

The Puzzle of the Briar Pipe
by Stuart Palmer

Uncle Abner
by Melville Davisson Post

CHILDREN

Master Skylark
by John Bennett (*£1.80*)

Mother West Wind's Children
by Thornton W. Burgess (*£1.70*)

Old Mother West Wind
by Thornton W. Burgess (*£1.70*)

The Cozy Lion
by Frances Hodgson Burnett (*£1.30*)

Racketty-Packetty House
by Frances Hodgson Burnett (*£1.30*)

The Spring Cleaning
by Frances Hodgson Burnett (£*1.00*)

The Tapestry Room
by Mrs. Molesworth (*£1.50*)

The Merry Adventures of Robin Hood
by Howard Pyle (*£2.25*)

The Pelican and the Kangaroo
by E. M. Silvanus (*£1.80*)

The Ugly Dachshund
by G. B. Stern (*£1.20*)

The Hired Man's Elephant
by Phil Stong (*£1.40*)

Knock Three Times!
by Marion St John Webb (£*1.75*)

Tom Stacey Reprints Ltd
28–29 Maiden Lane, London WC2E 7JP